Advance Praise for *Tasa*

Tasa's Song is a story of love and survival. World War II Poland provides the backdrop for this delicately rendered tale of a young woman, her music, and the beauty that persists even in times of great cruelty. Linda Kass writes with a sure and loving hand in this memorable debut novel, one that portrays the strength of the human spirit and how it can rise above the base and ignoble designs of our lesser kind.

—**Lee Martin**, author of *Turning Bones* and
The Bright Forever, a finalist for the
2006 Pulitzer Prize for Fiction

Tasa's Song is a sweeping historical drama about a young Jewish musician growing up in eastern Poland during World War II. As Tasa faces the horrors of the Holocaust with a bow and violin, Linda Kass weaves a sensuous, poetic narrative, both heartbreaking and melodic. It is the kind of book that makes you feel like you are reading by candlelight, no matter where you are, and at times the pages seemed to hum with music. This is a poignant, brave novel that book clubs and readers of all kinds will adore.

—**Matt Bondurant**, author of *The Night Swimmer*,
The Wettest County in the World, and *The Third Translation*

Tasa's Song fills your head with a symphony of family, friendship, and love against the tragic backdrop of war. Brimming with the sights and sounds of a world gone by, incredibly detailed and authentic, this book is razor sharp in its insights, and soaring in its lyric evocation of the past. Tasa herself steps out of history and into the world of unforgettable heroines.

—**Ann Kirschner**, author of *Sala's Gift*
and *Lady at the OK Corral*

Tasa's Song is a beautiful ode to all of the light and darkness history has to offer her children. Linda Kass has written a lasting tribute to life during wartime, including the hardships and triumphs that define the true nature of grace and resilience.

—**Amber Dermont**, author of The New York Times
bestseller *The Starboard Sea*

In showing us the transcendence of classical music against the horrors of the Holocaust, Linda Kass has given us a necessary and indispensable volume that details the evil and the beauty we as a species are capable of. *Tasa's Song* is a hauntingly heavenly melody heard in a darkness most terrifying, a novel at once harrowing and hopeful. I am as beguiled by its artistry as I am bedeviled by its theme.

—**Lee K. Abbott**, author of seven collections of
short stories, including *All Things, All at Once*

Linda Kass's moving debut novel brings vividly to life a Jewish family's struggle to survive World War II in eastern Poland, caught between the Nazi threat to the west and the Soviets to the east. Tasa, a gifted violinist, comes of age in the shadow of encroaching war, finding redemption in her music and through deep love despite the horrors that steadily draw near. Meticulously researched, *Tasa's Song* illuminates the day-to-day experience of war—the uncertainty and dawning horror, the devastating losses, and the small acts of grace.

—**Margot Singer**, author of *The Pale of Settlement*,
winner of the 2007 Flannery O'Connor
Award for Short Fiction

Tasa's Song is an intimate, evocative, deeply moving novel of devotion, love, and loss in the face of unspeakable evil. Read it for the powerful story it tells, the lives it honors, and the profoundly important lessons it teaches.

—**Kevin Boyle**, author of *Arc of Justice: A Saga of Race,
Civil Rights, and Murder in the Jazz Age*,
winner of the 2004 National Book Award for Nonfiction

Tasa's Song

Tasa's Song

A Novel

Linda Kass

Published 2016
Printed in the United States of America
ISBN: 978-1-63152-064-8 paperback
      978-1-63152-065-5 ebook
Library of Congress Control Number: 2015956235

For information, address:
She Writes Press
1563 Solano Ave #546
Berkeley, CA 94707

She Writes Press is a division of SparkPoint Studio, LLC.

This is a work of fiction. Names, characters, places, and incidents either are the product of the author's imagination or are used fictitiously. Any resemblance to actual persons, living or dead, is entirely coincidental.

For Aurelia Rosaminer Stern

Although the world is full of suffering, it is full also of the over-coming of it.

—Helen Keller

In the Blackness of the Night
Eastern Poland, March 1943

It was a night like others she had shared with Danik. He came to Tasa's bed after everyone was slumbering and the house beat with silence. The two of them whispered their feelings and fears, relishing the comfort of their stolen privacy. She knew that just before dawn, Danik would rouse himself and leave her to awaken alone, the imprint of his body still fresh beside her, but for now they drifted in each other's arms.

She'd just begun to float away when a rush of footsteps pulled her back. Her father burst into the bedroom; the shock on his face told her he was not there out of suspicion. His eyes, wide with another urgency, settled on Danik before he spoke. His voice was sharp. "We have fifteen minutes to gather our belongings. Take only what you absolutely need. Make sure you're wearing and packing warm clothes—as much as you can carry. We must leave before the Germans come for us." At that, Salomon stamped out the door.

Tasa stared into Danik's eyes, her heart pounding. Neither moved right away. She planted a quick kiss on his cheek before she pushed him from the room. Foggy from sleep, her head began spinning. Her father's brisk orders pulsated in her ears.

She tried to organize her thoughts, to focus on the task at hand. The village was buried in a deep layer of snow and ice. She pulled on her thickest corduroy pants, heaviest sweater, and warmest socks, put

1

aside her winter jacket, snow boots, and sheepskin *ushanka* hat. Into a large burlap satchel, she began stuffing an assortment of warm clothes, socks, flannel nightgowns. She looked around her room. What was she missing? In a moment of sudden clarity, she slid open her desk drawer to collect her journal and pen, the final note from her mother, the old family photo she had long ago found in her attic, a hairbrush. She eyed the blue enamel box atop her nightstand with her collection of letters and added it to her bag.

She scanned the room one last time. Her violin rested next to the nightstand. She froze at that instant, stunned by her lapse. How could she not have considered it before all else? Her body trembled at the thought of what might have happened—that she could lose the one possession she found most precious. She seized her instrument and slung the satchel's strap across her shoulder.

Rushing out to the hallway, she nearly bumped into Aunt Sascha and Cousin Tolek. The three of them joined her father, uncle, and Danik in the interior parlor, all of them engulfed in their heaviest hats and coats. She felt the anxiety in the air as she scanned their faces. For a moment she locked eyes with Danik, then spun back to her father. "What's going on, Papa? Where are—"

"We need to move quickly and quietly. You have to trust me—we'll be safe. I'll explain once we get far enough away from the village. Just follow me. And stay close!"

At that, her father strode to the kitchen and they trailed behind. "I'm going to lead. We'll walk single file, and I want you, Danik, to be in the back." He reached for a small dust broom at the side door and handed it to Danik. "Use this to sweep the snow and erase our footprints." He turned to the others, softening his gaze at Tolek. "I'm counting on you to be our bravest soldier. Stay close to me." Then to everyone, "Are we ready?"

Their silent march was invigorating at first. The cold air removed any fatigue Tasa still felt, despite how weighed down she was, how weighed down they all were. The trek seemed to her almost dreamlike, the blackness of the night their cover, only a sliver of moon casting a path for them as they slogged through the forest. She looked back at Danik as he brushed away the imprint of their feet on the snow, erasing each step as they moved farther from their past. She resumed her steady pace, retreating into her own thoughts, mulling over what had happened earlier. She glanced at her father, trying to discern any shift in his response to her.

After nearly two hours, their footsteps were the only sound amid the eerie stillness surrounding them. Her father motioned for them to stop as they approached a fallen tree, the six using the trunk as their resting spot while they chewed on grains and dried fruit he'd brought with him.

"I'm proud of you, Tolek. You're a brave young man." Salomon offered him a boiled egg, which the boy took quickly, mumbling his thanks.

Despite his slight frame, the onerous hike seemed to be less daunting for Tolek than for the others. And he didn't fret or complain. Tasa wondered what Sascha or Jakov discussed with their son through the ordeal of war, how a boy of not quite thirteen had grown up in spite of the past four years of conflict. He'd overcome his panic of a year earlier and managed to keep his wits at times like these. She reached for his hand and squeezed it, smiling through the darkness.

"We're close to our destination." Her father packed up the remaining food. "We'll be staying on Josef Gnyp's property, near Litovyshche. Josef's built a reinforced shelter to hide us." His words caught in his throat. "He's risking his . . . his family's lives to save us."

No one spoke. Tasa exhaled a mist of frost into the air. Josef Gnyp was Catholic and had worked for her father since before she was born. He had helped Papa construct the windmills that brought electricity to their village and build their grand home at a time when others, more knowing, were fleeing the country. He had a wife and daughter of his own. Tasa recalled the endless hours she'd followed Josef and his puppy, Theo, around their property in Podkamien, the summer days she and Danik would ride their horses to visit the Gnyps, swimming in the lake near their house, picnicking with them. Tasa closed her eyes, overcome by emotion. She knew the death penalties the Germans had recently established for anyone hiding or assisting Jews. Josef Gnyp had turned out to be the one person who could save them and was willing to risk all to do so.

The harsh cold kept them from resting for long. They resumed hiking, reenergized by the food and the knowledge that their destination was near. In just under an hour, Tasa glimpsed the outline of a horse and carriage, and a man standing at the isolated edge of the woods. She blinked back tears as she pointed toward the distant shapes.

In the years since she'd seen him, he had grown thinner and now wore a beard. His dark-blond hair was tinged with gray. Josef offered his arm to Tasa, who mounted the wagon first. Salomon handed her each of their bundled possessions before the others climbed up. Gunfire sounded in the distance as Josef explained how his peaceful village was the war's front line and how fluid that line between the Germans and Soviets had become. Even though long stretches of fertile fields separated his property from the center of town, fighting was close enough at times that they would need to exercise care and good judgment, he told them.

Their ride continued on a narrow and jagged path, stretching through fields dotted sparsely with houses. As they approached the Gnyps' property, Tasa felt its familiarity, although it looked bare now in winter and even more isolated—the wooden plank above a tiny creek leading to the stone cottage-style house, the brown shutters, the single rocker on a small porch. While the scenery was less picturesque and the Gnyp house far more modest, Tasa thought about her childhood estate in Podkamien, with its open land and abundant crops, grateful that here, too, they could be self-sufficient despite the war. She looked toward the sound of clucking hens and saw chicken coops inside a red shed whose door hung partially open, revealing several wooden plows.

Josef directed the horses to the right of the house and shed, where the barn and stables were attached, easing the wagon to a halt. Jumping down to the frozen earth, Tasa heard Theo's low-pitched barks before she spotted Jaga and Stefania standing at the barn's entrance. The dog trotted over to her as if there hadn't been a day's separation. She kneeled down to nuzzle him. He'd filled out, and his whiskers had turned salt and pepper. Tasa held his head in her hands, staring into his huge eyes through his long, shaggy mop of fur.

Tolek ran up to greet the dog as his parents and Salomon stepped from the wagon. The sheepdog's tail swished back and forth like a fan, his attention now on Tolek as Tasa hugged Jaga and Stefania. Josef guided all of them inside the stable, pushed away layers of hay in the middle of the barn to reveal the bunker's opening—a single panel he lifted to expose a stepladder. One by one, they lowered themselves into the shelter below.

Josef held a match to the wick of several kerosene lanterns, apologizing for the crude lighting and limited electrical current going to the barn. But the lamps adequately brightened this roomy refuge and Tasa immediately saw the great care he had taken to make it as comfortable as possible. Josef had placed cots in various areas, provided partitions for privacy, and arranged a central space with seating and a few tables that could allow the family to come together. She was astonished by what he had created. The hiding place had a fake entrance and openings made with pipes for ventilation.

Notwithstanding her gratitude and relief, she was overcome by a sickening feeling. This was where they would all be living now. Where her violin must remain silent. Where intimacy with Danik would be curtailed. In rote fashion, Tasa selected her cot and her space and began putting away her meager belongings as they all did, noiselessly, caught inside their own emotions. She lay on the narrow bed, atop its wool blanket. She felt the kind of chill that reached into her hair roots and tingled in her scalp. Taking in a breath, she caught the musty smell of the earth. She almost wanted to laugh, although it would be shrill if she allowed herself that release—her ceiling the floor of a barn covered with hay, her floor the soil that would someday serve as her everlasting place of rest. How was this to be?

Her eyes strained to adjust to the dimness. She could make out the shadowy shape of Danik sitting motionless on his own cot not far from her. Shivering, she slid underneath the blanket, pulled it tightly up to her chin, and closed her eyes. The day's events trailed backward, through the months of fear, to a time when her world felt whole and filled with promise. Backward to the dirt path she took with her mother to the village center and the house of her grandfather, and then with Danik to her tiny schoolhouse as the villagers greeted them along the way. All the way back to the pastoral view from her attic window. Within the silence she could hear the lyrical melody of Tchaikovsky's *Souvenir d'un Lieu Cher*, its echo of a beloved place blurring into her own memories.

Part One

To see a World in a Grain of Sand
And a Heaven in a Wild Flower,
Hold Infinity in the palm of your hand
And Eternity in an hour.

—William Blake

Podkamien
January 1933

Tasa tiptoed toward the narrow attic window. The floor chilled her bare feet. She pulled up on her flannel nightgown, trying not to trip over the dusty objects in her path, then stepped onto a wooden chest set between angled beams. Eyes closed, she held her face toward the rising sun and pretended it was summer: purple bellflowers dotting the countryside, the wind whispering in the grass.

"What are you staring at?" Danik's voice, although a quiet murmur, startled her. "You're always daydreaming."

She found it difficult to tell her older cousin, who was more like her best friend, all the fuzzy thoughts swirling through her head. Things she wished for. Music that played over and over in her mind.

"Come look. It's my favorite view of Podkamien." Tasa reached over to Danik and pulled at his flannel nightshirt. He had spent the night since Uncle Judah and Aunt Ella were visiting Albert at some important school in Paris.

Danik stepped forward and rested his head on Tasa's shoulder to peek out the window. And in a sassy tone he asked, "And why's that?"

Her cousin could be downright annoying. There were times she looked forward to his leaving next fall, when he would begin attending *gimnazjum* in the next, larger town of Brody, since schooling in their village ended at sixth level. Then she could be the oldest, the most accomplished, the smartest of her cousins still left in Podkamien.

No longer the little cousin who tagged along, the easiest one to tease. At least until she'd join Danik in two years, boarding with one of Mama's old friends—Frau something.

But then Tasa remembered how her head had felt heavy and her stomach had tied in knots when she'd first learned about Danik's departure. Who would meet up with her on school mornings after Mama walked her up the dirt road and left her to make her way? Who would finish the *pierniczki* she'd get at Kuchar's Bakery, linger with her to collect pine cones along their path, or pick the small yellow flowers from the dense clusters of sweet alyssum until they had to run, laughing, to beat the last tolling of the schoolhouse bell? Who would stay on the lookout when she chose to ride Cairo bareback or listen to her idle complaints or amuse her with his jokes and infectious laughter? She wondered why her feelings always pulled her in different directions and sent her moping.

It was about the time she'd been anticipating her loneliness without Danik around when Mama invented a game they'd play in the orchard. Her mother named it after their rural shtetl, since she'd conceal a golden zloty coin under one of the many different-sized stones arranged around the lavender shrubs for Tasa to find. "Under a stone" was the literal meaning of Podkamien, and Mama would tell her that their town was a lot like life, with many things hidden and awaiting discovery.

"Danik, our whole world is right out here!" Tasa took in her surroundings, refusing to let Danik cramp her dawn ritual. The morning frost glazed clumps of grass just under the window. Peering through the spires of evergreens and an early mist, she could see beyond to the village center and its outline of roofs, since nothing was far in Podkamien. There was one long street, the houses facing each other, the seemingly endless forest stretching beyond. This was the street where Danik and her other relatives lived, where Grampa Abram lived, where Podkamien's three synagogues and half a dozen Catholic churches anchored the townspeople, all with their peculiar beliefs and habits, like a spiritual cluster.

Glancing to the north, past the land and the stable and barn, Tasa fixed on the small lake that marked the end of her family's property. This swath of open countryside offered her the smell of pine and spruce and the promise of what would grow from the soil.

"I can hardly wait until springtime, Danik." Tasa could almost hear the deep, croaking frog calls and clucking of hens that would replace the hush of winter.

"Me neither." Danik moved away from the window, accidentally brushing against the toothed metal knob of a kerosene lamp. He looked around the dingy space. "So, what do you want to do up here?"

Tasa stepped toward him, finding herself facing a smeary full-length mirror. Her thick black braids were still in place, parted down the middle, like Mama, who always wrapped her hair in a bun. She surveyed her many hoarded possessions. Danik bent over to pick up the impaired violin she'd found during her latest attic adventure. It was missing a string and had a small crack at the edge. The remaining strings were lax.

"This looks too old to have been yours. Whose was it?" Danik held out the damaged instrument.

Tasa took the aged relic from him. She loved the feel of the violin, its hourglass shape and arched top and back. It was made of maple, like her own, but it was a full-size Ruggieri and felt weighty in her hands. She'd gotten her first violin four years earlier, just a few months before her sixth birthday, a present from Grampa Abram. He was the only person she allowed to call her Anastasia, her given name. Her stature was so small—even now she stood barely higher than the kitchen sink—that Abram had ordered her a miniature violin measuring only twenty centimeters.

"I think Gramma Ruth used to play."

"That explains where you got your talent." Danik had a twinkle in his eye.

Tasa's teacher showed her how to use as much of the bow as possible, with her arm all the way in the frog position, then moving to the lighter, tip end of the bow. She hated the scratchy sounds she made in the beginning and worked especially hard to keep the bow straight, parallel to the bridge of her violin, and not apply too much pressure. Having perfected Beethoven's "Ode to Joy" and Strauss's waltz "The Blue Danube," she was now learning some simple versions of Tchaikovsky concertos.

Tasa ran her hand along the chipped ebony fingerboard, moving toward the lower strings and the instrument's more pronounced concavity. In her mind she could hear Niccolo Paganini's *24th Caprice*, which Grampa said was the North Star for any violinist, since it contained the entire arsenal of technique within its measures. She closed her eyes, imagining herself playing this piece, bringing forth the double and triple stops and lively staccatos. But Paganini's masterpiece contained many difficult intervals for the left hand, including the parallel tenths, a range she worried her stubby fingers could never master. She opened her eyes and frowned.

Tasa saw Danik's impish grin as he regarded her, and decided to strike first. "At least I work at my music, while you just loaf around." Tasa knew Danik wasn't lazy, but she couldn't resist taunting him.

"Come on, Tasa. I'm not a total musical failure. I liked the Chopin mazurkas and polonaises playing on the radio last night, even hummed along."

"And you liked the *Koziolek Matolek* comic books Papa brought home, too." Tasa baited him in return, although she actually liked the far-fetched adventures of Matolek, the billy goat who was searching for the town of Pacanow, where, he heard, they made goat shoes.

While giggling over the story with Danik in the kitchen the previous evening, she had glanced down the hall and watched as her father grasped her mother's waist between his large hands, pulling her to him. She saw a look between them that was different from how they were in front of her. Later, a man's voice on the radio hastily reported on an election in Germany. After her parents clicked off the radio, there was a lingering silence, then hushed conversation.

Now she tried to remember where Germany sat on the map of central Europe that covered an entire wall in her fourth-year classroom. Their village was very close to the Czechoslovakian and Soviet borders. At least she knew that much geography.

She placed the delicate instrument down, next to a box of letters and photographs. "Look at this, Danik!" A dated, sepia-colored image of a gathering of people caught her eye. She picked it up and began inspecting the faces; "1921" was written on the front corner. She turned the photo over, reading the neat handwriting: *Halina and Salomon at their engagement with me and Abram, the children and grandchildren.*

Danik grabbed the photo from Tasa and stared at the family portrait. "There's my father. His suspenders give him away."

"Your mother's holding a baby . . ." Tasa peered more closely. "That's you, Danik. How silly you look! In an outfit more fitting for a baby girl!"

The sound of her parents' voices from the kitchen below interrupted their laughter. Fixing her eyes on Danik, Tasa put her finger to her lips. She carefully replaced the photograph and practically held her breath so her parents would continue talking as she strained to hear their muffled words.

"I don't know what it means . . . naming him chancellor . . ."

"Frau Rothstein was lucky to get out of Germany . . ."

Tasa tiptoed along the outer edge of the musty attic, and Danik followed. A creaking board gave them away, initially silencing her parents.

Halina's crisp voice called up. "Tasa, Daniel. Come down for breakfast."

"Yes, Mama, we're coming." Tasa looked at Danik and mouthed the words "caught again." She was hungry, happy for the break from their morning adventure. She took two steps at a time as she descended the stairs, landing with a bounce on both feet, facing her parents as they sat at opposite ends of their tiny butcher-block kitchen table. Danik strutted ahead of her, then stood there sheepishly.

"What trouble have you two been causing this morning?" Salomon wore his plaid flannel pajamas, his unshaven whiskers casting a dark shadow around his face.

Halina brushed her lips across Tasa's forehead and stood back, her arms crossed, her mouth smiling. She was still in her dressing gown, her hair trailing in a thin braid down her back. "Children, wash your hands. I can only imagine what you've been into."

Tasa did as she was told and stepped toward the sink. After rubbing her hands dry with the soft cloth Mama handed her, she dropped into a ladder-back chair, its wood slats hard against her spine. Her mother prepared their substantial breakfast—putting eggs to boil in a pot of water on the stove, slicing a loaf of sourdough rye bread, and, from the icebox, gathering a jug of milk and an assortment of cheeses. Tasa was so hungry she knew she wouldn't have any trouble that morning finishing everything on her plate, something Mama insisted on at every meal.

A ray of light fell across the braided jute rug that covered the kitchen floor. The table sat against a double-paned window adorned with an upper tier of red-checkered curtains. Tasa felt the sun's warmth on her cheeks. Her mother reached for stoneware stacked on an open shelf and took out four dishes, handing them to Tasa to set atop the burlap place mats. She loved the painted rooster at the center of each dish and often moved her food along the perimeter so she could admire the red crest on the bird's head and his bushy tail arced like a rainbow. A rooster's loud crowing was to proclaim his territory, Papa had told her. Tasa was hearing the sound of the bird's distinctive call in her head when Mama interrupted her musing.

"How long were you two playing in the attic?" Her mother began slicing apples at the wooden counter, plucking them out of a wire basket that also held potatoes, beets, and onions.

Tasa turned toward her mother to respond, but Danik answered first. "Maybe an hour."

"We found a photograph of you and Papa when you were young. Everyone was in the picture, Mama. Danik was a baby and looked very silly." Tasa looked over at Danik and crinkled her nose. He returned a playful glare she pretended to ignore. "There were aunts and uncles I've never met. Where are all of them?"

Tasa could tell she annoyed her parents with her many questions. But their answers helped her piece the puzzle of their lives together. She had learned about her parents' courtship in Vienna—her mother a student, her father a soldier in the Austrian army during the Great War. Both had come from Podkamien and known each other since childhood, their families having settled in her village all the way back in the late 1800s, when it was Austrian Poland led by Emperor Franz Joseph. In conveying the complicated history of Poland, Tasa's schoolteacher used Podkamien as an example when she said you could live and die in one spot and occupy four different countries, because this part of Poland was constantly being invaded and carved up, then "liberated" by somebody.

Tasa bit into an apple wedge she'd taken from the counter. Once, she'd asked her parents why she was an only child when they had so many sisters and brothers. She didn't remember their exact answer but supposed that staying together as a family must have seemed to her parents much easier with just the three of them.

"The war changed things," her mother answered. "It always does. Many people looked for what they thought might be better lives elsewhere. Like your uncle Walter, Papa's brother." Halina brought the platter of sliced apples to the table. "He lives in the United States and is married, with two small children. So you have American cousins, Tasa! Maybe we can go to America someday to meet them."

Tasa was still thinking about that when her father changed the subject. "Halina, Kornel Makuszynski just created a comic-book series the children read last night. You liked this, no?" Salomon looked from Danik to Tasa.

"Matolek was a funny goat, but it was sad he couldn't find his home, Papa." She hadn't thought about that fact until just now.

"Salomon, why don't you buy Tasa more advanced books? Like *King Macius the First*?"

Tasa rolled her eyes so only her father and Danik could see. Papa winked back at them, careful that Mama didn't notice.

"We found an old violin this morning. Tasa thought it had been Gramma Ruth's." Danik scooted his chair closer to the table and put his napkin on his lap. Tasa widened her eyes, surprised by his good manners.

15

"She played the violin beautifully." Halina spread butter on a slice of bread. "I think that's why Grampa Abram takes such pride in Tasa's playing."

"Mama, I want so badly to play like Paganini. Grampa Abram told me Paganini could play three octaves across four strings in a hand span!" Tasa looked down at her small hands, spreading apart her short fingers, suddenly discouraged.

"You will grow, my love. You'll be tall enough to reach for the stars someday." Her mother put a piece of bread on each of their plates, along with an egg, some cheese, and slices of apple. "Both of you children need to be patient. You have your whole lives ahead of you." She poured each of them a cup of black tea.

"Aunt Halina, what was that news report you listened to on the radio last night?"

Tasa's parents looked at each other. They weren't smiling.

Salomon spoke first, his voice subdued. "Just political reports from Germany. Many people have been out of work, have done poorly since the end of the Great War. They elected a new leader, hoping he'll make their lives better."

Halina cut in. "He has made many promises to the people, changes he says will unify them as a country." She abruptly lowered the teakettle onto the counter, and it landed with a smack.

Tasa stopped eating and shifted in her chair. She picked at the rest of the food on her plate, not really listening to her mother. Lifting the bread into her mouth, she chewed the grainy bite slowly, staring at the red rooster emerging in the background next to her hard-boiled egg. She began to use her fork to move the remaining bread and cheese and apple pieces to the edge so she could see the entire bird, imagining him sitting calmly on the fence outside, grasping the wood with his large, spurred feet, looking out for his flock of hens from his high perch. The rooster's bright crest standing tall, his shiny black coat reflecting the light, his long, feathered tail curling up, then down, ready to sound his distinctive alarm at the first approach of a predator.

Frau Rothstein
1935

The twenty-three-kilometer journey to Brody by horse and wagon zigzagged north and west along a jagged road. Tasa, Danik, and Salomon didn't leave Podkamien until the late afternoon. In the August heat, the horses required a slow pace and frequent stops for rest and water. The humidity turned Tasa's skin sticky.

For the first hour she said nothing, distressed from the tearful exchange with her mother and grandfather that had capped off weeks of wide-ranging emotions. She couldn't help but finally notice the utilitarian beauty in the fertile fields of corn and potatoes, beets and oats steadily unfurling along their route.

It was near dusk when they reached Brody. The small city was set in the valley of the upper Styr River but seemed to rise in the distance above the continuous plains blanketed in glowing orange and pink. At first glance, the town felt large and alien. Her mother had told her it was nearly ten times the size of Podkamien, about twenty-two thousand people. Tasa apprehensively surveyed the expansive Market Square as her father eased their vehicle into a wagon yard already tightly packed with horses and carriages. A tailor's shop and tavern were open for business.

"Tasa, you'll want to go to Dudek's Tavern." Danik began to speak rapidly, a wide grin on his face. "Food's great. My friend's father owns the watch store in the square, and there's a great pastry shop just a few doors away."

Her past worries began to drift away as her eyes wandered the square. A number of Jewish men donned long black jackets, their trousers tucked into high black socks. They had uncut sideburns and wore tall, narrow hats. The Jewish women dressed like Gramma Ruth had, with dark skirts that swirled around their ankles, but many also wore wigs pulled forward over part of their upper foreheads, while others covered their heads with scarves. She heard them speaking in different languages. One sounded similar to German, probably Yiddish, but another she'd never heard before. A young man wearing a beret and holding a child's hand nodded at her father and mumbled a greeting in Polish. Several open-air stalls—canvas covers held up by posts—revealed people peddling clothes and hats. Just beyond the square, tucked behind the trunks of birch, elm, and oaks that surrounded the narrow openings of cobblestone streets, stood the houses of central Brody in variations of gray and brown, stone and wood.

Tasa hesitated in stepping out of the carriage as a smiling, large-busted, middle-aged woman with dark, wavy hair approached her father, her sturdy arms enclosing him in a bear hug.

"Guten abend, Salomon! *Willkommen!"*

Earlier, Danik had told her Frau Rothstein was born in Berlin and never learned Polish well, that she was embarrassed to speak the language although she understood it completely. So he talked to her in Polish and she answered in German. Tasa was glad she and Danik had learned German and Czech in lower school. Between her sixth-level Polish history class and her parents' efforts to prepare her for Brody, she also knew that a large contingent of Jews lived there—ten thousand. They'd fled from persecution in several European countries over the years, and the most Orthodox spoke only Yiddish.

"Schones kind." Frau held out her arms to Tasa, her eyes gleaming as she kept telling Salomon what a beautiful girl Tasa was. Tasa felt herself blushing. "You will like it here. The school is close, not even one kilometer. You will make friends, and we will get along just fine."

Papa addressed Frau by her given name, Greta, as he answered her questions about Mama. Frau inquired about Danik's older brother, one of her first boarders, as she took several of Tasa's smaller suitcases from the carriage and carried them up the steps of her two-story brick house.

Tasa turned, admiring the last sliver of sun, as Danik walked up to her. "You'll have me to hassle again, Tasa." He tilted his head just slightly, and, despite the dusk, she could see the mischief in his eyes. The moon and light from several lamps illuminated a pale yellow path as she entered what would be her home for the next six years. The time stretched incomprehensively ahead of her like Poland's never-ending fields of beets and potatoes. And yet it felt tantalizing as well.

After her father's departure, Tasa explored the cozy house room by room. There were three bedrooms on the upper floor. The master bedroom and bath were at one end, separated by a small library and a hallway from the other two rooms where Frau's two sons had grown up, rooms she and Danik would occupy.

Roaming the living room with Danik, Tasa picked up a framed photo of Albert Riesmann on the fireplace mantel.

"That's Marten Rothstein standing next to my brother," Danik said. "He teaches mathematics at our school."

"Look at this!" Tasa had never seen a gramophone.

Frau entered the room, placing a plate of cookies on the side table. "There's a small music shop in Brody's town center where I purchase recordings of my favorite composers. I recently bought the first European recording of Rachmaninoff's Piano Concerto no. 3." She pulled out an album from a walnut cabinet next to the phonograph to show them.

Tasa knew Rachmaninoff's concerto was one of the most technically difficult pieces ever written for the piano. "I believe this piece is piano's equivalent of Paganini's *24 Caprices.*" She instantly felt quite clever.

"Frau is a part-time music teacher and pianist." Danik helped himself to a cookie, his eyes twinkling as he bit into the raspberry filling at its center.

Tasa ran her hand across the polished ebony finish of the grand piano. "Well, that explains this beautiful Bösendorfer."

"I'd love to work with you on the violin, Tasa. I'll find violin and piano music we can play together—Bach, Viotti, Chopin, Schubert, Smetana. Yes?"

"That would be wonderful!" Tasa sat down on the piano bench, rubbing its velvet covering. "I'm not good enough yet, but soon I can try more difficult pieces by Tchaikovsky and Sibelius. And, of course, Paganini."

Frau beamed broadly, a youthful dimple emerging from her right cheek.

Later in the evening, Tasa visited the wood-paneled library upstairs. She discovered works in German, Russian, and Polish, some of the volumes leather-bound and weighty. She slid each book off the shelf to examine its contents, always replacing it in its exact spot. She selected the books that seemed to her the most intriguing, perhaps because she'd heard the authors' names mentioned by her parents or other adults: Freud and Goethe, Hesse and Babel, Chekhov and Tolstoy. Her parents' library was much more limited, mostly books by Poles. Here she could be exposed to new writers and different points of view. The thought of a world beyond her insular village aroused her curiosity.

Tasa inhaled the buttery aromas of the first batch of raspberry-walnut pastry seeping from the oven, its warmth welcome on this chilly Friday in December. A light coating of flour covered the counter. Frau's black bib smock was caked with its own markings of the white powder from the many times she rubbed her sticky hands against her ample hips as she kneaded balls of cream-cheese dough, smoothing and flattening them onto wax paper and into a three-quarter-inch disk that she would wrap, then chill for several hours. Tasa watched with admiration. They'd gone through several rounds of rugelach preparations for tomorrow's Hanukkah festivities. She knew to roll the dough into precise twelve-inch circles on a sheet of lightly floured waxed paper, and to dust the dough with flour so the wooden pin wouldn't stick.

"Slide the pastry and paper onto a baking sheet, Tasa." Frau methodically chopped walnuts and raisins with a sharp butcher cleaver, beads of perspiration beginning to form on her forehead. The final step was the most fun, as they cut the dough into a dozen pie-shaped wedges, rolling up each wedge like a rug, molding each piece with a slight bend at its center.

If the bite-size crescent-shaped rugelach were the traditional baked treat for Hanukkah, Frau Rothstein's nine-branched brass candelabrum was the universal symbol of a holiday that marked the religious freedom of the Jewish community. In anticipation, Frau's Menorah already held a candle in the ninth *shamash* holder, as well as one in the far-right holder for the first of eight nights of this Festival of Lights. And, as in the home of Frau's Catholic neighbors, the Jankowskis, readying for Christmas, a short fir tree stood in the corner of her living room.

The early afternoon sun streamed through the kitchen window as the small radiator cranked heat into the room. Winter remained half the year in Poland, snow beginning in October and not subsiding until April ran into May, when the packed layers gradually thawed.

Frau untied her smock from the back and lifted the bib's halter over her head, revealing a floral, short-sleeved, round-collared dress. She wore black crepe-soled shoes to cushion those hours spent on her feet in the kitchen. She had a German orderliness about her and kept to a strict routine of domestic chores all week.

Frau was just removing the last of the rugelach from the oven when the front door slammed. Moments later, Danik appeared in the kitchen doorway, his eyes widening at the baking scene in front of him. In only four months since their arrival, a growth spurt had left him a clear foot taller than Tasa. His tan winter field jacket was unbuttoned, his brown wool sweater a contrast with his almost-reddish mop of hair. He flashed his most winning smile as he gave Frau a quick shoulder squeeze and reached for a still-warm pastry from the plateful now sitting on the kitchen table.

"That's for tomorrow, Danik," Tasa chided, as she pushed her cousin's hand away.

"Maybe if you eat more, you'll grow a little," Danik retorted, and puffed out his cheeks. Tasa gently punched him in the stomach, glancing quickly at Frau who stood back, her dimple deepening.

"Danik, take off your boots. The melting ice is dripping on the floor. I'll get your coat." Frau hung it on the back of a kitchen chair, then reached for two plates in the light birch cabinet against the far wall. "You can both have a few pieces with a glass of milk. Then I need you to run an errand for me before we lose daylight. One head of cabbage, a small bag of rice, and two onions. Also cabbage rolls and borscht for tonight's dinner. And I need some buckwheat honey."

"What's that for?"

"I'm making a *babka* for the Janowskis' Christmas Eve dinner."

Tasa slept late and lay in bed for several minutes, trying to shake off her sluggishness. Buttery aromas permeated the entire house; that meant Frau had risen early to make the *babka*, as she always began her day the moment the sun swarmed through the white lace bedroom curtains. No matter that it was Sunday.

Lifting her pillow up against the wall, Tasa sat upright as her stomach began to gurgle softly. She reached over to the small night table and opened a blue enamel box, removing an envelope. As she closed the lid, Tasa slid her fingers across the smooth surface, then lifted the box to her lips, kissing it gently as a parent might kiss the top of a child's head. Rereading her mother's letters had become a ritual. This one had arrived ten days earlier. Tasa took the letter out of the envelope and carefully unfolded the white parchment, examining the exacting script of her mother's pen.

December 11, 1935

Dearest Tasa,

It was so nice to visit last month and see how you are set-tling into your life in Brody. I miss having you here, but that's what is so good about our letters to each other.

My first piece of news is that Aunt Ella got a long letter from Albert. He finished his schooling at the Sorbonne and now lives with Aunt Roza and her new husband in Palestine while he studies engineering at Technion University.

Last week we heard from Papa's brother in America. Uncle Walter said he's begun finding work at reasonable wages and hopes to soon buy and manage a parking lot with his sav-ings. He wrote about the inspired leadership of their president, Franklin Roosevelt. Uncle Walter would love if we could find a way to cross the vast Atlantic Ocean and visit them next summer. I doubt we could afford such a trip, especially since Papa is talking more seriously about building a new house for us, closer to the lake but a bit farther from the barn and stables. With Mr. Gnyp's help in construction and carpentry, Papa wants to make it two stories and brick. I must say, the idea of having a modernized kitchen is something I'm excited about. Papa thinks we can stay in this house while he takes his time to construct a "palace" on the other end of Cairo's grazing field.

Speaking of Cairo, his winter coat has grown in since you saw him in August, so he looks almost fat now! Every morn-ing when Papa or Mr. Gnyp goes to the barn to feed him, he seems disappointed not to see you. Don't worry, we're trying to make up for your absence by giving him more attention and sometimes invite Tolek over to walk him around the field (with supervision). Now that Tolek has begun first level at school this year, he's actually become somewhat precocious. His vocabulary is quite advanced, according to his teachers, but Aunt Sascha says the boy has been difficult to contain when he comes home from school and Uncle Jakov is still seeing patients.

Grampa Abram wants to know if you're playing your violin and says he looks forward to new songs you can play for him after a year of lessons, practice, and growing fingers. He misses you terribly, as we all do.

Aunt Ella and Uncle Judah are our constant companions, since they, too, are childless, with Danik there and Albert in Haifa. Uncle Judah's legal practice keeps him very busy. Aunt Ella and I are taking an embroidery class in town. I hope to finish some special pillow covers for your room by the time you come home for your break next month.

I hope you like the Hanukkah gift I sent along. It can be a place to keep your most precious, but small, possessions.

Please give Danik and Frau Rothstein our love. And most of all to you, my dear child.

Mama (and Papa)

Tasa wasn't sure if the pangs she felt were from hunger or from the emptiness that always followed the reading of her mother's letters. As the Hanukkah festivities neared, she felt a growing malaise she fought to contain. She would answer the letter after breakfast. She rolled out of bed and into the hall, first peeking into Danik's room. He was sleeping deeply, only parts of his hair exposed, the pillow covering most of his head. She carefully closed his door and headed down to the kitchen.

As always, Frau Rothstein greeted her with a hug. *"Guten morgen!"* Stepping away, Frau met Tasa's eyes. "Missing your family today, yes?" She held Tasa's chin softly in her hand. "It's okay to be sad, *kinder*. We want those we love most to be with us." She embraced Tasa again, holding her tightly as Tasa trembled through several sobs. "I know, *kinder*." Tasa took in a gulp of air and wiped her eyes dry.

"Let's get the cake out of the oven, fix you some breakfast, then play some music together!" Frau added.

December 21, 1935
Dear Mama and Papa,

I was so happy to receive your letter and the beautiful enamel case, where I now keep all the letters you've sent me. I miss you and Grampa Abram so much! When I get homesick, Frau Rothstein helps me feel better. She is so kind to me in every way, and I've already grown to love her.

Please tell Grampa Abram that I'm practicing violin every day and that Frau found some wonderful music written for both violin and piano. We started with Bach's Violin Concerto in E Major. There are many sonatas by Viotti that we play, but my favorite piece is Chopin's Nocturne no. 2 (the one in E-flat) arranged for violin and piano. The melody makes me think of you and of Podkamien because it goes from feeling sad and gentle to being hopeful and exhilarating near the end. I love its rhythmic freedom. You would be proud of how well I play the trills and high registers. It took lots of practice!

I will pass along all of your news to Danik if he ever gets up. Half the day goes by on weekends before he is awake. It is exciting that Papa will be building us a new house and you will get a bigger kitchen. Frau Rothstein is teaching me how to bake, and I, too, would like us to have a bigger kitchen so I can bake with you. I hope Cairo has somebody other than Tolek giving him exercise. Please find someone to ride him and make sure he has a blanket during these frigid months.

Tonight we begin our Hanukkah celebrations. Tuesday will be our last day of school before the new year.

Hugs and kisses to you!
Tasa

Monday morning was crisp and clear, the landscape bearing a glow as farmers and lumbermen made their way into town. Tasa crossed the square with Danik. She wore her warmest overcoat, a thick hat and scarf covering most of her head and face. Squeals and the chatter of children mixed with the clip-clops of horse hooves on the cobblestone street. Customers paused to peek inside stores along the market perimeter, sometimes bumping into shop owners as they swept snow from their entries. The two strolled alongside the Gothic town hall on the south side of the square, and Tasa slowed to admire the Renaissance mural paintings that adorned its outside walls. The cousins passed rows of narrow, multistoried trader houses with red tile roofs and dormers, while Tasa envisioned the late-spring sprouting of colorful flowers that would fill the empty wooden boxes lining their lower-floor windows.

Despite the bitter cold, the open-air market was bustling with shoppers, and she and Danik moved rapidly among the many trading stalls. Townspeople, buying everything from hats to bagels at this early hour, entered the center of Brody from a labyrinth of narrow alleys that spread from the square to their dense rows of brick and stone houses.

Tasa stopped in front of a baroque fountain as loud voices caught her attention. Danik pivoted toward the sound, and the two walked closer together toward the general store.

A middle-aged Polish woman stood at the checkout counter, scowling as she pounded the wooden surface. "You overcharged me! I bought only three jars of horseradish and some canned apricots."

The Hasidic shopkeeper bowed his head and spoke quietly. "Please, ma'am . . . These products are priced reasonably. I'm sorry you—"

"Hitler is right about you people." She shoved a few coins across the counter, grabbed her goods, and stamped out, bumping hard into Danik so that he momentarily lost his balance.

Tasa felt the color rise in her face. She shifted her book bag and tightened her neck scarf. Danik steadied himself, his expression blank except for a look she'd never seen on him. His eyes glared, like he was angry and maybe scared, as she was. The two began walking in silence past the town center and the Church of the Nativity of the Virgin Mary, approaching the Jewish quarter.

Tasa hadn't taken notice of the Orthodox Jewish community in her tiny village as she had in Brody. In Podkamien, everyone was familiar and accepted. Here, while a vibrant and distinctive Jewish world existed—the landmark Old Synagogue and the Jewish cemetery, the echo of conversations in Yiddish—it was more often contained within the Jewish quarter. It was a separate world; at least, that was how she saw it now. Tasa and Danik passed women in wigs and men with sideburn curls wearing black garb and carrying books of the Talmud—a sharp contrast with the Polish Catholics they'd watched flowing into the spacious church courtyard the previous day. All Tasa could hear was the steady rhythm of her and Danik's steps, the silence between them unbearable.

"That woman was . . . she acted so different from the way the Janowskis are with us. The shopkeeper didn't even do anything. Why was she so agitated?"

Danik looked uncomfortable, like he was struggling to find the words to answer her. He took in a gulp of air and quickly exhaled. "Frau Rothstein was listening to Polskie Radio the other day when I was fixing myself a sandwich. The announcer was talking about Adolf Hitler's leadership of Germany. And he described some new laws in Germany—Nuremberg Laws, I think they said."

Danik slowed his pace. "I asked Frau what they were. She said many people were afraid of Hitler. That he hated Jews."

"Hated Jews?" Tasa looked at Danik in disbelief.

"Yes, that's what she said." He stopped and locked eyes with Tasa. "The laws would *marginalize* the Jews—that was how she put it—but then she said that no one would let a man like that stay in power, and not to worry."

Tasa took in his words, thinking back to the first time she'd heard about Hitler, how the mention of his name in her home had provoked tension and silence. It hadn't meant anything to her then.

She and Danik continued their walk in silence. A stray black cat crossed their path as the cousins left the Jewish quarter on their route to Brody Catholic Gimnazjum.

Gypsy Airs
Spring 1937

S itting next to the window in the back row of third-period science class, Tasa gazed at the emerging signs of spring outside. The swath of white baby's breath, an array of Siberian iris in blue and purple, and the red blooms of the corn poppy all reminded her of home, of Podkamien.

She turned her head as her teacher erased the chemical notations he'd written on the blackboard. The symbols disappeared from the smooth surface, just as Professor Rothstein had wiped off the math equations last period and Professor Gorka had removed the list of four Latin verb conjugations in first-period Languages. At Brody Catholic Gimnazjum, the students stayed put while the teachers moved from classroom to classroom throughout the day. Religious study was the only subject requiring students to leave their "home" room.

Bartek Boraski, stout and full-faced, walked stiffly around his imposing rectangular wooden desk, plucking up a sheet of paper. His booming voice began calling the names of her Roman Catholic class-mates. "Ania Dudek, Maria Grabowski, Dora Landau, Lucia Mazur, and Felka Sawacki. Head to the first-floor chapel with Father Szach."

Having taken in a deep gulp of air, Professor Boraski exhaled slowly as he looked down again at his student roster. "Lopa Berkowicz, Helga and Paulina Lisewitz, Anastasia Rosinski, Irina Zalenski. Report to Professor Fishel in room twenty-six."

Tasa felt her face redden at the sound of her formal name. At nearly fourteen, she seemed to blush about a lot of things—all of which she could share with her closest friend, Irina. Tasa listened to the names of the last group, the Greek Catholic girls, called to join their designated religion class for fourth period.

Religion was also the only class that segregated students by their respective beliefs. She still felt a twinge of discomfort about being different, being Jewish at a Catholic school, but it came from what the outside world of Brody brought into her school, rather than from how the school actually operated. Just the day before at lunch, Ania Dudek, whose family owned one of the popular taverns in town, had told Tasa that her father was concerned that the proximity of the Hasidic synagogue to his pub was hurting business.

"Why does he think that?" Tasa had asked Ania.

"He said his customers can get pretty loud as the evening goes on, and he overheard some things." Ania took a bite of her cheese sandwich and washed it down with some milk before continuing. "Some men talk about how strangely the Hasids dress and how they speak in another language to each other and it makes them uncomfortable. And it seems they refer to all the Jews as one group." Ania's oval face seemed to take on a strained expression, and her voice grew in volume. "I mean, you're Jewish and you don't act like the Hasids."

Tasa knew Ania was trying to compliment her, but she still felt unnerved. Deep down, she knew there was something wrong with being exempted from a growing attitude in Brody about "the Jews" because of her lack of strict observance and assimilated physical appearance. Danik said he noticed the same thing in upper school. He and Tasa talked about how they were more at ease at school than they were walking the streets of Brody, where they'd begun to see and hear more intolerance. But inevitably some comment or tone or outright insult—directed mostly at the large number of observant Jews—would seep into the school's previously impenetrable walls.

"What does a Hasid *act* like?" Tasa had tried to contain her emotions, realizing Ania meant no harm. "I mean, they're regular

29

people—shopkeepers, tailors, parents. They're human beings with a certain attire that singles them out. That's not different from a monk's habit, is it?"

Ania was quiet at first, then nodded in agreement. "I know that. My words just came out all wrong. I'm sorry."

Lost in her thoughts, Tasa was now startled by a clanging noise and looked up to see Professor Boraski jiggling the wooden handle of the hand bell to alert the formal closure of third period.

$$\int \, \natural$$

Room 26 was not a typical classroom. It was spacious enough to hold Tasa's thirty middle-school peers for religion, as well as the seventy-five students from all lower and upper schools of both divisions who competed to gain entrance to Brody Catholic Orchestra, where Tasa played first violin. Orchestra students thought nothing of the giant chart of the Hebrew alphabet, whose layout reminded Tasa of the periodic table that Professor Boraski brought with him to science class when he taught the unit on chemistry.

"*Shalom*, Irina. *Shalom*, Tasa." Professor Joshua Fishel put out his hand and greeted each student at the door. His trim black beard, *kippa* fastened atop his head of short curls, and dark suit were in stark contrast to Professor Boraski's close-cropped blond hair, brown pants, white shirt, and bow tie. As the students took their seats, Professor Fishel walked to his desk and clasped his hand bell to get the girls' attention. He moved to the blackboard, picked up a piece of chalk, and wrote, "Leviticus 19:16–17," and next to that the words "judging your neighbor." He turned around and faced the class.

"The book of Leviticus in the Hebrew Bible contains codes of laws and directives that instruct people to judge one another fairly and with loving-kindness." Two girls in the back continued chattering, prompting Fishel to walk several steps forward and direct his gaze toward that part of the room. He cleared the gravel in his throat and continued. "This passage citation is particularly important because we are being judged by some and we may judge others in turn." Tasa sat up straighter in her seat and looked over to Irina, who returned a knowing smile. Tasa had told Irina about Ania's comment as the two walked into town with Danik after school yesterday.

Professor Fishel began reading the passage from a *Chumash* at his desk. "'Do not favor the poor or show deference to the rich; judge your neighbor fairly . . . You shall not hate your kinsman in your heart . . . Love your neighbor as yourself. I am the Lord.' Ladies, what does this passage say to you?" He closed the book of scriptures and walked around to the front of his desk. "Can you cite others from your readings that may further express the message being conveyed here?"

Lopa was the first to raise her hand. Like her friends, Tasa resented how Lopa seemed to talk down to them in class, like she knew more than they did. They all gossiped about Lopa behind her back. The girl shifted in her chair, adjusting her eyeglasses as Professor Fishel called on her. "Maimonides suggests all people are believed to have goodness inside them, and that one who judges is obliged to look for those good qualities."

Tasa knew she had been judging Lopa and felt guilty at that instant. She tried to consider the girl's positive traits.

"Lopa has offered an important aspect of what the Bible suggests as practical advice for everyday behavior. The Jewish philosopher Maimonides certainly expands our understanding. Anyone else?"

Tasa's hand shot up. "Hillel says not to judge your fellow human being until you've stood in his shoes."

Professor Fishel smiled at Tasa. "I'm glad you brought a rabbinic sage like Hillel to our attention, Tasa. As we think about judging one another, what about how we judge ourselves?"

She excitedly quoted directly from Hillel. "'If I am not for myself, who will be for me? And when I am for myself, what am I?' Does that say we must believe in ourselves but believe just the same in those around us?" Tasa suddenly thought about some of the Poles in town who she felt would judge Professor Fishel's wearing a *kippa* on his head. "What if those around us are wrong, Professor Fishel?"

After he walked closer to the left section of the room, where Tasa sat, the professor stroked his beard for several moments, seeming to be lost in thought. "Alongside the ancient scholars' interpretations exists an evolving wisdom that judgments are flawed and consequently must be carried out with care and empathy." He moved directly next to Tasa's desk. "This notion Tasa mentioned of refraining 'until you have reached that person's place' is a caution for all of us to take into account a person's situation as you evaluate his or her behavior."

Professor Fishel scanned the room. Most of the students paid close attention. Paulina Liesewitz hesitantly raised her hand. "Perhaps this is saying we should err toward the positive in judging others?"

"What about when people . . ." Lopa's voice was almost too soft to hear at first, and she paused to rephrase her question. "What about all the people who are judging us as Jews?"

The professor's face grew pensive, and the room took on an uncomfortable silence. He began pacing along the perimeter. A full minute passed before he stopped suddenly, as if an idea had popped into his head.

"Throughout history, people of various religious beliefs, if they are different from the majority, have been judged and sometimes persecuted, the Jewish people particularly. Let's not look at this personally for a minute and think about what causes this negative judgment."

Several students spoke at once.

"Being different can cause fear for those who don't understand certain practices," Paulina's cousin, Helga, suggested.

"If a person behaves differently than what one is used to, he might be judged badly," Irina said. "Especially if the group is a minority group."

Professor Fishel nodded. "Yes, many groups may be feared and mistrusted because of their different customs and religious beliefs. But also from their race or their economic situation. A farmer and a landowner may each judge the other in negative ways. So, what must we learn from this?"

Lopa raised her hand. "Doesn't this go back to scriptures and the

Leviticus passage? To love your neighbor as yourself, to 'do unto others' as you want others to treat you?" She looked over at Tasa and smiled. Tasa, feeling uncomfortably conflicted, smiled back weakly.

"Exactly. Which brings me to another group that has a history of persecution, the culture we know as gypsies. They call themselves Roma. The world has long regarded the Romani people with both curiosity and suspicion."

Professor Fishel strode to the front of the room and approached the chalkboard. "Their nomadic lifestyle has caused them always to be outsiders, belonging to no country, their origins shrouded in mystery. They have migrated to both Poland and Russia, where they have been more accepted, and actually . . ."

At that, the professor wrote out the Hebrew letters *kli*, followed by 'a useful or prepared instrument or tool,' and *zemer*, 'to make music'—*k'li zemer*. "This literally means 'vessels of song' or 'instruments of music.' 'Klezmer.' Our Jewish klezmer melodies have been most influenced by the culture and tradition of the Romani people, who have always been highly musical. So here we see the very positive side of a people that has been judged as undesirable, as we follow the rule of Leviticus." He put down the piece of chalk he was using, eying his words on the board.

Tasa knew klezmer music, so often played in Podkamien celebrations. Grampa Abram once took her to a wedding held at his synagogue, the smallest of the three in their village, where he was president. He wanted her to see the itinerant Jewish troubadours, known as *klezmorim*, perform, since the violin was typically their instrument of choice. She'd never seen such a joyful and expressive display of dance. It felt unpredictable to her—and exciting. First was the klezmer *doina*, a violin tune of free rhythm, with the performer stretching the notes to accommodate his mood and imagination. A wonderful circle dance called the hora followed, engaging the entire wedding party. The women and men gathered separately, each group holding hands, their feet rapidly stepping one over the other, two concentric circles forming, swirling in a fast-paced motion to the right, then abruptly shifting left. More circles. Faster. Around and around.

Professor Fishel's voice interrupted Tasa's daydream, as he was again standing very close to her seat. "This may be of greater interest to those of you in my orchestra class." An accomplished violinist himself, he also taught Music Performance and directed the well-regarded orchestra, choirs, and glee ensembles. "I've selected a famous piece for our concluding school recital that was inspired by gypsy music, Pablo de Sarasate's *Gypsy Airs*."

April 24, 1937

Dearest Grampa Abram,

I don't know how to begin to express what I felt when Frau Rothstein told me a package arrived from you today, on my exact birth date!! That you marked the outside "fragile" just added to the suspense, and I nearly fainted when I set my eyes on the precious Johann Kulik violin!! The workmanship and wood are extraordinary. I can't imagine what you must have gone through to get a violin of this quality, and from Prague. The tiny engraving shows it was made in 1869—nearly sixty years ago! This gift makes what I am about to tell you even more exciting. (And please share this letter with Mama and Papa.)

Brody Catholic Orchestra's public recital for the close of our school year will feature several wonderful pieces, among them Sarasate's Zigeunerweisen (Gypsy Airs). Professor Fishel held auditions for the solo violinist a few weeks ago, and I was selected, Grampa!!! I can hardly believe it! And now I will play this extraordinary instrument in my first solo public recital. I'm still pinching myself at my good fortune. And it is all because of you that I am at this point in my ability.

As you know more than anyone, this is a most challenging

composition. The improvisational quality of the mournful lento 4/4 section of Gypsy Airs is demanding, to say the least, like the flying spiccato where I have to bounce my bow lightly on the string to create those short, distinct notes. Frau Rothstein is working with me every free moment after dinner. Professor Fishel is also spending extra time every day after school for practice.

The fast pace at the end of this piece and its left-hand plucking are new to me. I certainly have much practice ahead to do justice to this virtuosic piece of music, but having an instrument of this caliber gives me much added confidence. I am determined to master this composition.

I'm so glad the recital comes during warmer weather so you can accompany Mama and Papa to Brody to hear me perform. I've missed you so much, Grampa, and I so look forward to our summer together in Podkamien.

Much love,

Tasa

∫ ♫

Tasa couldn't wait to play her new violin and could think of little else on her way to school the next day. As Danik chattered on about some bet he had with one of his friends, she was thinking through how she would play a particularly challenging section of harmonics in *Gypsy Airs*. She nearly bumped into Lopa in the hall on her way to homeroom.

"Oh . . . so sorry, I—" Jolted from her reverie, Tasa stopped midsentence when she came face-to-face with Lopa, eyeing the dark blue bruises around her left cheekbone and scratches along her chin. "Lopa, what happened to you?"

Lopa spoke in a low voice and avoided eye contact. "It . . . it's nothing."

"What do you mean, nothing? You look like you've been in a fight, Lopa." Tasa spoke more gently. She felt a surge of sympathy for the girl.

"You can't say anything. They said they'd hurt me worse if I told on them." Lopa's voice broke.

Tasa nodded. She knew Lopa was an easy target for some of the rougher boys at school. She'd seen them bully her during the lunch hour when the girls' and boys' divisions ate together. "Of course."

"Some of the older boys followed me after school yesterday. They just taunted me at first but started slapping at me when I ignored them. Like they wanted me to cry. Their beating didn't hurt as much as what they said to me."

"What did they say?" Tasa leaned forward to hear Lopa above the noisy hallway, now filling with students on their way to classes.

"They called me an ugly Jew girl." A single tear glided underneath Lopa's glasses and down her cheek. The clanging of hand bells could be heard from adjacent classrooms. Tasa squeezed Lopa's shoulder and took her hand, and the two hurried to homeroom.

$$\int \wr$$

Tasa remained quieter than usual during dinner that evening, mulling over the incident with Lopa, ashamed of her own superior behavior toward her classmate. She now saw herself as a target and realized that any of her Jewish friends could be similarly abused. She felt Frau's eyes on her and tried to appear as if all was normal, even though it wasn't.

"Let's play a duo this evening. I want to try out my new violin." Given the weather and time of year, Tasa suggested Beethoven's *Spring* Sonata.

"Wonderful choice!" Frau appeared relieved to resume their musical routine. "Beethoven's violin sonatas are among the first ever written that give the violin a voice equal to the piano's." After a quick dinner cleanup, the two took their places in the living room. As Tasa tuned her violin, Frau Rothstein opened her sheet music to the second of the piece's four movements: the adagio.

Tasa loved to learn as much as she could about the history of each piece of music, as well as anecdotes from the life of the composer, a curiosity that Abram had instilled in her when she was a young child. The more she understood—when the music was written, what the composer might have intended—the more she was able to put herself inside the melody and find her own voice in playing it. She loved the *Spring* Sonata's second movement because it was played *molto espressivo* and that directive encouraged even physical expression by the performer to convey the mood of the piece.

As she began playing, Tasa imagined a gentle bird flying up and around dense-leafed trees shading a peaceful orchard, the flowers bursting forth in full color, birds soaring together against a calm wind and brilliant sky, then retreating to their branches, calling to one another, settling finally at day's end.

This sonata was a musical dance between the violin and the piano. While she had some liberty in how loudly and softly she played the various sections and how she articulated the notes, the composition required not just perfect timing and tone between the two instruments, but a unity in styles.

"Frau, I don't know if this makes sense." Tasa lowered her bow. "But when we play this piece and approach the . . . I guess you might call it the symmetry—what I think was intended by Beethoven—I feel a sort of freedom unlike anything I've ever experienced."

Frau Rothstein smiled. "Tasa, your playing is at such a level, it's a gift you have. You're able to interpret and express what the composer created, a connection only the very best musicians make." She scooted the piano bench away from the keyboard and turned to face Tasa. "Your parents and grandfather will be very proud of your rapid progress when they hear your *Gypsy Airs* solo."

"I don't know what I'd do without my music, Frau." Tasa's mind suddenly filled with the jumble of her earlier conversation, mixed with a diffuse sense of fear and homesickness. "Sometimes I hear things that scare me, things that are directed more and more toward the Jews. Playing my violin helps me forget all that."

"What do you hear, child?" Frau furrowed her brows. "Has someone said something to hurt you?"

"Everyone treats me with much kindness." Tasa put her bow and violin aside and sat next to Frau. "But I see how Hasids are regarded. And I hear stories from my friends."

Frau took Tasa's hands in her own. Her mouth tightened as she spoke. "You're right about what you see. There's increasing pressure by Poland's political parties to pass laws restrictive against Polish Jews." Frau paused for a moment and locked eyes with Tasa. "Some of this has already happened with Polish professional organizations excluding Jews. But I don't think this kind of hatred can take hold throughout an entire country."

Tasa was about to reference other discriminatory practices, like the quotas for Jews in some universities, when she heard Danik in the foyer and the front door slamming behind him. She picked up her violin and bow to continue their practice but felt unsettled by the untimely ending to the conversation.

$$\int \wr$$

By late spring, rain dampened the soil and the grass grew a vibrant green. Time seemed to slow as daylight lingered and the end of the academic year approached. Tasa was finishing her second year of lower school and Danik his first of upper school, and both had prominent roles in the year-end recital: Danik was the baritone soloist in the boys' choir, and Tasa was the youngest of any of the performing musicians. The two had spent most late afternoons of the past six weeks together in rehearsals, along with girls and boys in both upper and lower schools. Danik began to introduce Tasa to more of his friends who also sang in choir, but mostly boys her own age, like Jakub Hirsch and Michail Wechsler. She'd already gotten to know Danik's best friend, Sidor Zalenski, Irina's older brother, who played cello in the orchestra.

One afternoon in late May, Tasa heard distant horse clips and, anticipating the arrival of her parents and grandfather, raced outside to Frau Rothstein's front steps. Papa sat on an elevated perch, a wide smile on his face while he concentrated on pulling in the reins. Tasa tugged the door open before the wagon came to a full stop. Her mother wore her trademark low bun and a casual cotton blouse and matching tapered trousers, her hair and attire impeccable despite their hours of travel. Overdressed in a dark suit, Grampa Abram took a handkerchief to wipe his brow as he slowly stepped from the carriage after her mother.

Mama was uncharacteristically tongue-tied, making a great fuss over Tasa's recent growth spurt. Papa jumped down from his post, and, it seemed, all three hugged her at once. After Danik and Frau Rothstein burst from the house, the greetings and hugs and excited talk all began to blur together. Within the hour, Aunt Ella and Uncle Judah arrived. Tasa felt a jubilance that she realized had been absent from her life in Brody.

Grampa Abram wanted to know all the details about her violin progress. Aunt Ella and Uncle Judah were flabbergasted at how much Danik had "filled out." Their excited chatter continued through the dinner feast Frau Rothstein prepared and well into the night.

The next morning, Tasa took great care in getting dressed for the concert. Professor Fishel asked that all performers wear white tops, with dark skirts for the girls and dark pants for the boys. She finished buttoning her favorite white blouse, its short, capped sleeves allowing her greater arm movement. As Tasa smoothed her long black skirt with her hands, her mother came into her room, a comb and brush in hand. Within a few minutes, she meticulously secured Tasa's thick black hair into a low bun.

"There! What do you think?" Mama held up a mirror. Tasa loved the effect, knowing she could never get her hair to look this way.

"Here, I want you to wear this." Her mother plucked a dainty pearl necklace from her pocket and fastened it around Tasa's neck. "This is a special occasion, after all." At that, she took out some rouge and faintly dabbed pink blush on Tasa's cheeks, then applied a pale blotting of red lipstick. Tasa hugged her mother in gratitude.

After Mama left, Tasa stood for several minutes, studying her image in the mirror—turning one way and another, smiling, bowing, pretending she was holding her violin, blotting the lipstick and noting its odd sensation—taking in this new reflection of herself. Interrupted by a knock on her bedroom door, she froze in place as Danik poked his head into her bedroom. He had on dark trousers, his white shirt untucked and not fully buttoned. He hadn't yet shaved and had reddish stubble on his face. Usually teasing and always talkative, he was now speechless.

"You look so . . . so pretty, Tasa," he finally stammered. "I wanted to wish you luck at the concert."

Her already-blushed cheeks reddened even further, and she felt a fluttering in the pit of her stomach.

The day was perfect—sunny, clear, not too hot. Tasa walked alone to school, ahead of the others. This was her first public recital, and she needed to prepare for it mentally. A few families strolled through the streets, admiring the bustle of commerce, enjoying the breeze and the array of scents that filled the air. Sunlight swarmed around the sturdy pillar-like trunks of blossoming linden trees, the sweet smell of lemon and honey overpowering even the enormous, wafting blooms of wisteria.

Later, she stood backstage with her violin, alone with her memory of the morning. The buzzing of conversation captured her attention as the performance hall began to fill. Trying to keep her mind off the approaching concert, she pictured the crowds of family and friends making their way through the Market Square, the Jewish quarter, and the church courtyards of Brody, and up the steps of the massive limestone school building. As they entered the spacious atrium shared by the girls' and boys' *gimnazjum* and *liceum* divisions of her school, they'd likely take notice of the white-and-crimson Polish flag flanking one side, the photograph of late Polish statesman Jozef Pilsudski at the other. Connected to the entryway, the school's performance auditorium was sizable, with its deep concert stage and seating for hundreds. Tasa could make out distinct voices of the audience in the front rows. She looked across the stage to watch her fellow orchestra members take their designated seats. Risers stood in front of the orchestra to allow a seamless transition from the instrumental to the vocal performances.

She was so lost in thought that Professor Fishel's hand on her forearm startled her. "Are you ready, Tasa?" Wearing a black tuxedo with tails, the *kippa* firmly atop his head, he smiled down at her and squeezed her arm. "I don't need to offer good luck to you, young lady. You have truly mastered this difficult composition." At that, he walked out to the center of the stage.

"Welcome friends and family of Brody Catholic Academy to our highly anticipated year-end school recital! My name is Joshua Fishel and I direct the school's music groups." He paused, as the performance auditorium settled into a quiet, broken only by an occasional cough. "The students have been practicing all spring, and we have quite a treat in store for you. Our orchestra will first play *Zigeunerweisen*, Opus 20, best known as *Gypsy Airs*. The piece was written in 1878 by the Spanish composer and virtuoso Pablo de Sarasate and premiered the same year in Leipzig."

Professor Fishel turned his head slightly toward Tasa as he continued. "It is now my distinct pleasure to introduce a fourteen-year-old with the musical gifts of one much older. She's a brilliant violinist with a promising future, and, to quote those who know her best, 'a little girl with a big voice.' Please welcome Anastasia Rosinski!" Fishel turned to face Tasa as she walked to center stage. She acknowledged his approving wink as she stepped to her designated position for the performance, keenly aware of the audience's eyes on her.

Hearing the applause and seeing the large crowd at first made her self-conscious, aware of how panic could seize her, how a single mistake could interrupt the dream of her playing. She drew a deep breath and focused on adjusting the pegs of her violin, sounding several notes out with her bow. Satisfied, she looked to Professor Fishel, now her conductor, who raised his rosewood baton and, with a downward stroke, signaled the orchestra to begin the imposing introduction of *Gypsy Airs*, with its slow, majestic energy that built steadily to Tasa's cue. She put her violin to her chin and raised her bow up, elbow high, placing it against the strings. Closing her eyes for a moment, she made her dramatic entrance, the echoing of the orchestra's mournful passage.

She moved along the span of the fingerboard, from the deepest valleys to the highest pitch like a single bird in song, a quick pluck of her strings, then plunging downward again. Her brisk fingering, plucking, bowing, and articulation, the pulsating rhythm, vibrato trill, and force of the double stops, transported her to a Podkamien wedding at the center of a spirited dancing circle. She felt the wild freedom of gypsies dancing, of the *klezmorim* playing their violins. The emotional range of the music oscillated like a seesaw, from longing to laughter, yearning to teasing, singing to crying and back to singing again, the orchestra answering each rousing emotion. She felt a thin trickle of sweat, dripping slowly along her neck during the rapid-fire culminating section, *allegro molto vivace*. She could imagine the gypsies in their colorful garb dancing faster and faster, almost spiraling out of control until the orchestra's final chord.

As she slowed her breathing, Tasa felt herself letting go, as if alone in an open space, rays of luminous light crossing in front of her. The audience's deafening applause shocked her back to the present. Surrounding her was a crowd, clapping wildly, in her school's auditorium. She saw her proud parents and grandfather. She turned to make contact with Professor Fishel, who was beaming, saw her fellow orchestra members joining the applause. She told herself to bow, to smile. It was as though she'd just awakened.

Instinctively, she turned toward the far side of the stage. Still behind the curtain but in her full view was Danik, about to perform his solo with the boys' choir. Their eyes expressed to each other an understanding of this moment—her personal triumph and his to come—but also something more, something much larger than either one of them.

Denial
June 1938

The sun baked throughout the early afternoon while Tasa attempted to lounge in the orchard. The air was motionless except for an occasional breeze that fluttered across her face. Trying to cool off, she had just taken her second bath of the day, then slipped into a light yellow summer dress. Her hair, still damp, was in a ponytail as black and shiny as the feathers of the two sparrows she admired from her resting spot. Perched on the low red brick wall enclosing the orchard, the birds were glistening in the sun from their dips in the small pond Papa had dug in the far corner of the orchard, adjacent to the squared-off formal garden where Mama planted purple geraniums and red poppies.

Tasa felt the sun's rays on her face and bare arms and legs. She closed her eyes, her mind traveling back to Brody and her stirring duet performance with Sidor at her second school recital. The singing of birds and fluttering whir of insects blurred into their two musical voices joining as one: her violin's melodic wandering and guiding, his cello steady, the lower notes echoing and following her precise fingering as she climbed upward in pitch until her final note died away.

She nearly jumped from the chaise as two large, clammy hands covered her eyes like a blindfold. She grabbed the wrists of her intruder, only to find Danik standing above her, blocking the sun.

"You're such a troublemaker, Danik! Couldn't you see I was sleeping?"

Tasa couldn't keep from smiling. Danik seemed pleased with himself, chuckling as Tasa concluded, "Some things never change. Remember all the tricks you played on me when we were little?"

"Yes, but you were always beating back, Tasa."

"Really? What about all the times you held on to my braid until I cried or you tackled me?" She remembered their play as if it had happened yesterday. "I had bruises to show for it!"

"You had more bruises falling off Cairo than anything I did." Danik began rolling up his shirtsleeves. Tasa noticed his muscular forearms and became suddenly self-conscious, quickly looking away as Danik continued. "But if you want to drum up the past, I seem to recall your fingernails digging into my hand, the twisting of my ears, and a few bites you shamelessly took to my leg."

It had been just two weeks since the two had returned from Brody. While missing Frau Rothstein and her friends, Tasa was happy to be back in Podkamien, jesting with Danik. Her feelings for him altered somehow, leaving her often flustered by his presence.

"Is sleeping going to occupy all your time now that school is out?" Danik pulled over the nearby lounge chair and eased himself into it.

"Look who's talking—you're the one who didn't wake up most weekends before noon. And I can see *you're* being highly productive right now." Tasa sat up, taking in the sweeping view from the orchard, before she wiped away beads of sweat from her forehead. "Seriously, aren't you tired from this heat? The air's so damp it's hard to breathe."

"I know. I don't have much energy for much of anything today." Danik stifled a yawn. "I was going to practice some vocal exercises Professor Fishel wants me to master over the summer, but I didn't have it in me."

"What songs does he have you working on?" Danik's role in the Brody Catholic boys' choir had become more prominent since his first solo performance in the school's recital. He had a commanding presence and expressiveness in his delivery. In the past year, his voice had matured into a rich, warm-textured baritone with a wide range that almost reached into a high, lyrical tenor. Frau Rothstein had found music that included piano, violin, and baritone vocalist, and they all practiced together.

"Schubert's *Die Schöne Müllerin*. Its twenty songs are based on the poems of Wilhelm Müller that my humanities class was studying." Danik slapped a fly that hovered over his knee. "I left a set of piano music with Frau so we could work on them when we go back in August."

"I can't believe next year will be your last year of high school." Tasa tried to keep the gloominess she felt out of her voice. "But my friends and I will finally be in upper school, so it won't be so embarrassing for you, Sidor, and your other friends to spend time with us, right?" Conveniently, Irina and her brother were, respectively, best friends with Tasa and Danik, and the foursome often joined up after school to get pastries in Brody's Market Square. Tasa thought Irina had a crush on Danik, and it bothered her.

"You're already flirting with all of my friends, Tasa," Danik teased. "You're not very subtle."

"You don't know what you're talking about!" Tasa suddenly remembered the dream she'd been having when Danik had abruptly woken her. It was Kodály's Duo for Violin and Cello, which she had practiced every day the month before with Sidor, until they'd gotten it perfect. "I don't have *that* kind of interest in your friends, Danik."

They chattered on in this way, the tone light and bantering, yet the thought of being separated from Danik, even though it was still a year away, stirred an emptiness inside her that she couldn't shake off. But here they were, after all, together and back in Podkamien. And while the day was stifling hot, she was living amid the countryside in the new dream home that Papa had built on their property with the help of Josef Gnyp. The entire family was expected to be together in just a couple of hours, including Danik's brother, who was visiting from Palestine.

The Rosinskis' new house was two stories and spacious. The red brick was dusted with a light coat of white paint that gave it a rosy hue. White shutters adorned the front windows, all opened during this unseasonable hot spell. Mama got her new, modernized kitchen and full dining room. Since their house was now fifty yards north of where the old one had stood, closer to the lake, the space between the house and the barn and stables opened up, offering an expansive panorama of the land and its surroundings. Papa had positioned the house on the property so there was a beautiful view to admire from literally every window.

Aunt Sascha and Uncle Jakov arrived first with Tolek who was now eight. Tasa held back a grin as she observed how high the boy pulled up his shorts and socks, making his growing legs look rangy. Aunt Sophia and Uncle Ehud arrived moments later with Dalila and Mela. Both girls had red hair like paprika and pale, freckled skin. Dalila was already taller than Tolek, even though she was a full year younger. Mela's eyes were large for a two-year-old, and dark, and they glistened each time she smiled. The Rosinskis' housemaid, Julia, gathered the children and found some games to occupy them while Tasa and her mother took Sascha and Sophia on a tour around the new house. The living room was more like an intimate den, covered in wood panels, with book-filled shelves and family photographs dispersed among several highly polished walnut side tables. Several cushioned arm-chairs in tan, a love seat, and a full-size sofa were arranged atop a large brown-and-gold Oriental rug. An upright piano stood in the corner.

Her mother led Tasa's two aunts upstairs. Tasa followed close behind, running her hand along the curved and smooth mahogany stair railing on their way to the four bedrooms, each anointed with varnished rosewood dressers and all looking out over the back fields. Pausing to gaze out each window, she admired the rows of linden trees Josef had recently planted. Just beyond, she watched Cairo, lazy in his movements, stretching his neck to the ground, taking in mouthfuls of sweet grass, the sun beating on his black, silky coat. Small, white-tiled bathrooms adjoined two of the bedrooms, with a third, larger bathroom at the other end of the hallway, each one with brass-footed tubs and toilets operated by a pull chain mounted from above.

"This is really quite grand, Halina. Salomon didn't miss a detail." Tasa thought she detected an odd tone in Aunt Sascha's words, then a look between Sascha and Aunt Sophia. "Jakov's medical practice doesn't seem to offer us much savings."

Over the chatter, Tasa recognized a particular voice from downstairs. She excused herself and raced down the steps.

"Albert! I can't believe it's you." Her oldest cousin stood on the porch with his parents and Danik. Tasa had seen Aunt Ella and Uncle Judah on her second day home, but Albert had arrived only yesterday, his first time back to Poland and their village in a full year. When she was a young child, he could get her to blush crimson by announcing she'd grow into a beautiful woman some day. Papa always said Albert was very smart and someday would take care of all of them. Albert affectionately pinched Tasa's cheek and then gave her a big hug, picking her up off the ground. Even at fifteen, she was barely five feet tall.

"You and Danik now resemble each other more than ever, except for this." She put her hand against Albert's close-cropped beard. Tasa thought it made him look older than his twenty-three years, or maybe just more distinguished. Albert was broad-shouldered and tall, like Danik, with a light complexion and reddish-brown hair, but she thought Danik the more handsome. "So, you still live with Aunt Roza, right? When do you finish your studies?"

"Soon, dear Tasa. Less than a year. Maybe then I can have a place of my own and start my own family." Albert eyed an adjacent chair and slid into it, motioning Tasa to sit. "I've missed you, little one, but I keep up with all you are doing through Danik and my parents."

Ella and Judah looked on, smiles on their faces, while her father brought several chairs out to the porch. Her mother, back downstairs by now, brought out a tray with fresh lemonade. Aunt Norah and Uncle Levi, married just two years, arrived with Grampa Abram. She gave her aunt and uncle a kiss, then circled her arms around her grandfather's waist.

Despite how late it was in the day, the heat was unrelenting. Mama began pouring the lemonade and passing glasses around, wiping her hands on her apron before she sat next to Papa. Tasa watched her father take a cloth from the back pocket of his trousers to wipe his brow. Uncle Judah's suspenders pressed his white shirt, damp with sweat, against his chest. The ceiling fan kept circulating hot air, its din muting the squeals of the smaller children playing with Julia in the orchard.

"So I hear we have true musicians in the family." Albert, his hands in his pockets, looked cooler than most in his seersucker trousers and short-sleeved linen shirt. Tasa blushed and Danik grinned. "Could we have a performance if the evening cools down?"

Ella spoke first. "Your brother has surprised all of us with his vocal talent, Albert. I'm sure Tasa has been an influence. Right, Tasa?"

"Danik has his own ability, Aunt Ella, and he's worked hard to further his gifts." Tasa gazed briefly toward Danik, then looked back at her aunt. "There's so much wonderful culture in Brody, and our school has a fine reputation in music performance. Along with Frau Rothstein as a music teacher, we're fortunate."

"Yes, you are fortunate in many ways, my dear," Uncle Judah agreed. "Your loving parents, your father's hard work, this fine house and landscape—"

"Dear Uncle," Albert spoke up, directing his comments to Salomon. "I don't want to diminish the glory of what you have built here, but why are you deepening your roots in Podkamien—in Poland, for that matter?" Albert was close with her father and always candid and sincere in his conversations with him, as he was with everyone in the family. But Tasa saw Aunt Ella give Albert a look. Then her aunt glanced over at her and Danik.

Her mother turned to Papa and murmured something in his ear. Papa slightly shook his head no and leaned forward in his chair. "What are you saying, Albert?"

Tasa felt the gravity of the conversation begin to take hold. She looked over at Danik and could see he was sitting on the edge of his seat and likely shared her surprise that the adults were about to carry on a political discussion in their company.

"With all due respect to you, Uncle, and to everyone here, I must be frank. And I apologize in advance if what I am going to say makes anyone uncomfortable." Albert took a gulp of his lemonade before continuing. "You live amid the countryside, the lushness of the land, the serenity of summer nights, Uncle Salomon. I fear you've become out of touch with the growing conflict of the world around us.

"When Hitler was named chancellor of Germany five years ago, we had no idea the power he was amassing, the control he would assert, and how his twisted views and anti-Semitism would spread—"

Her mother interrupted Albert. "I'm not sure this is a conversation we ought to be having with the children." She looked over to Grampa Abram, his nod barely noticeable but his eyes expressing agreement.

Tasa winced. "Mama, we're not children! And if you think that Danik and I are oblivious to what Albert is saying, then you, too, are out of touch." Immediately realizing she had been disrespectful, she felt her face reddening. "I don't mean to be rude, Mama—but we have witnessed much while in Brody, and you need to know that."

Her mother glared at her, then quickly looked away.

Tasa wouldn't be quieted. "Mama, just in walking from Frau Rothstein's to our school, we've seen how Jews, particularly Jews who wear their religion in their appearance, even a simple *kippa*, are being judged and marginalized." She looked over at Danik, nodding for him to continue.

"We know about Germany's Nuremburg Laws and our own variations of them right here in Poland." Danik looked over at his older brother. "Take Professor Fishel, our music and Jewish religion teacher. He's obviously Jewish, and he can't teach in Polish public schools. Albert, you're still in touch with Marten Rothstein, aren't you? He must have shared that with you."

At this point, Jakov and Judah began to speak at once, Jakov blurting out, "Jewish doctors and lawyers are banned from Polish professional organizations and have been for at least two or three years."

"And while that is discriminatory and humiliating to us as professionals," Judah added, "Jews and open-minded Poles still frequent our practices." He turned to Jakov. "Has it hurt the number of patients you see?"

Albert spoke again, but more emphatically. "This is not about business being diminished, Papa. This is much graver than that."

He put his glass down and leaned forward in his chair. "The annexation of Austria into the German Third Reich just three months ago is a clarion call for what lies ahead. The Anschluss might literally mean unification, and Hitler may portray himself as a liberator, rather than a tyrant, but that's a facade. Evil exists in the world, and Hitler is the embodiment of evil. What's happening is all around you. You may choose to deny it. But there will be another war. And Poland will be caught in the middle, without power, as it always has been."

The silence that followed was as stifling as the oppressive heat. It was clear to Tasa that Albert was willing to spoil the mood of the get-together in order to inject a dose of reality into their family's thinking. She didn't want this conversation to be cut short before she understood more of what her enlightened and worldly cousin knew.

"How is it that you know so much and yet you are so far away in Palestine, Albert?"

"I study with people from all over Eastern Europe, Tasa. A girl I'm very friendly with is from Berlin. While much information is censored in the press, Bernice still receives letters from her parents. They live in fear. They talk about decrees being set by National Socialists systematically forcing Jews out of daily life, robbing them of their basic rights. Just recently, a decree was passed forbidding Aryan and Jewish children to play together. Jews have designated benches in public parks where they can sit; Jewish doctors are no longer allowed to practice medicine, which is clearly more severe than the lesser laws our Polish government is currently ordering."

Albert was talking rapidly now. "Don't think these atrocities won't happen here. Bernice said her family was skeptical when the initial decrees came out, shortly after Hitler took over Germany. But more and more restrictions kept being added. Now the Jews can shop only in groceries at designated times. They're forbidden to convert. And all film centers, opera houses, and theaters are marked *verboten* to them." The full weight of Albert's words, and his certainty of tone, cast a pall over the room. Tasa wanted to disagree with him, although she knew what he said was far from folly.

Her father sat forward, locking eyes with Albert. "How can this be true? Why wouldn't we hear of all this, read of this in the newspapers?"

"Papa, Podkamien is isolated. And everyone knows and likes one another. The Jews and non-Jews have lived together for a long while. I remember Mama telling me everyone called you the unofficial town mayor after you brought electricity to Podkamien. It's just so peaceful here." Tasa's words had no sooner left her mouth than she grasped their truth. She felt suddenly light-headed.

Albert broke in. "Uncle, it's difficult for the reality in Germany and Austria to filter outside, especially to the remote rural villages of Poland. Hitler is exerting tight control of the Nazi propaganda machine, and news gets out only in bits and pieces." Albert sat back, looking suddenly exhausted.

Tasa's mother spoke up softly, but her words hung heavy. "I heard from Salomon's brother, Walter. He says the US Congress seems immovable on raising the quota on immigrants. So, as people may want to leave Germany and Austria, it's becoming harder to get into America."

Levi, who had remained quiet up to this point, leaned forward in his chair. "You know of this new 'citizenship law' in Poland? It was passed about the same time as the Anschluss took place. Later this year, the passports of Polish citizens who have lived abroad for more than five years will be revoked if those citizens haven't maintained contact here. This affects you, Albert, and I also think this is a way for Poland to rid itself of the tens of thousands of Polish Jews residing elsewhere, particularly in Germany."

Levi edged back into his seat. "I do believe Poland is acting broadly to reduce the number of Jews here. So I take what you say, Albert, and see a need to act. I've already talked quietly to some people about finding a way to emigrate to the United States—perhaps by way of Romania—before it's too late."

Tasa looked over to her parents, her mother tightly clasping her hands on her lap, her father shaking his head in what seemed stubborn denial. "Papa, what will become of us if there's another war?"

Her father again wiped his brow and took in a deep breath, which he calmly and slowly exhaled. "I think there are certainly issues with which we must be concerned and, as Jews, must be vigilant in learning more about. But I see our talk is nearing panic. What is being discussed is very far from our experiences here in Podkamien. I don't believe we are under immediate threat or that war is imminent. Albert, you're a smart young man and I don't take your words lightly, nor should any of us. But let us all take a bit of a break from this difficult and worrisome conversation. I, for one, am both tense and hungry. Let's go inside and have dinner, shall we?"

At that, her father stood up, opened the door into the house, and motioned to her mother, who began gathering the empty glasses onto a tray. Aunt Ella helped her, and Aunt Norah followed them into the house. Aunt Sascha and Aunt Sophia walked around to the orchard to check on Tolek, Dalila, and Mela.

The rest of the family moved quietly into the house. Inside it was bright, despite the near onset of evening, the sun banking low into the distant clouds. The windows were open, and with the outside heat came the shrill of cicadas. Salomon began pouring red wine, and Halina served various Polish cheeses, passing black bread around the table where Tasa sat among twelve adults and three children.

As her mother turned the radio on to some light mazurkas, Tasa heard what she thought was the hum of planes flying overhead in the distance.

Kristallnacht
November 1938

Happily distracted by the melody thrumming from the radio, Tasa had barely touched her bowl of buckwheat porridge. She mindlessly buttered the piece of warm rye bread Frau set on her plate. Danik poked her arm with a platter of Polish cheeses—*bundz, golka,* a mound of pot cheese, *oscypek*—but instead of helping herself to the food, she stared at her plate, lost in a musical reverie.

"Have you lost your appetite, child?" Frau brought the pot full of *kasza gryczana* to the table and began refilling Danik's empty bowl. "You need to nourish yourself like Danik does."

And now a piece by Spanish composer Pablo de Sarasate . . .

"Danik, Frau, listen!"

As the first notes of *Gypsy Airs* filled the room, Tasa was transported back to the concert hall and her own performance less than two years earlier. She absorbed the familiar refrain, while majestic images filled her head like a dream and she felt her mood drifting with the music. Its melancholy and gaiety. The teasing and laughter and dancing. The thrill. And hope. She closed her eyes and let the song take her.

Tasa's trance was broken by a crackling noise from the small receiver—carrying her back to her girlhood, when the radio first entered her tranquil rural life. The electric mill her father built—and the electricity it produced—powered everything from their wells to lamps and iceboxes and led to remarkable changes. Longer days as light extended into the night, water that tasted better, fresher food. But, of all these miracles, it was the radio that enthralled her the most, connecting her to mesmerizing music and mysterious voices and news from places outside Podkamien. In her insular child's view, the one-foot-square wooden box seemed to have almost magical powers.

That magic had a dark side sometimes. The brusque and ominous words now echoing from the speaker invaded the peaceful kitchen, the music dissipating into bursts of phrases that landed like a series of smacks.

Savage nightlong attacks . . . Nazi storm troopers and German civilians burning and looting . . . thousands of Jewish-owned businesses . . . hundreds of synagogues.

Tasa reached for Danik's hand, clasped her fingers tightly around his. Frau Rothstein stood behind them both, pressing against their shoulders as the three listened. The commentator said the attacks were planned and coordinated and directed at Jews. Throughout Germany and parts of Austria, German authorities watched the brutality but didn't intervene. The streets were left littered with shards from the windows of all the homes and schools and hospitals and stores that were ransacked. So much broken glass, they were calling it Kristallnacht.

Indignation seemed to seize the reporter, his voice shrill, his cadence projecting panic.

Mob law ruled in Berlin throughout the afternoon and evening as hordes of hooligans indulged in an orgy of destruction. I have seen several anti-Jewish outbreaks in Germany during the last five years, but never anything as nauseating as this. Racial hatred and hysteria seemed to have taken complete hold of otherwise decent people. I saw fashionably dressed women clapping their hands and screaming with glee, while respectable middle-class mothers held up their babies to see the fun.

By this time, Frau had slid into the empty kitchen chair. The three sat in a stupor. How could these atrocities have happened? Tasa tried to make sense of this terrifying reality, flinching at the shocking details. Synagogues, along with thousands of prayer halls and schools, had been set on fire at precisely the same time, and fire brigades and police all over Germany were not allowed to leave their quarters unless an express command to that effect had been given. As she listened, Tasa could almost hear the crashing of overturned furniture, the breaking of glass, and the trampling of heavy boots as drunken mobs forced their way into homes.

Make this stop, Tasa wanted to tell Frau, but her voice was as irretrievable as the life they had known just minutes earlier. Frau must have felt the same terror. She switched off the radio.

A few weeks after Kristallnacht, Tasa and Danik arrived back from school to find Frau staring into an American newspaper article.

"What is this?" Tasa could see only the *New York Times* masthead and the bold headline: "Nazis Smash, Loot and Burn Jewish Shops and Temples Until Goebbels Calls a Halt."

"Your father sent this. He received it from your uncle Walter. Thank God this brutality is being reported in America." Frau folded and unfolded the article as she spoke, her voice unnaturally high-pitched.

Tasa stroked Frau's arm, calming herself as she recalled the shattering episode she had shoved to the back of her mind, retrieving the truth of it once again. Frau offered Tasa the article, and, for that moment, Tasa regretted having chosen English last year for her language elective.

The words began to blur on the page as if her mind refused to take them in. She sucked in a deep breath and squeezed her eyes shut, trying to bring forth some kind of stoicism so she could read the information without feeling its emotional toll.

"It says the assaults were made on 'defenseless and innocent people.'

Calls them 'repugnant' and a 'disgrace' to Germany." Tasa began to translate parts of the article for Danik. She told him that all twenty-one synagogues in Vienna were attacked, that fires and bombs destroyed most of them.

Danik remained silent. His face expressed a seething anger. Of course he was enraged. They all were. But she couldn't stop reading. "Jews were severely beaten. Furniture and goods were flung from homes and stores—"

"I don't want to hear any more. I can't." Danik turned away.

"Children, this is good news. Don't you see?" Frau's face relaxed as she spoke. She paused and nodded as if to herself. "The world won't stand for this. It's just a matter of time before Poland's own government will *have* to distance itself from Nazi brutalities."

Except for the evergreens, all the trees had shed their leaves and the hours of daylight continued to shrink. Snow dusted the roads and fields. By the time they finished their dinner and washed the last of the dishes, it seemed late, although it was only half past six. Tasa, Frau, and Danik moved to the living room for tea and pastry. It was an evening routine Tasa savored—dessert and laughter and music.

Frau suggested they play a duo for violin and piano from Smetana's symphonic poems, *From My Homeland*. Danik eased back into the couch. Tasa smiled at him coyly as she stood several steps behind Frau, whose hands were already poised on the keyboard of her Bösendorfer. Frau nodded as she began the piece's distinct opening notes. Tasa gently stretched her neck side to side as she listened to Frau's introduction, signaling her cue. Closing her eyes, she brought the butt of her instrument up toward her chin, resting the lower back of it on her collarbone, and began drawing her bow across the strings.

The tempo was fast at first, the notes high, and she drew long strokes. The song grew softer, then sped up, became lusty, then hushed and peaceful. The Czech composer used music to paint the landscapes of his native land. Tasa inhabited the melody's delicate and pastoral scene, that countryside she could see from her attic window as a child. She could feel the summer heat even now as she played, could hear the early-dawn crowing of roosters and, later, the shrill of cicadas filling the evening quiet as the moon and stars glowed above. She felt herself back in the fields around her house with Danik, chasing the intermittent glow of fireflies, cupping them in her hand, only to see another flash above her head, dancing and circling and illuminating the pitch-black background. She swayed and dipped, fingering and plucking the strings, lost in Smetana's world, gliding her hand along the fingerboard, until the rapid finale ended with Danik's hearty "Bravo!" and applause.

In bed that evening, Tasa remained in the vivid countryside of her rural village, her mind filled with memories. Of Shabbos dinners with aunts and uncles and cousins, their plentiful meals of mushroom-filled pierogi, boiled chicken, and steamed cabbage that left her stomach aching. Of the stories her father would read to her to lull her to sleep—far-fetched adventures of a goat searching for his home.

A foggy image emerged that she couldn't place. The image of a plate with a painted rooster at the center—the rooster's proud stance, red crest, and arced tail. The sound of crowing at this late hour.

They Shall Have Music
August 1939

The horses plodded forward sluggishly in the noon heat. Danik pulled left on the reins, then tightened his grip, directing the pair to the side of the jagged road as he eased the wagon to a halt. "Let's stop here, give them water and eat our sandwiches." He jumped down from the carriage and held his hand out to Tasa.

It was a bittersweet journey, so different from the first trip to Brody that she and Danik had made together with her father four years earlier. Everything about this jaunt seemed more like an ending than a beginning. When Tasa looked ahead, all she could see were goodbyes. Danik had come with her to visit with Frau Rothstein and several others in Brody before he would go alone to Lwow and his university studies, some ninety kilometers to the southwest. So they had made plans to leave Podkamien on this first day of August, eager to enjoy each other's company for several more weeks before they, too, would part ways. Now eighteen, Danik was given permission to drive the carriage and keep it in Lwow.

Tasa tried to mask her sense of hollowness and wondered if Danik shared similar feelings. She could deal with the separation from her parents, her grandfather, her village, and all that was most familiar to her during her years in Brody, because Danik was ever-present— at Frau Rothstein's, at school, and during their joint music lessons. This transition to a life in Brody without Danik was something she'd fretted over in solitude through much of the summer, feeding her apprehension of loss as she obsessively played the slow, lyrical passages of Tchaikovsky's *Sérénade Mélancolique*.

"It's so peaceful out here. We seem to have this road to ourselves every time we travel back and forth." As she took Danik's hand, she again thought back to that first excursion from Podkamien to Brody, recalling another set of emotions, that of her first separation from her family and village, and how her fear had kept her from noticing the beauty around her. Now, she observed the lushness of the land as she scanned the seemingly endless and dense fields of sugar beets, their rosettes of leaves spreading upward. She could barely make out the outline of a lone farmer in the distance, distracted by the whinny of the horses as Danik set out their water.

"I suppose we should enjoy the quiet now because Brody is always abuzz with activity. I'm going to miss it."

Still standing beside the carriage, Tasa studied Danik's face. This was the first hint of such feelings he'd given. "What will you miss most?"

"Everything. I've gotten so comfortable in Brody. I love Frau. Brody Catholic has been great—my friends, the teachers, Professor Fishel especially. And, of course, I'll miss not having you around to annoy." Wearing his usual sly grin, Danik eased himself onto the platform at the rear of the carriage. As he unwrapped his sandwich, she found herself at eye level with him, despite their height difference. He locked eyes with her for a moment. "You know I'll miss you, Tasa."

Feeling her face redden, Tasa avoided eye contact as she spoke. "When you graduated last May, I was so happy for you, so proud of all your accomplishments." She offered a limp smile and looked away. "But I can't help feeling sad right now. Left behind, I guess."

Lost. That would have been closer to the truth of it. Missing loved ones was a familiar companion that went back almost as far as she could remember—what with Gramma Ruth's death, Albert leaving for college, Aunt Roza moving to Palestine, Aunt Norah and Levi departing a year ago for Romania in hopes of getting to America. And now Tasa anticipated the separation from Danik, her steadiest companion.

Her homesick pangs had never lessened. She told herself she was fortunate, coming from a rural town where most children ended their education by seventh grade because their families were unable to afford the outlying secondary schools. But that didn't keep her from yearning for a time that seemed long ago, when everyone was together in Podkamien. It was why she held on to the family photograph she had found years earlier. The picture asserted her roots. Just like the window of her attic revealed her world and everyone in it—all of her relatives, the open land around her, her little village and its close-knit feel. It was solid, familiar, secure. It was home.

"Do you miss the way it was when we were little, Danik, when the whole family was still in the village? When all we had to do was drum up games in the orchard or get into trouble on our way to school?" She looked at her cousin, trying to read his thoughts.

"I think about it . . . I do. But Brody's been good for us. And our summers have been full yet undemanding. Look how much fun we've had swimming in the lake near the Gnyps."

Tasa smiled, genuinely this time. Mr. Gnyp lived just ten kilometers west of Podkamien where Papa owned several mills and where he had first met his longtime handyman. She and Danik had visited Josef and Jaga Gnyp every weekend, lunching picnic-style with them and their young daughter, Stefania. They'd romp around with Theo, the Gnyps' Polish lowland sheepdog, before grabbing their swimwear and cooling off in the lake. Tasa was a hesitant swimmer, but Danik largely ignored her fear of deep water, taking pleasure in dunking her head below the surface at every opportunity. "Fight your fear," he'd say to her, as her splashing led to continued taunts, ending only when she'd swallowed large gulps of water and was consumed by coughing fits. Still, she did have Danik to thank for what little confidence she had gained as a swimmer.

"And I've had great times with my parents." Danik ate the last bite of his sandwich and bunched the paper into a ball. "Papa has shared a lot about his legal work with me lately. He's been back and forth to Lwow since last spring. Defending a college student arrested for publicly protesting the hiring of a humanities professor at the university."

Danik stopped for a moment, as though realizing he might have been going into too much detail and losing her interest. Tasa nodded him on. "I guess the professor was a full-fledged communist who shared his views openly in class. So the student began holding anti-communist rallies that drew a lot of attention. He was detained without a warrant from a legal authority, not to mention the violation of his right to freely express himself."

"Do you want to study law, like your father?"

"I think his work is interesting." Danik jumped down from the carriage footboard and began readying the horses for the final leg of their journey. "By the way, Papa spent one night in Lwow when Aunt Sascha and Uncle Janek were visiting a close friend of theirs last month. The friend is who I'll board with in Lwow, sort of like Frau Rothstein."

The two traveled in comfortable silence for much of the rest of their trip. Tasa took in the last few stretches of open land and fertile fields. Upon their arrival in Brody, Tasa felt a general tension in the air, palpable like the heat. The escalating commotion and noise level as they approached the city were a stark contrast with the quiet and insular atmosphere they had left in Podkamien.

As Danik maneuvered the horse and carriage into the wagon yard, Tasa's attention was drawn to shouts from the Market Square. The two quickly dismounted, Danik hurriedly securing the carriage to a post. Tasa followed Danik's clipped steps toward the perimeter shops, where a crowd was forming. There, in plain view, several young Polish thugs were roughing up a Jewish tradesman. The Hasid's tall black hat and long jacket had been trampled on the ground, his shirt torn.

Tasa held on to Danik's arm as she felt him begin to push forward. "You can't get in the middle of this, Danik! You'll get hurt!"

Several older shopkeepers pulled the assailants away just as a Polish police officer lackadaisically entered the circle to break up the cluster of onlookers. Tasa urged Danik to the other side of the market, passing the open-air stalls where the peddling of hats and clothes was a daily ritual. Several other hoodlums were bullying Polish peasants, preventing them from approaching kiosks owned by Jewish peddlers.

Tasa held Danik's arm firmly, using the force of her entire body to steer him across the square as quickly as she could toward Frau Rothstein's house, feeling his resistance as he kept looking back. Her heart was pounding.

♪ ♩

Frau Rothstein had prepared a scrumptious dinner for their arrival. As a special treat, she invited Marten and his wife, Sonya, and Joshua Fishel to join them. Still wearing her cooking smock, she brought a large platter of brisket into the dining room.

"*Matka*, come sit down; we have a feast here." Marten rose halfway from his seat, pulling out the chair next to him for his mother. Frau quickly slipped the black bib garment over her head and hung it behind the kitchen door before taking her place at the head of the table.

"Well, well!" Frau took a deep breath, then smiled broadly. Her brown eyes sparkled. "Most of my children are here now, and that makes me very happy. I want to hear everything you all have been up to these last few months." The tension from the afternoon began to melt away. Tasa loved that she and Danik were considered family and knew Frau missed her younger son, Moses, who'd stayed in Krakow after finishing university studies there five years earlier.

"I'm sure Mother also wants to make sure the two of you practiced your music during your summer away." With his right arm, Marten gestured the movement of an imaginary bow playing against violin strings to tease Tasa. Then he turned toward Danik. "And I know Joshua has more than a passing interest in *your* progress as well."

"I can't speak for Tasa, but you all know her discipline when it comes to practicing." Danik gently elbowed Tasa, who had seconds earlier pinched his arm under the table. "I worked on a variety of choral compositions, but so much of the great work is sacred music, masses—like Mozart's Requiem in D Minor. Even Szymanowski's choral masterpiece, *Stabat Mater*, pairs Polish musical elements with a liturgical text."

"What about the cantatas, Danik? There are secular pieces that can challenge your vocal range, as can, certainly, eighteenth-century opera." Professor Fishel first discovered Danik's rich baritone and had selected him for most solos in the school's choir. "I, for one, would like to see you continue as a choral scholar in Lwow."

"I'm conflicted about whether to further my musical studies or focus on the law and political thought." Danik stopped for a moment, as though excited by a new idea. "I think that's why I'm so taken with *The Magic Flute*. Musically, the opera is a masterpiece, and its story speaks to my desire for enlightened government." He grinned broadly. "Couldn't you see me playing Papageno?"

Tasa couldn't help but giggle at the image of Danik as this comic character, singing of his job as a bird catcher and longing for a wife or, at least, a girlfriend. "Yes, Danik, I can see you covered with bird feathers."

As the guests joined her in laughter, she wondered if they all felt like she did—desperate to escape into humor. She and Sonya rose to help Frau clear the table, and she brought out a plate of rugelach and a lemon cake just in time to hear a shift in the conversation.

"Your desire for a more rational government, Danik, is a fanciful hope right now." Joshua Fishel shifted in his chair. "You've seen the economic situation in Poland deteriorate, and those in power seem ready to blame this on the Jews, taking a page from our ugly neighbor." He paused to reach for a pastry. "Polish leaders knew full well that Germany was invalidating the passports of Polish Jews living in

Germany and Austria a year ago. But instead of allowing them entry, Poland did the opposite."

"Joshua and I have learned appalling details about *many* questionable activities of our government leaders." Marten quickly glanced at his wife and mother. "I'm not sure everyone fully understands what's been happening here." He swilled down a large mouthful of wine. "Do you realize more than twelve thousand Polish-born Jews were taken from their homes in Germany last fall—on Hitler's orders, of course—and put on trains going to the Polish border? Our own border guards actually stopped them and sent them back over the river into Germany. The stalemate continued for days, in pouring rain, until Poland finally granted entry to a third of them."

"What . . . what happened to the rest?" Tasa was incredulous. "It's frightening how much we're hated."

Danik nodded at her and turned to the others. "Earlier today, a Hasid was being beaten right in the open in the Market Square and hardly anyone stepped forward, not even the Polish police."

"I'm afraid what you saw is not an isolated case." Marten looked at his mother as he spoke. "The German assault on the Jews since Hitler came to power is well known—their intimidation, boycotts, random violence, and restrictive legislation. Now it's seeped into the towns and cities of Poland."

"Since Kristallnacht, everyone knows the evil of Hitler's Germany." Tasa detected a restrained agitation in Frau Rothstein's unwavering voice. "That horror was reported throughout the world. Civilized nations won't tolerate the brutality and violence of the Nazi government or its anti-Semitism. World opinion will turn sharply against Hitler's regime. Just wait and see."

Tasa remembered that same reaction from Frau months earlier and wondered how she had pushed the horror of Kristallnacht from her mind since then. She'd gotten caught up in school, the orchestra, and her friends. Then she was back in Podkamien over the summer. At times, everything in her life seemed normal. Or maybe she was just too self-absorbed.

The afternoon before Danik would leave for Lwow, the cousins decided to go to the cinema to see a film. *They Shall Have Music* featured famed violinist Jascha Heifetz as himself in a story about a young runaway finding his purpose in life after hearing the virtuoso performance of Heifetz. The narrative, the way Heifetz stepped in to save a music school for poor children from foreclosure, was pleasant enough, but Tasa was mesmerized as she watched her idol, dressed in a white tuxedo and black bow tie, playing Camille Saint-Saens' Introduction and Rondo Capriccioso on his priceless Stradivarius.

The music's connection to Sarasate and its style of Spanish dance music, similar to the vivacity of *Gypsy Airs*, was not lost on her. Nor was the Paganini-like jump in octaves and intricate fingering. After a passionate and lyrical opening, the excitability of this piece grew into its predominantly wistful mood. It mimicked her tremulous emotions—abstract and confusing.

To her, the music was anything but abstract; its melody and rhythm had a clear and brilliant structure that she followed line by line. At times, she found herself holding her breath while listening to the fast-paced, crisp succession of staccato notes and triple stops. Only Heifetz could carry off this feat so flawlessly, she thought, using the whole bow from the tip to the frog with full movement of his entire arm. During the trills and octave jumps in the solo, she looked over at Danik, wondering if he found the music as exhilarating as she did. She could measure his reaction in the way his eyes fixed forward, stirred as she was by the pleading melody of the violin as it changed from a single line of 2/4 to a two-voice double-stop passage, as it climbed into the higher register of the instrument just to snap back to a quick 6/8. Beyond the electrifying performance, Tasa found the music soothing, its power comforting her at that moment.

After the film, Tasa and Danik walked aimlessly along the perimeter of the square. With the shops closed and town center nearly empty, only the sound of their footsteps on the cobblestone broke the stillness. Tasa hooked her arm around Danik's elbow. She couldn't tell if he shared the inner turmoil she felt, knowing they would part ways the next day amid the uncertainty of the world around them.

"Brody won't be the same without you, Danik." Tasa searched for the right words to express her free-floating emotions. "Sometimes thinking about life here, with all the unrest and you gone, I feel overwhelmed."

Danik looked down at Tasa as they slowed their pace. "I understand what you mean. I feel that way about relocating to Lwow. I'll miss being here, and being with you." Danik pulled a handkerchief from his pocket with his free hand, blotting the back of his neck, the August heat still thick into the evening. "I'm scared, too. There's something happening here, or *about* to happen here, and even though you've got Frau to turn to, I worry about you, and for all of us."

"Do you think there'll be war?" Tasa felt her heart quicken as she put the words to her fear.

"It's hard to know. But we need to keep our heads clear and be smart."

She felt her eyes begin to tear up, unable to hold off a swift wave of undefined feelings. So much was going through her mind, and everything seemed to be happening so fast. Was this swell of feelings for Danik? Or was it just fear? Or a bit of both? The idea of Danik visiting her in Brody suddenly seemed a fantasy, overshadowed by some larger premonition that was taking hold of her. A change was near, and it was beyond Danik's departure the next morning. Something enormous and terrible, much darker than the navy sky. Tasa shivered with a sudden chill of apprehension. She tightened her hold on Danik's arm, even as she could feel him slipping away from her.

Part Two

"*And ever has it been that love knows not its own depth until the hour of separation.*"

—Kahlil Gibran

Poland 1939-1941

LITHUANIA

Vilna

GERMANY

Danzig

GERMANY

USSR

Poznań

Pińsk

Warsaw

Łódź

POLAND

Lublin

Równe

Brody
Podkamien
Krakow
Lvov
Gnyp
Bunker

CZECHOSLOVAKIA

USSR

ROMANIA

Eastern Poland annexed by Germany
in 1939 to the Soviet Union

SIBERIA

RUSSIAN
FEDERATION

Ural
Mtns.

Chelyabinsk

2980.5 km / 1863 mi

2002.8 km / 1252 mi

POLAND

Podkamien

UKRAINE

KAZAKHSTAN

4200.4 km / 2625 mi

Shymkent

A Secret Pact
September—November 1939

Tasa awoke to loud reverberations. She opened her curtains to the pink light of dawn and a swarm of airplanes overhead. Shrieking, she ran into Frau Rothstein's bedroom, fixing her eyes on her guardian, who was tightening a robe over her nightgown. Frau took Tasa's hand and gave it a tight squeeze, and the two scurried down the stairs to the kitchen.

The radio sat, cold and still, in the center of the table until Frau clicked on the receiver. Harsh, hissing sounds mixed with the shrill voice of a news reporter. The loud whirr of airplanes and thunder-like booms resounded in the background. Frantic knocking shook Tasa from her transfixed state. She opened the door to find their neighbors, the Janowskis, still in their sleepwear, the color drained from their faces.

Near nine that morning, a crackled announcement confirmed their worst fear. The Germans had marched into Poland. Tasa spent the blur of the next few days listening to news reports. Afraid to look the others in the eye or say aloud what she was thinking, she felt her anxiety grating like the static over the airwaves.

They later pieced together what had happened: Squadrons of planes had unloaded bombs and wreaked destruction on cities and villages in western Poland, as the German onslaught moved east, toward them on one side, while the Soviet army approached Brody in its push westward. Artillery blasted into Polish towns and shtetls and cities, burning synagogues and demolishing homes west and north of Brody. On the morning of September 3, the Kresowa Cavalry Brigade, stationed near the Market Square, merged with other Polish army units defending the town from German tanks. That same day, just before the transmission broke off, Polskie Radio announced that France and Great Britain, allies of Poland, had declared war on Germany.

For seventeen days after the initial attack, at the very edges of their city, the noise of gunfire was deafening. Tasa was filled with dread, despite Frau's solid presence. What had become of her village of Podkamien, of her parents, her grandfather? What about Danik? Frau kept her wits, despite what Tasa realized was a deep concern—that Frau's younger son, Moses, was in Krakow. Units of the Third Reich were directly clashing with the Red Army. Everyone expected the Germans to succeed and take over Poland.

Then the sounds of war went silent. Suddenly, the German army made its exit west and the Soviet army remained in Brody. What became clear was that the Germans and Soviets had made some kind of secret pact that would divide and annex the whole of Poland. The villages and cities of eastern Poland—including Brody, Podkamien, and Lwow—fell to the Soviets. Tasa now lived in the Ukrainian Republic, part of the Soviet Union. Poland, an independent nation since 1918, no longer existed.

The November day was unseasonably warm, but even worse was how stifling the atmosphere felt. The lack of air movement on the third floor of the school seemed another sign of all that was seriously wrong in Tasa's life right now. There were new rules and regulations about everything. Soldiers were snooping around. Even the curriculum had changed. The classroom's open windows invited an unwelcome din of traffic noise and voices as Aleksey Vetrov's lecture on Russian literature droned on and on.

Irina sat near the front with her typically erect posture while Ivan Gorski, one row ahead of Tasa, was asleep at his desk. Tasa felt like putting her head down as well. If only Vetrov would stop talking, she could get to lunch. If only she could unwrap the rugelach she'd brought without making noise. Looking out to the street below, she noticed the chestnut trees still bore a few of their rust-colored leaves, occasionally glistening when the sun broke free from the veil of clouds. At the right moment and angle, she could turn them into sparkling stars, instead of focusing on the military truck slowing as it neared the school building, a dusty tarp partially pulled back to fit a half dozen soldiers in its bed.

It appeared as though the entire city of Brody sat passively under a layer of dust. Or perhaps it just took on an ashen pall in her mind's eye. Tasa now saw only gray stucco facades of houses on her walk to and from school through the Market Square, a route she often took alone since Danik had left for Lwow, that city likely under its own siege. Instead of taking pleasure in the children at play or in the bustle of Brody residents in the market—little of that went on now anyway—she focused on the ruts in the road and stretches of uneven gravel along her path and replayed the events that had suddenly turned everything in her world upside down.

She nearly jumped in her seat as she saw two soldiers enter the classroom. They were dressed identically in olive-green tunics and trousers, their round brown helmets unbuckled. Sunlight caught all the shiny buttons on their uniforms—buttons even adorning external breast pockets. The Soviets carried bayonets, hanging on their hips, held by a brown leather strap across their shoulders.

Professor Vetrov stopped writing on the blackboard and stepped backward awkwardly, almost losing his balance. Tasa was surprised to see his unease; she would have thought that as a Soviet citizen, he would be used to this scene. The soldiers began to walk the aisles from desk to desk, much like Professor Vetrov was known to do, but their heavy black boots clomped where Vetrov, despite his heft, treaded silently.

Tasa's violin case stuck out from under her desk into the aisle, and she worried the men would step on it. Her heart began to pound. She leaned down surreptitiously and maneuvered the case but saw that one of the soldiers noticed her. She froze in her seat, trying to fix her eyes on a neutral spot. The other soldier handed a piece of paper to Professor Vetrov, who stared at it for a moment.

Not lifting his head, the teacher intoned, "Lopa Berkowicz."

Lopa sat in a desk adjacent to Tasa's. Even though Lopa had been in most of her classes over the years, they had never become close, so Tasa didn't know much about the girl's background. She thought back to just a few years earlier, how her friends had teased Lopa, how Tasa had silently been part of that catty group until an anti-Semitic beating of the awkward girl by older boys in their school had taught Tasa that to some, she might be no different. Lopa glanced over at Tasa now, desperation in her eyes as she slowly raised her hand to identify herself to the soldier. As the soldier with the note moved toward their desks, Lopa reached out to grab Tasa's hand, but Tasa put her hands on her lap and looked down at the floor. It was then that she saw a thin rivulet of pale yellow inching toward her feet. Her eyes followed the stream back to where it swelled into a puddle under Lopa's desk.

The scraping of Lopa's metal chair against the hard floor and a blast of horns outside made Tasa jerk as she watched Lopa being led out of the classroom. This was the second time in the past week that soldiers had entered the school unannounced, without warning. So far, half a dozen students had been singled out and had strangely disappeared. Hushed conversations in private offered a consistent reason for their absence: their parents were associated with enemies of the state, a term that covered a broad group of Poles, Ukrainians, and Jews. Who else would be targeted? Was she next? What about Irina and Ania? Was Frau safe?

Instinctively, Tasa began to take in deep breaths, trying to tamp down her growing panic. *Steady . . . Inhale, exhale. Shut your mind off. Don't stand out. Steady.* She numbly understood at that moment that she would never see or hear from Lopa, or any of the arrested students, again.

The second soldier stayed in the classroom, his eyes fixed on the blackboard. A frozen silence in the room intensified the throbbing in Tasa's head. Her classmates sat anchored to their wooden seats, their faces blank, averting their eyes from one another. Professor Vetrov cleared his throat and finally returned to his notes, but when he spoke, his voice was halting.

"We . . . we need to go forward in our lesson. I have only"—he glanced at his wrist—"a few more minutes of class time." With some effort, he moved from behind his desk, where he had safely stationed himself during the terrorizing interruption. His thick gut gave him a slovenly appearance, his shirt buttons pulling and the back of his creased shirt partially untucked. Only his suspenders were solidly in place.

"While the last century produced notable Russian poetry, prose, and drama, in this class we will focus mostly on literature consistent with Stalin's policy of socialist realism." With his pudgy hand, Vetrov smoothed away several oily hairs that had strayed over his forehead. Tasa strained to pay attention. "The leading figure in twentieth-century literature is Maxim Gorky, and we will cover his work in great detail. The realism in his work is typified in his 1925 book, *Artmanov Business*, as it depicts the decay and inevitable downfall of Russia's ruling class."

Vetrov paused and scanned the students' faces for reactions. Tasa's frozen return stare belied the churning in her gut. She could barely focus on his words, as they became a muddle of compressed sounds— an unceasing meld of drumming and rumbling echoing in her head. He assigned a much earlier book by Gorky—*Mother*, written in 1906. "This book lays the foundation for a new period in Russian literature . . ." He faltered for a moment, cleared his throat as the second soldier turned to leave. "That period . . . we now embrace." He reached for his hand bell. Her body tensed at its harsh, clanging cry.

Tasa certainly wasn't embracing this new literary era. She'd been excited about taking a class in Russian literature as she'd come back to school this year, hoping to delve into her nineteenth-century favorites: Pushkin, Leskov, and Turgenev; Tolstoy and Dostoyevsky; Ukrainian-born novelist Nikolai Gogol; and her most beloved Russian author, Anton Chekhov. She had read—actually, devoured—*The Cherry Orchard* over the summer. Just thinking about the play made Tasa nostalgic for her own orchard in Podkamien. She thought about the fate of Madame Ranevskaya's estate and her downfall. What would become of her own home, its land? And what would happen to Lopa?

Professor Vetrov's voice interrupted her thoughts. "May I have a word with you, Tasa?" She was carrying her violin case—her book bag slung over her shoulder—so he took her free arm and held it as he walked with her down the hall. Unnerved by being singled out, she could only fix her gaze on his bushy mustache when he spoke.

"Your Russian is pretty good. What is your background that you have such a facility with the language?"

Tasa mumbled something about her ease with languages, that she also spoke German and Czech. She knew she had to find a way to skirt his inquiry, how discreet she now had to be with everyone—even a hapless puppet like Vetrov.

She hated the abrupt changes that had been made, almost immediately, after the Soviets took over. It was difficult for her to understand how some held an ideological affinity with the communists, how they saw Soviet rule as an opportunity. Certain Polish activists had actually welcomed the Red Army just two months earlier. LONG LIVE THE GREAT THEORY OF MARX, ENGELS, LENIN AND STALIN, one banner read. The Poles and Jews Tasa knew were alienated from such expressions of joy and distressed by the spectacles of flowers strewn at soldiers' feet when they marched into Brody.

Staged elections just a month earlier had put a legal stamp on the Soviet control of eastern Poland, dismantling Polish administrative offices and other institutions. Jews with communist affiliations were initially favored over Poles in high positions, an act that further alienated the two groups. Tasa had a brief respite from school as it closed to incorporate the new policies. Now the high school was coeducational, with Soviet-appointed supervisors running the show. Communism permeated the curriculum—especially in history and humanities classes. Children of Soviet officials became classmates. Russian replaced Polish as the official language and was a required subject. Certain books that she loved disappeared, especially the work of Polish writers. School uniforms were abolished, but strict rules governed the dress code.

The insipid conformity in all things—how they dressed, what they thought—was ubiquitous. In her new assigned readings, the thematic focus was on Soviet convictions and the glorification of the working class, the denouncing of all things considered "bourgeois" or even mildly materialistic or conventional. Frau Rothstein had told Tasa that Russia's nationalistic fixation already had its impact on musical compositions, since music, like all art, was being used as a tool to further a political agenda. Under the Soviets, art was valued for its social function in support of the people, rather than as creative expression for its own sake, or for the individual artist's pleasure. Work by composers she adored, like Rachmaninoff, Chopin, and Tchaikovsky, didn't fit into this manifesto.

But Soviet indoctrination went far beyond art. Since religious education was forbidden, students were no longer separated into thirds—the distinct sections for Roman Catholics, Greek Catholics, and Jews—as was the case when the school was a private Catholic academy. Professor Fishel, contrary to his principles, removed his skullcap and kept his job as a music teacher. Tasa learned that staying neutral was key. Teachers suspected of anticommunist tendencies were monitored in their classrooms and quickly replaced with new Soviet instructors, like Aleksey Vetrov. Bulletins warned that "informants for the enemy" would be punished.

Tasa felt an ever-present shadow of fear, now growing by the direct inquiry of Professor Vetrov. Everyone was being watched. Better to say little to keep from saying something that might be used against her. She said nothing about her family. Clearly not communist sympathizers, they could easily be targeted. She was an orphan as far as anyone knew. That was what Frau had discussed with her during those early days of September.

She longed for the smothering attention and strict rules of her childhood. In place of her family, she carried a raw emptiness and apprehension. Albert's predictions of war on that sweltering summer night in Podkamien had been accurate, unlike her father's long-ago suggestion that Albert would someday take care of them. Albert was in Palestine, Danik was in Lwow, and, except for the stable companionship of Frau Rothstein and several friends, Tasa was navigating each encounter, like this one, by herself.

"So, you speak many languages, Tasa?" Professor Vetrov's curiosity seemed to Tasa more than mere interest.

"Yes, but Russian is now my language of choice. I enjoy much of your country's musical and literary heritage, so I look forward to your class, Professor Vetrov."

"Ah, and who might be your favorite Russian author, young lady?"

Fingering her braid, Tasa pondered an appropriate answer. "Why, everyone's favorite is Alexander Pushkin. He is credited, by many, much more knowledgeable than I, as the founder of modern Russian literature."

Vetrov's face offered little reaction, but he began to twist the tips of his mustache before he probed further, as if immersed in thought. "And I assume your affection for *Eugene Onegin*?"

Tasa carefully chose her words. "I found Pushkin's theme of the relationship between fiction and real life intriguing, especially the way he portrays how people are often shaped by art."

She observed Vetrov's face for any reaction. He nodded slowly, his eyes turning toward an approaching student. She was satisfied she had pulled off the charade, at least this time.

After Professor Vetrov was finished questioning her and his oversize figure disappeared around the corner, Tasa realized all she wanted to do was practice her violin. The lunch period nearly over, she opened her bag, took out the rugelach she'd brought from Frau's latest batch, and bit into it, relishing the tartness of the raspberry in her mouth as she headed down the hall toward the music room.

No one was in the cavernous classroom. Each wooden chair was empty, every metal stand bare. She scanned its stark white walls, focusing on the gaping space where the giant chart of the Hebrew alphabet once stood. She walked to the back and opened her leather violin case, lifting her treasured Johann Kulik as if it were a delicate baby. She adjusted the pegs and with her bow drew out several notes. Softly, she began practicing Szymanowski's first violin concerto and then moved on to her favorite Chopin nocturne, disappearing in a melody that made her think of her family and home. After several minutes, she sensed a presence and looked up. Standing inside the doorway was one of the soldiers who'd been in her classroom that morning.

She lowered her bow and froze, holding the instrument tightly to her chest.

As he approached, his clipped steps resounded on the concrete floor. His steely black eyes bore into her. He reached his hand toward her expectantly.

She kept a neutral affect. "Do you want to hold my violin?"

"*Da.*"

Tasa looked down at the floor, willing herself not to race from the room. She took in a silent gulp of air and carefully handed over the instrument.

The soldier grasped the violin clumsily by its neck before he used both his hands to level it, balancing one hand underneath. He began to slide his thick fingers down the ebony neck and along its strings. His index finger was missing the top knuckle. With it, he started to carelessly pluck several strings, which fell flat. Tasa tensed up and gritted her teeth to keep from saying something reckless.

He asked her, "What music were you playing?"

Her heart hammered in her ears as she watched how loosely he was holding the violin. She wanted to grab it back from him. He slowly began swinging the instrument.

"I was practicing Shostakovich." Tasa instinctively knew what she should say, looking the man in the eye as she spoke. She took a chance that he didn't know one composer from another. He held the instrument more tightly. She thought he might break it. In her worked-up state, she began to perspire and hoped it wasn't obvious. Several moments passed in silence. The soldier's left eyelid twitched as he handed her back her violin.

After school, Tasa asked Irina to go with her to the market for pastries. She desperately needed to do something normal, like get some hot tea and a piece of *sernik*. She especially liked her cheesecake baked in the oven and prepared on a layer of crumbly cake.

"And let's go see my papa at work afterward. Sidor may be with him." Irina's older brother had planned to attend the university in Lwow with Danik, but when their mother got ill, he'd decided to work in his father's watch store for the year and concentrate on playing his cello.

As they entered the market, a brisk wind made Tasa's eyes water. Irina tugged at her scarf, tightening it around her neck to keep the hood of her coat from flopping down on her shoulders. The past commotion and excitement of the open-air market was absent that afternoon, something Tasa had noticed more and more often since the war began and the Soviets took control of the city. Some of the wooden legs on trading stalls were broken, their canvas roofs caved into what had been spaces for the active exchange of goods. The girls stopped in front of a large placard affixed to a building wall, showing Stalin and Hitler embracing each other. Tasa had seen others attached to fences on her way to school.

"That says it all, doesn't it? I think I've lost my appetite." The sober awareness of the reality they faced was as permanent as the identification card she now carried with her everywhere.

"Oh, Tasa, let's try to enjoy ourselves." Irina had reason to avoid political discussion, given the battle going on between her father and brother. Irina had shared with Tasa that Sidor, like many Polish youths, had turned to communism. It had driven a wedge between him and his family. Nightly arguments between father and son centered on what the father called "pathological" oppression by the Soviets. He pointed to the control by Moscow of their media, how all agriculture was made collective. Sidor spoke of state schooling that offered greater access. He suggested he might be supported as a musician in a way that was difficult under the Polish economy. Max Zalenski would shout to his son that all he was listening to was communist propaganda, and he told Irina he feared her brother's next decision would be to join the Soviet army. With her mother not well, Irina had a troubled home life.

"See, look at these new street names." Irina pointed upward. "Pushkin Street, Gogol Street, Turgenev Street. I think it's a nice touch."

The shiny metal signs nailed to the buildings' outer walls proclaimed the new Russian street names—another Soviet mutation instituted after the takeover. Tasa thought it an affront to the great authors' memories to assign them to the now-defiled Brody streets. As if the Soviet soldiers cared about literature. They'd closed the bookshop, burned down the library, and shut down all Polish publishers in their wholesale and strict enforcement of censorship.

"If the Russians like writers so much, why did they have to destroy this statue?" Tasa couldn't help drawing Irina's attention to the hole in the center of the square's baroque fountain where the sculpture of one of Poland's most famous writers and poets, Adam Mickiewicz, had stood. The statue had been destroyed, along with all monuments or records that celebrated Polish culture and politics, like the life-size photograph of the late Polish statesman Jozef Pilsudski that had hung in her school lobby and the white-and-crimson Polish flag. The Gothic town hall on the south side of the square had been damaged, its spire removed, and the Renaissance mural paintings that adorned its outside walls were painted over. The rows of narrow trader houses stood empty, their red-tile roofs and dormers the only color left on the street.

Nearing the pastry shop, Tasa stared at the desecration of the Church of the Nativity of the Virgin Mary, only the courtyard remaining intact. How ecumenical the Soviet destruction had been, she thought bitterly; the sacred buildings of the Jewish quarter had been similarly vandalized. Hasidim were relegated to private praying, and they now congregated away from the eyes of Soviets who persecuted any organized religion. Headstones at the Jewish cemetery had been knocked down. Even the ringing of church bells was banned. While abandoned, the old synagogue of Brody was left standing and now served as Soviet offices. *Another ironic twist*, Tasa thought.

As they lingered, sipping their tea, Tasa kept staring into her cup, unnerved by what remained unspoken between her and Irina, who'd sat silently in Vetrov's class through Lopa's ordeal, as had all the rest of them.

"You seem agitated, Tasa."

"And you're not? How can you sit there and pretend everything is okay when it's anything but?" Tasa felt her tone punitive, her voice cracking. But she couldn't believe Irina's facade of normalcy when she was seething inside. Was this what it meant to survive? To ignore reality, to stop thinking? What would they be turning into then?

Tasa felt shame at how she had turned away from Lopa that morning. But did she have a choice? The incident confirmed the many rumors circulating about censored or lost mail that was followed by arrests. Writing to anyone was fraught with risk, so Tasa shared her closely held thoughts and feelings only with Frau, and she believed she could do the same with Irina. But now she stopped herself from telling Irina what had happened in the orchestra room and how she was afraid to play her violin at school.

Irina pursed her lips and looked away. "Nothing we say or do will make a difference, Tasa." She reached for her wool hat and scrunched it over her curly mop of hair, then wrapped her scarf around her neck so many times, her facial features were barely visible. "Let's get out of here."

The girls had only a half-block walk to reach the shop of Max Zalenski. Irina gave a warm kiss to her father, whose eyes lit up when he saw her. Tasa placed a soft peck on both of the watchmaker's hollow cheeks and, as she stood back, noticed his wan smile and strained expression. The war had been particularly difficult for shopkeepers, especially over the past few months, as commerce diminished. But it seemed they had caught Mr. Zalenski at a difficult moment.

"Did you hear what else the communists did to us?"

Tasa worried that Mr. Zalenski's open agitation could get him in trouble, even though no one else came into his tiny shop after the girls arrived.

"Their plan is to withdraw the zloty from circulation, replace it with the worthless ruble. But the Soviets will give the Russian currency equal value."

Tasa and Irina looked at each other, their eyes widening.

"Do you understand what this means?" Mr. Zalenski hit his fist forcefully on the counter, his worn face registering the pain. "My life savings will be wiped out by the end of this year. Every Pole's life savings will be worthless!"

Tasa's mind flashed to her own family. What would this mean for them—for their savings? She recalled the childhood game with her mother and the hidden zloty coin that, to her, had meant hopefulness and discovery. Suddenly she was overcome with a sense of loss—of being separated from her family, of not having Danik with her in Brody, of the diminished intensity and joy that used to come from the things she cared about most.

Her attention returned to the Zalenskis. All at once it made sense to her—Irina's need to ignore what was happening around them, with her mother's illness and the family tension. Now this. She regretted her outburst at the café. She reached over to squeeze Irina's hand. Irina returned a grateful glance, conveying their unspoken pact to stick together no matter what the future held.

The Thrill of Anxiety
Winter 1939–40

It was still dark when Tasa woke up. A vague but troubling dream left her feeling wretched and panicky, her body drenched with sweat. There was something claustrophobic about the vision stuck in her mind—a dim sense of walls pressing in around her, a sort of confinement. It was elusive, as were most of her dreams, whose details would disappear into a veil of darkness. Why did she wake so often in the predawn hours, her mind filled with confusing thoughts? She much preferred the mornings when a melody brought her to consciousness, but that hadn't been the case since the war had become her life's inescapable backdrop.

She pulled out Danik's letter and reread it.

December 15, 1939

Dear Tasa,

I can't imagine what life in Brody must be like, what your schooling now offers you. Lwow has been renamed Lvov. Like Brody, it is now part of the Soviet empire.

After the invasions of last September, the university kept operating in the prewar Polish system and classes continued. Then, in October, the Polish rector was dismissed, replaced by a prominent Ukrainian historian, Mykhailo Marchenko, who was determined to transform the University of Lwow into the Ukrainian National University.

Polish professors and administrative assistants are being fired and replaced by Ukrainians or Russians specializing in Marxism, Leninism, and political economics, as well as Ukrainian and Soviet literature, history, and geography. Departments relating to religion, free-market economics, capitalism, or the West in general have been closed. The tuition was abolished (not a bad thing), and several new chairs were opened, particularly the chairs of Russian language and literature. Polish literature and language were dissolved. I'm sure that's the case at Brody Catholic, which must now be a state school.

I think about you often, Tasa. I feel very alone here, although my solitary existence may be for the best. Less trouble to get into, like the mischief you and I could stir up in Podkamien and Brody. I have no one to harass or embarrass—do you miss that? Few of my old friends are here, and it's difficult to get to know people in the current climate.

I'm hoping there is some way I can come to Brody to see you and Frau Rothstein. I miss our family, and I'm worried about them and you. I haven't heard from anyone. Have you?

Be well, Tasa.

Love,

Danik

Looking out her window, she saw that a new layer of snow covered the streets and the glow of the nearly full moon illuminated the sidewalks below. The idea of a walk outside to get some fresh air appealed to her, despite the freezing temperature. After slipping into her warmest wool sweater and a pair of lined corduroy pants and pulling thick socks over her feet, she tiptoed across the hall and down the stairs, careful not to awaken Frau.

In the foyer, Tasa donned her overcoat, boots, gloves, and beret and silently opened, then closed, the front door. A wave of excitement ran through her as she stepped into the empty street. The city was asleep, the world around her still. All Tasa could hear was the beating of her own heart and the rhythmic sound of the tree branches moving with the wind. Her steps were also silent, cushioned by the loosely packed snow, glistening now under the muted light of the street lamps as she approached the town center. She stopped for a moment, focusing on the double towers of the Gothic church in the distance, rising above the roofs, knowing that when she got closer she would see the church disfigured, abandoned. She found the shops and stalls dark, and the Market Square empty but for a single soldier in the distance, leaning against an iron railing.

She looked up at the dark sky, the clouds sparse enough to expose the glimmer of stars. She watched the frost of her exhalation before breathing in the wintry air and catching a whiff of several odors—tobacco, burnt wood, perhaps animals. She observed the lamplit rooms of homes from the street and felt a deeper chill standing there, wondering what would become of the people inside and what would come of their dreams. Her steps now sounded hollow on the exposed cobblestones as she passed the darkened storefronts of Max Zalenski Watches, the pastry shop, Dudek's Tavern, Brody Tailor.

She thought about her letter from Danik, how careful he was in sharing his experience, how cautious they all had to be to communicate. She had no way to reveal her feelings to any of her family. Yet she'd felt Danik in the room with her when she read his words. God, how she missed him, missed those happier days when they both lived with Frau. When she peeked into his room on weekend mornings, eager to explore Brody, instead finding his covers kicked aside and his face buried beneath his pillow, wisps of his tousled hair visible, the sound of his deep breathing synchronized with the rise of the sheet covering his chest. Or the morning of her debut school performance when he first saw her so dressed up—his loss of words, the hint of attraction in his eyes. She held on to that image of a younger, more carefree Danik in her mind, instead of the older, more solemn young man he might now be.

Street lamps started to dim as the sun began to rise, its yellow circle conjuring a different memory for her—that of the golden zloty she often searched for amid the spring blooms in her orchard.

It was finally winter break. Tasa stayed with Frau Rothstein in Brody. There wasn't any other choice. Where would she go? She told herself she was lucky, she was safe—given the circumstances. But the war's presence was never far from her mind, and she often felt like its prisoner. Frau had suggested she have some girls over. Irina, Ania, Pauline, and Lucia were now sitting on her bed, combing each other's long hair. Having them around kept her from feeling so homesick, tamped down her creeping fear.

"I think Ivan likes you, Ania." Tasa could see how most boys became infatuated with Ania, who was tall, blond, and large-breasted.

"Don't be silly! Ivan's been having eyes for Lucia." Ania giggled as she winked at Irina and Pauline. "Ivan has roving eyes—I'll say that."

"He pulled a crazy stunt in Professor Rothstein's math class yesterday." Irina paused for effect as the girls gave her their full attention. "When Rothstein erased the Russian literature notes on the board, Ivan frantically raised his hand and said Professor Vetrov had specifically asked that the notes on the left side of the board stay there until the next day. Professor Rothstein believed him. He actually looked frightened, as though he'd done something terribly wrong."

Marten Rothstein's and Joshua Fishel's command of the Russian language, and their deference to the Soviets in charge of the school, had protected them from the fate of most of their colleagues, who had been summarily fired. Tasa was incensed that any her classmates was stupid enough to make light of the situation.

"Ivan can be insensitive and cruel." She stood up, stretched her arms outward, and rolled her head in one direction and then the other, as if that would release the nagging knots she felt in her neck and shoulders. "All the new Soviet faculty take advantage of the few Polish professors we've got left because they can. Vetrov's no exception. Ivan's 'joke' was absolutely plausible. No wonder Professor Rothstein was scared."

"What do you think of Professor Vetrov? I find him annoying, and he has bad breath." Lucia pinched her nose for effect, getting the girls to snicker.

"I think he's just a busybody with more bark than bite." Tasa thought back to how he reacted to the soldiers' having entered her class last month, the memory triggering a sudden unease. "He's kind of pathetic, actually."

"That's for sure." Pauline was typically the last to weigh in. "Is anybody hungry? What time is it, anyway?"

"Let's go to my father's tavern for dinner. Thanks to the free vodka he gives Soviet soldiers, he has more than ample supplies of food and drink."

Tasa appreciated Ania's offer. Anything to break up the restlessness and tedium of their days. "I need to tell Frau." She marched down the stairs with her friends following close behind. They donned their coats and boots and headed out into the chilly air, the last vestiges of daylight remaining.

As they approached the Market Square, Ania pointed to the assembly of their favorite boys from school and quickly caught up with them. "Hey, Jan, where's Dora?"

Tasa admired Ania's social ease. She knew exactly how to get the boys' attention. Jan Landau's twin sister was not one of Ania's favorites, but inquiring about her now seemed genuine. As usual, Jan was with Ivan Gorski. Tonight, Jakub Hirsch and Michail Wechsler tagged along. Tasa had known both of them since the years they were in choir with Danik. Tasa thought the evening was turning out well, even though she preferred being with Danik and Sidor to the boys in her class.

"We're going to my father's tavern for dinner. Do you guys want to join us?"

The group of nine struck out together across the town's central square. Despite the approaching darkness, it was still early and

Dudek's Tavern wasn't crowded. Ania motioned for the friends to sit at a large booth, and they all squeezed in, Ivan making sure he was next to Ania. Tasa caught Ania's gaze and widened her eyes, as if to say, *I told you so*. A waitress approached the table, and Ivan ordered a pitcher of Zywiec.

"I can't believe it's the last day of the year." Tasa was usually less talkative in larger groups and often felt ill at ease with the boys around. But tonight, as she scanned the faces of her peers, she felt closer to all of them. What an anomaly they were—Polish Jews and Catholics, together. And yet how much tighter their bond had become since the Soviets took away their common citizenship. "We've been through so much change on one hand. Yet it feels like time has stood still. It's weird."

Ivan wore a pensive expression and began playing with his napkin, tearing it into long strips. Jan kept his eyes on the empty place setting in front of him but nodded in agreement. No one seemed to want to talk about the war. Lucia twirled a strand of hair that fell across her cheek and was about to speak, when the waitress plunked down a pitcher of beer and took their food orders.

As the glasses were poured and passed, Ania was the first to respond. "I think time has stopped for us in terms of considering the future. I mean, I'm not thinking about university. I don't believe any of us is looking into what we want to do with our life right now." She spoke her next words directly to Tasa. "But I don't think it's weird. Time for us is in the moment."

"There's a lot of speculation about what's going to happen among customers in my father's shop." Irina sipped her drink. "My parents are always fretful, especially with Sidor. But they refuse to talk about what lies ahead."

"Look at you, Tasa, with your violin. You were going somewhere." Jakub was about to say more just as the waitress arrived with bowls of mushroom-barley soup.

Wistful about Jakub's deeper implication, Tasa welcomed the interruption. All she had ever wanted was to play her violin like her idol, Niccolo Paganini. Music transported her to another world, one that had not only beauty but also order and clarity. And she could express her own voice while playing and feel utterly free.

"I'm with Ania. We have now. Let's make the most of it." Ivan refilled his mug with the Polish lager and raised it in the air. "Here's to our violin prodigy. Here's to swimming naked in the Styr River." At that, Michail, Ania, and Lucia began giggling. "Here's to breaking some rules to get back at the bad guys. And here's to one Polish custom they haven't yet outlawed." At that, Ivan guzzled half the beer in his mug, then wiped his mouth on his sleeve.

The reference to the group's past escapade didn't seem to be lost on Jan, also on his second mug of beer, its pale yellow topped with a good-size head. "I'm all for fun and games. So what's up for tonight?"

"We could keep drinking here. At least it's warm." Tasa was beginning to feel the lager, enjoying its light, carbonated, and almost-sweet taste, aware of its strong aroma of honey, clover, and malt. She felt a thrill alongside her general anxiety. She'd relived what had happened to Lopa Berkowicz a hundred times in her head, her memory of last month's incident suffocating at times. Getting back at the Soviets sounded just fine.

One waitress cleared the soup as another brought plates of stuffed cabbage rolls, pierogi, kielbasa, and cabbage and corned beef to their table. Still cautious, Tasa scanned the tavern. Her eyes froze on a couple of Russian teachers from their school eating nearby, several bowls of borscht and piroshki, along with a large helping of rye bread, in front of them. Ivan made another toast about the survival of Polish food, his voice getting louder. Pauline told him to keep it down.

Looking at all the food, Tasa thought of Danik's hearty appetite during their many dinners at Frau's. She wondered what and where he was eating this evening, whether he was alone, and felt guilty for the plentiful food and camaraderie. Jakub interrupted her thoughts as he passed her the plate of stuffed cabbage and called to the waitress for another pitcher.

"I think we have a major opportunity tonight." Ivan took a swig of his beer.

"What do you have in mind?" Michail perked up from his singular attention on the sausage.

Ivan lowered his voice, his eyes taking in the growing crowd at the pub. "Look, these Russians like their vodka. Half of them are stone drunk every night."

"Ivan's right." Michail stopped eating for a moment, a forkful in the air. "They don't run the tightest operation. And I heard they're easily bribable."

"Sidor told me they often come into my papa's watch store and swoon over the merchandise. Sidor says they ask lots of questions, that they're obsessed with watches."

Tasa was surprised—pleasantly—that Irina was joining what seemed to be a developing plot, hoping that this time the group actually *did* something. One Friday afternoon the month before, several of them had sat for hours, talking about a prank that involved putting hot peppers in Professor Stanislaw's lunch food. It was rumored that the Russian history professor kept to a bland diet because of an ulcer— ironic because most students thought the professor *caused* ulcers, his classroom rules were so ridiculously rigid. Details had been gathered about when he went to lunch, with whom he ate, who would divert his attention, and who would actually carry out the caper. But it was just talk. By that Monday, the plan had lost steam.

But now Tasa could feel trouble in store, and she savored the thought of it. "Irina would know. I've seen a lot of them wearing a number of watches on one arm." She turned toward Ivan. "Whatever you have in mind, bribing them with watches is a good strategy."

"And they don't always enforce curfew. You see the cracks in their surveillance mostly at night, when we can do pretty much what we want. Ivan's also right about their drinking habits." Jan pushed his empty plate aside.

"Okay. So this is what I think needs to happen." Ivan took a deep breath as the group huddled together more closely. "I want to seri- ously impair their military fleet. You know, so the trucks won't start. Do you see where I'm heading?"

The night's plan started to take shape. Ivan smiled widely, scanning each of the friends. "So, are we all in this together? It can be our way to officially honor the arrival of 1940."

Jan, Michail, and Irina gave a thumbs-up. Ania nodded excitedly, as did Lucia. Even Pauline agreed.

"What do we have to lose? I mean, what matters anymore?"

Jakub's questions hung in the smoky air of the tavern. Tasa wasn't sure she could counter them. And yet she hesitated, some inner voice of reason stopping her. After all, this was no lunch-food prank. And getting drunk and swimming naked in the Styr was a rite of passage. Tonight's plotting felt different—desperate. She wondered what she was turning into, what they were all becoming here. They sounded like a bunch of hoodlums. "You know, what we're talking about is not just risky; it's breaking laws."

"Come on, Tasa. Whose laws are we talking about?" Jakub sat up straighter.

Tasa studied the faces of her friends. Who *was* making the rules for them? Soviet soldiers threatened her classmates every time they entered the door of the school building. All Poles lived with terror now. She experienced it firsthand. They all did. And they looked away in self-protection as classmates from targeted families were removed from their school without warning. So who could blame them for striking back?

"You're right. This is payback for Lopa and all the other arrests. It's an eye for an eye." Still carrying an undercurrent of fear, Tasa was determined to make sure their strategy was smart and safe, that they got the job done right.

No one spoke. Tasa broke the silence. "I have an idea of how this can work."

When she finished outlining the scheme, the group reviewed each element several times, gaining confidence. Ivan grabbed Tasa then and kissed her smack on the lips, catching her completely off guard. Everyone laughed as she felt the color rise in her face and Ivan declared Tasa and her plan simply brilliant.

Their first piece of luck was finding only two soldiers, instead of the usual four, on surveillance at the Market Square, and neither seemed older than twenty. Ania and Lucia, in their role as decoys, sauntered up to where the men stood at the south end of the square. From where Tasa was hiding at the far corner, along with Irina and Pauline, she could see the other girls approach the soldiers and begin a conversation. She knew that, according to plan, Ania was complaining about some boys following them and was asking for the officers' protection.

Ania would tell Tasa later that the young Soviets had clearly been drinking, the sweet-and-sour smell of what was probably cheap vodka lingering on their breath. Lucia then did as she'd been instructed. She pulled up her sleeve, revealing a showy watch that Irina had earlier removed from a drawer in her father's shop—one she had promised Mr. Zalenski wouldn't miss. The soldiers appeared to be animated over the watch, and Lucia took it off her wrist and handed it to one of them.

"Now she's got to be telling him all those facts you gave her, Irina." Barely whispering, Tasa couldn't help ticking off these important steps of the plan to Irina and Pauline as she watched from afar, wishing she were right there, listening to Lucia's description of the inner workings of the timepiece, the result of Irina's strong coaching.

Tasa observed the entire plot unfold. Ivan and Jan now silently walked around the perimeter, away from the yellow glow of the street lamps, to what had been Brody's Old Synagogue. Several military trucks sat out front. Jakub and Michail stood directly across the Market Square, also able to view the girls interacting with the soldiers while keeping a line of sight on the activity around the vehicles and on Tasa, Irina, and Pauline, whose roles were to watch Ania and Lucia in case reinforcement was needed.

Ania preoccupied the guards on duty with such ease that Tasa couldn't help but silently chuckle. One pulled out a flask and offered it to Ania and Lucia. From this distance, the four looked like old friends.

Tasa motioned a sign to Jakub, who in turn gave an okay signal to Jan. She kept her eyes on Ivan as he carefully opened the first truck's door, got in, and lowered himself onto the floorboards, his legs dangling from the driver's side. She saw the light of his flashlight and knew he would soon be disconnecting the engine wiring. He moved quickly from one truck to another.

The nine friends met up afterward along a cobblestone alley beyond the square, opposite the direction the unsuspecting soldiers had taken.

"We pulled it off!" Ivan practically spit out his words, his eyes gleaming.

"Did you see how smoothly I gave the signal to Jan?" Jakub was slurring his words, his teeth chattering.

"Those Soviet guys were all over Ania. And she set me up perfectly."

"Lucia, you should talk. It was like you were a watch expert, the way you spouted off." Ania gave Lucia a squeeze.

"We could see the whole scene from our lookout post." Irina turned to face Lucia. "I think you have something for me." Irina held out her wrist for the watch her father had unwittingly loaned them.

Tasa took in her friends' slaps and words of congratulations with a knowing smile. Her strategy had worked perfectly. It was close to midnight by the time the group wished one another a happy new year and went their separate ways. As Tasa walked home, she thought that the only way the evening could have been better would have been if Danik had been there to be part of the ruse. How her bold behavior would have surprised him.

She woke up late on New Year's Day to hear the account of the chaotic scene that had taken place that morning. A handful of soldiers had piled into the disabled vehicles, clearly in a hurry to take off. Each driver's attempt to start his truck was met with the grinding of a dead engine. According to several shopkeepers, including Sidor and his father, there was much shouting of obscenities in Russian to the drivers, who kept pumping the gas pedals, trying to get the motors to turn over. Tasa felt a brief wave of satisfaction before the emptiness washed back in to fill her. In the end, nothing she and her classmates did would change anything.

After the prank and a disorganized investigation that went nowhere, a loose calm developed. In the days and weeks that followed, Ivan, as ringleader, made deals with select Soviet guards known to frequent the Zalenski watch shop. A cheap watch bought extra time for the pack of classmates to loiter past curfew in the Market Square. The group continued to relive and relish their success, a distraction that Tasa welcomed.

"Tasa, your father is here!"

Tasa jumped from her desk upstairs at Frau Rothstein's unexpected announcement, her heart leaping as she practically flew into her father's arms. She hadn't seen Papa in nearly six months. The only communication she'd had with her parents since she'd arrived in August was through messengers. Even then, the letters were neutral on the chance they'd be intercepted. The family's clear philosophical distance from communism was well known in Podkamien. Tasa realized what a threat this posed.

"My beautiful Tasa! To see you, to see you're safe. I've missed you so." Her father embraced her, holding her tightly for several minutes.

Tasa closed her eyes, hugging him back, not wanting to let go. Finally, she looked up at his face and took a step backward to inspect the whole image of her father. He seemed thinner, his hair grayer, his mouth tense. "Why are you here now, Papa? Is everything all right?"

"It's not good." He then blurted out, "Uncle Judah has been arrested! So have many attorneys. All have had a case against a communist at one time or another."

"Oh my God!" Tasa burst into tears, the sobs choking her words. "I . . . I don't understand . . ." She thought of an image of her last visit with Uncle Judah, in late summer, and felt a stab of heartache at the shocking news. "What does this mean, Papa? Where did they take him?

What about Danik? Does he know?" Tasa shivered as she realized it could have been her father, and she reached out for him again. "Oh, Papa, I'm so glad you're here."

"Have they arrested anyone else in your family?" Frau's face darkened.

"No, but I'm a target." He turned to Tasa. "Your mother fears that all men in Podkamien, especially a wealthy landowner like me, will soon be arrested. And she's likely right. There've been stories of Soviets beginning to deport Poles and Jews to the far north—anyone thought to be involved in counterrevolutionary activity. I need to find a more secure place, I'm afraid."

"Why don't you stay with the family boarding Danik in Lwow?" Her father's eyes widened at Frau's suggestion. "Staying with Danik would be safe for you, and a big help to Danik."

"I need to get false papers, and must do this quickly. At the same time, I'm concerned what the Soviets' next move might be."

"You'll stay here overnight, Salomon, and I'll get you in touch with the right people to help you."

"You're an angel, Frau. I couldn't be more grateful." Then, to Tasa, "Thank God you have Frau. Now, tell me everything. We have much to catch up on."

The three talked late into the night, Tasa's mind racing forward and back. She needed and wanted her father near her, but hated the reason for his visit. Uncle Judah was imprisoned by the Soviets, her father was now a fugitive, and the rest of her family—Mama, Aunt Ella, Grampa Abram, and the others—were alone in Podkamien.

That night, she was unable to sleep and thought back to the last occasion her extended family had been together—two summers earlier, just after her father had finished building their new house. The tension that evening and Albert's talk of war seemed almost a fantasy, so safe they had all felt then. She recalled when, later that evening, after the night air replaced the stifling heat, she and Danik had performed for the family.

They had chosen a song by the German composer Louis Spohr,

inspired by a poem and written for baritone, violin, and piano, one they'd practiced for months with Frau. It was called *Abendfeier*, which translated as "celebration of the evening"—the perfect selection. Tasa remembered every detail of that moment, how interconnected she and Danik had been, mastering every musical nuance and expressing the euphoric message underlying each note and phrase of the song— as if violin and voice were one instrument.

The Note
February 1940

Tasa hurried across the icy central square, fighting a fierce winter wind that blurred her vision and resisted her forward movement. Lowering her head to keep her eyes from watering, she pulled the loose ends of her neck shawl inside her heavy field jacket and zipped the coat higher. She was returning from an afternoon at Irina's house. Now that Mrs. Zalenski's health had improved, the family's mood had lightened as well.

Today, everyone had played a role in preparing dinner using an old family recipe for *zupa ogorkowa*. Even Sidor and his father worked side by side, chopping carrots, leeks, onions, potatoes, and celery, setting aside their political bickerings. Irina and Tasa grated the pickles—sour kosher ones—from which the soup got its name. Mrs. Zalenski was at the stove, first sautéing the vegetables, then creating the thickened roux out of butter, flour, nutmeg, and milk. Making this hearty soup was a family affair, and Tasa relished the time she got to spend with them, thankful to have another loving home where she felt safe and welcome.

Since her father's surprise visit several weeks earlier, she had lived in a constant state of fretfulness. Papa, with Frau's help, had gotten a false passport and relocated to what they all now knew as Lvov. Before he departed, he told Tasa he would return to visit her late at night, but it was unclear exactly when that would happen. It was safer for all of them that way. Tasa shuddered to imagine the whereabouts of Uncle Judah, thinking of the students from school arrested by the Soviets and not heard from again. Her heart ached for Danik, the loss he must feel, and she drew comfort from the fact that her father was with him.

Other questions loomed. What was to become of Mama, Grampa Abram, and the others left in Podkamien? When would she see them again? Every time she agonized about them, she was overcome with a panic that made her heart race and her stomach queasy. Her refuge was an afternoon at Irina's or when her violin transported her somewhere far from this place and time. But then the darkness was always still there—the waiting, the not knowing, the fear, and her lack of control to do, or change, anything.

As the familiar outline of Frau's house came into view, Tasa's heartbeat slowed a bit. The image of Frau in her cooking smock, baking a fresh challah or pan-frying pierogi, brought a smile to her face. But when she opened the door, Tasa gasped in surprise.

"Julia! What are you doing here?"

Her mother's housemaid looked distraught, her dark brown eyes wide and shiny, filling her wan face, a fringed wrap still covering her head. Tasa turned to Frau, whose expression spoke volumes.

"Julia brings a note to you, Tasa. From your mother. Please. Take your coat off. Sit down." Frau pulled several chairs away from the kitchen table. "Let's all sit down."

"She wrote this last night, Tasa, and told me I must reach you." Julia's voice faltered as she began weeping. "They took the women, all the women . . . the children, too. In the middle of the night." Julia had difficulty drawing in enough air to expel her next set of words. "I overheard the officers say the women were being sent to a work camp. In Siberia . . . or Kazakhstan. A cattle train transported them."

Tasa sat motionless, too stunned to react. It was as though she was looking from the outside at this scene, at all of them, the three disconnected from one another. A hard moon poured blue light through the window, casting a chilled shadow across their faces, Julia's face swallowed by the burden she bore as the messenger, Frau easing her weary guest into a kitchen chair. Tasa sat immobilized as if by an external force, her eyes fixed on her family's housemaid. *This is not real*, she thought. If she blinked hard, she'd wake up from this nightmare.

Frau was holding a piece of folded parchment paper in front of her. Tasa saw that she was talking, but at first she heard Frau's voice as if muffled, the words reverberating but not joining together like they should. Frau sat down close to Tasa. She felt Frau's hands alongside her face, saw Frau staring directly into her eyes. Then Frau's words grew louder and clearer. "*Kinder*, look at me. Do you want me to read this to you? Or do you want to read it yourself?"

As if in a daydream, Tasa couldn't register or focus on the face in front of her. "It's going to be fine, *kinder*. Your mama will be fine. You need to read this letter. Now."

Frau placed the paper in Tasa's hands, holding on to it until Tasa's fingers actually grasped it. Tasa held the note in front of her for several moments, motionless. This wouldn't be true if she didn't read the words inside. Gingerly unfolding it, she noticed her mother's handwriting lacked its usual care; the letter was clearly scribbled in haste. Yesterday's date of February 9 was scratched out, and the 10th was written above it.

My dearest Tasa,

I don't want you to worry about me. I am fine. The Soviets are taking us north—I'm not sure where but will write when I arrive. I'll be traveling with Aunt Ella. Also Aunt Sophia and Dalila and Mela—so glad they didn't separate her from her young children. Many women are being sent with us, wives of Polish officers and attorneys and landowners. We'll receive various labor assignments but will be safe. I am concerned only about your protection now, and Papa's. Grampa Abram remains in Podkamien; the Soviets wouldn't transport someone his age. He'll stay with Uncle Jakov and his family, who are also safe; Jakov's medical skills are sought here.

You must stay close to Frau Rothstein and go on as you have been. I'm saddened you are growing up in a world where people can be forced from their home and family. All you have, dearest Tasa, is your mind and your heart. Stay in school and work hard. Play your violin and draw pleasure from your musical gift. Your mind and soul cannot be taken from you by anyone. Remember that.

Your father and Frau Rothstein will make sure you and Danik are safe.

Keep me in your heart until we come together again.
All my love,
Mama

∫ ∖

Tasa read and reread her mother's letter late into the evening, until she knew every single line by heart. She turned the words over and over in her mind as she fixed her eyes outside her bedroom window where the clouds hung low and dense, blustery winds announcing the arrival of another storm. Soon the snow came down in a white sheet, swirling and spiraling every which way.

Tasa sucked in the air and drew into herself. She imagined her mother's arms around her until it felt almost palpable, filling her with an unbearable longing. She had to keep her mother alive in her mind, to bring forth all her memories, not lose her tangible essence. She thought about memory itself and how she learned to remember the music she loved. How her repetition of violin pieces embedded that music in her mind, allowing her to call it up even months later. How she learned to feel the music more each time. She realized how much of her life over the last five years had taken her away from her mother. She closed her eyes, drew in a deep breath, and willed herself back to a childhood that seemed so long ago.

The smell of Mama's perfume. The small string of pearls Mama always wore when she got dressed up. The way Mama twisted her hair in a bun each day and how she carefully braided her long black hair each night.

How she helped Tasa choose her outfit to wear on her first trip to Brody to meet Frau Rothstein. How she meticulously packed Tasa's blouses and skirts, talking to her all the while about how Tasa would come home many weekends, how she'd be staying with Danik at Frau's house, reassuring her that she and Papa would come to see her often. Encouraging her earliest dreams.

"Mama, I want so badly to play like Paganini. Grampa Abram told me Paganini could play three octaves across four strings in a hand span! It's so hard for me to stretch my hands. They're so small, and my fingers are so short."

"You will grow, my love. You'll be tall enough to reach for the stars someday."

How she always promised Tasa that everything would be okay and Tasa believed her. How Mama started their hide-and-seek game in the orchard as a way to soothe Tasa's loneliness at Danik's departure.

It was then Tasa let her tears flow. And when she felt she might never stop, she thought about how brave her mother was, how positive and hopeful the letter she'd written. Tasa read the words yet again, until her eyes could no longer focus.

It was dark and still as Tasa opened her eyes, realizing she had fallen asleep. Her mother's note had been folded and placed on the night table, and Tasa found herself under her covers. Still groggy, she didn't move at first but slowly became conscious of a hollowness inside her, much deeper than hunger. Her eyes felt raw and gritty.

Like a gift, the opening harps in Smetana's first symphonic poem, *Vysehrad*, began playing in her head, soothing her. As a layered melody of horns and strings replaced the gentle world the harps created, a picture of rolling pastureland and a castle on a hill over the Vlatava River, the seat of the earliest Czech kings, built in her mind. The music's lyrical depiction of the Czech composer's native countryside and history resonated with her own yearning. The descending passage evoked the collapse of the castle, and she relived her own breakdown as the music fell silent. The returning harps reminded her of the castle's beauty; the ending notes painted for her the image of flowing water, the river surviving the castle's ruin.

Tasa flung the covers aside, noticing the crumpled shirt and pants she had on. Catching her disheveled image in the adjacent mirror, she walked over to it and peered more closely, only to find her eyes red and puffy, her braid half undone. As she stared at her gloomy reflection, the previous evening materialized from the fog of her sleep and another melody began playing in her mind, one that felt assured and steady. Tasa thought about her mother and focused on her courage, like that of the female warrior at the heart of Smetana's third movement, *Sarka*. From the height of cymbals crashing to a single melody, then a chorus of instruments converging into the deep tone of horns, Tasa sought, like the music, a satisfying resolution.

Bits of light appeared through her eyelet-lace curtains. She quickly changed her clothes and straightened her hair before sitting down at her desk to write back to her mother. As she sat staring at her blank sheet of parchment, she realized she had nowhere to send such a letter, no way to communicate. She put her head in her hands, but no tears would come, as if she were empty inside.

A tapping at the door made her jump, and she turned to see Frau Rothstein in a bathrobe. In an instant, Tasa found herself encircled in Frau's tight embrace. She caught the scent of sliced apples, which took her back to Podkamien and her mother. And her tears flowed again.

"I don't know what I would do without you, Frau. It feels like you're the only person I have left."

"There, there, *kinder*. I'm not going anywhere." Frau smoothed Tasa's hair and planted a kiss atop her head. "Your mother will be safe, and your father is not far. He will now come more often to visit you."

Tasa choked through several more sobs. "You've made your house into a home for me. I'm so grateful. But this sadness . . ." Tasa looked up at her confidant. "I feel so empty inside."

Frau sat back on Tasa's bed, motioning Tasa to sit next to her. "Your mother is a strong woman, and so are you. Both survivors, yes?"

Tasa nodded, a half smile wet with tears. She rested her head on Frau's shoulder, and they stayed like that for several minutes, as Frau stroked Tasa's hair. Finally, Frau moved slightly and tapped Tasa's knee. "Let's have breakfast. Enough crying for today."

Tasa offered Frau a brave face and occupied herself by listening to music on the radio while Frau cooked. Chopin's Minuet Waltz, a piano solo Frau had often played, captured her attention momentarily, but its brisk and frolicking tempo jarred her now. Like a small dog circularly chasing his tail, the notes cavorted and looped; their trills and gaiety assaulting, rather than comforting. Frau asked Tasa if she wanted to help her bake a lemon cake in the afternoon. Tasa shook her head numbly, though it wasn't as if she had other plans that day. As she mindlessly ate her breakfast, it suddenly dawned on her what she needed to do.

February 11, 1940

I think about the safety of a mother's arms as I write this letter, how those arms bring warmth to a child. How your arms, Mama, have always kept me feeling safe and secure even when we've been apart. I know my words cannot reach you now, that you are on a train heading far away from me. Julia arrived yesterday in Brody to give me this awful news. And I know you told me not to worry, but I can't shut out my feelings. I need to express them somehow to you, Mama. I need to tell you how much I want to run back to the safety of your arms, far away from the harm that's encircling us.

I hate this war. I hate that it keeps us apart. I hate that Papa has to be in hiding, that Uncle Judah has been arrested. That you will be at some kind of work camp (what does that mean?), and that Aunt Ella, Aunt Sophia, and her two little girls have also been deported to this place far north, where I know it will be colder than our Polyn. I am so maddened not knowing where you are, not knowing how to reach you. I want to believe you are all right.

I must believe this and hold on to it.

You told me to stay close to Frau, to stay in school, to focus on my music. I will do all these things, Mama. But I will still worry. I feel like a lost child, even with the love and protection of Frau, who is so very kind and good to me. Mama, I need you now more than ever.

Remember what you taught me when I was a small girl when we played our game in the orchard? When you hid a zloty under one of the stones around the shrubs for me to find, you said our town was a lot like life, with many things hidden, yet to be discovered. But the stones in our orchard eventually grew moss, didn't they? These green, flowerless, velvety plants need constant hydration, but they lack true roots. I am like the moss, Mama. I am thirsty for your love but lacking roots now. And what I have discovered is both good and bad.

I discovered the strength inside me that allows me to go beyond the growing fear and worry I carry each day this war continues and my family is away from me. I've also seen the ugliness and cruelty and violence that can be part of the human spirit. That sickens me. And I realized just how deep my grief is in your absence. I'm learning that this pain can't be ever present, Mama, or I won't be able to go on.

I wonder what it means now that the zloty we used for our special game no longer exists. I find myself filled with such frightening images sometimes. I try not to think of only dark thoughts, but writing them here may help me rid myself of them somehow.

I will keep you in my heart, Mama. I will make you present every day until we are back together. I will think of you in my music and in my dreams. And in these letters I will write to you that I wish could reach you, wherever you are.
I love you and miss you more than you can know.
Tasa

Just after dinner, Tasa searched for sheet music of Chopin's Nocturne in E-flat Major, the piece the Soviet soldier had caught her playing at school. She had considered quitting the orchestra after that encounter in protest, given the limited repertoire the ensemble was allowed to play. Instead, she held on to her anger and the tension she'd felt when the solider toyed with her violin, defiantly playing sections of Polish works in the moments before orchestra class began. It had been as if she were daring anyone to stop her. No one did.

She finally located Sarasate's arrangement of Chopin's nocturne for violin and piano, excited to occupy this time with Frau by escaping into music. Tasa became immersed immediately in the piece's gentle, melodic introduction, and she let the nocturne's reflective mood meet her own melancholy, then lift her as the music ascended into high notes that sang with passion. Their playing continued well into the evening, an antidote for her malaise.

Near midnight, Tasa and Frau Rothstein sat quietly, drinking hot tea in the kitchen, comfortable in their flannel sleeping gowns, exhausted from the last two days of intense emotions. The turn of the knob on the side door startled Tasa. Then, suddenly, Papa and Danik were there, materializing as if apparitions. Today of all days! She leaped out of her chair and threw her arms around both of them at once, almost knocking Danik against the stove. She held tightly to her father and cousin, not wanting to let go. The homecoming was bittersweet, she knew, the visit putting all of them at risk. She pushed those thoughts from her mind.

This time, Tasa shed tears of happiness. Everyone tried to speak at once, but in the end Frau won out. "Tasa, hang up their coats. Quickly. Salomon, Danik, let's all move to the inside of the house, where the lights won't be so noticeable at this hour. *Sich beeilen*—hurry!"

As Tasa rushed to join the others in the living room, she couldn't take her eyes off Danik, noticing so much at once—a gravity she could see, despite the love his face expressed at that moment, a new leanness to his muscular frame, a vulnerability in the way he carried himself. "Oh, Danik, I've been so worried about you!"

Their eyes met, and she felt the heat rising in her face despite the frigid cold outside, a sort of magnetic charge, as if the past six months of separation had been accumulating in her heart, slowly, only to surface at once, now, in this swell of ambiguous feelings. They understood each other. She knew that. They always had. And loved each other. They were family, after all. She moved closer to him, touching his shoulder without uttering a word. As they took a seat side by side on the couch, Tasa patted the empty space on her left for her father, whose cheek she gently kissed as he sat.

Frau walked in the room with a tray of tea and fresh lemon cake. She eased it down onto the table in front of them. "You must be starving. And cold. I'd put on a fire, but I don't want to draw attention to the house." She began pouring tea and handed the first cup to Salomon. "How long was your trip?"

He leaned forward for the tea and took a slice of cake. "We left Lvov just as the sun set. We never stopped and kept the horses at a fast clip."

Frau handed Danik a cup of tea and a plate of the cake before she sat down in the armchair next to Salomon. She looked at Tasa as she paused, as though stopping herself from saying her next words.

Only then did it hit Tasa. Her father and Danik didn't yet know, couldn't know, about Mama and Aunt Ella. Danik would be devastated, Papa distraught. Yet there was no way around telling them. Tasa nodded to Frau to take the lead.

"Salomon, you know trouble was underfoot in Podkamien and you would have been arrested had you not left." Frau looked from Salomon to Danik and back to Salomon, as Tasa was already up from the couch, heading toward the stairs. "We were paid a visit yesterday by your housemaid, Julia."

Returning to the parlor out of breath, Tasa handed the letter to her father, choosing her words carefully. "Papa, Mama says she is safe." She turned to Danik. "So is your mother. We must believe this."

As her father read Mama's letter, the color drained from his face.

"What is it, Uncle Salomon?" Danik's voice caught.

It felt like a long silence before her father spoke up, though it may have been just a moment. "Tasa is right. This may be a blessing in the end." He turned to Danik. "The women have been transported to a work camp in northern Siberia. Tasa's mother, your mother, Aunt Sophia, and her girls. I don't think the Soviets will hurt them as they would those they see as overt enemies of the state—people like me, a landowner."

Danik's mouth tightened, but his face remained deadpan. "I agree about the women, but . . ."

Tasa put her arm around his shoulder as they all again sat in silence for several minutes, before Danik spoke up again, anger in his voice. "The Soviets are bastards, but we're forgetting how much worse things could be if we were living in German-occupied Poland."

"What do you mean, Danik?" The words were out of Tasa's mouth before she was overcome with a desire *not* to know, with the wish to remain blissfully ignorant. The future was not what it used to be, for her or anyone.

"Have you heard of the *Einsatzgruppen*?" Danik looked hesitantly over at Salomon, who nodded for him to go on. Danik drew in a breath, then continued, his words clipped. "They're SS paramilitary death squads. They've been killing Jews, Gypsies, Soviet political operatives. All throughout the territory operated by the German armed forces. It's been going on since Germany attacked Poland last fall." Danik picked up his tea and cupped it between his hands.

"Danik, how do you know such details?" Frau was sitting on the edge of her seat, disbelief in her tone. Tasa felt her ears get hot.

"I told this story to Uncle Salomon on the trip over here. When I am finished, you will know that my sources are solid." Danik placed his cup back on the tray.

"The Germans have a plan called *Intelligenzaktion*, a plot to eliminate Polish intelligentsia. Last November, there was a meeting of nearly two hundred academics at a lecture hall at Jagiellonian University in

Krakow, at the invitation of the rector. The invitation said attendance was required, that they'd learn about Germany's plans for Polish education. So they all went.

"What they didn't know was that the Gestapo *commanded* the rector to send this invitation." Danik paused to let his words sink in. "Everyone there was frisked, kicked, slapped, hit with riffle butts, and arrested, then taken by train to some prison camp. But here's where it backfired. Many were well known beyond Poland. There was a loud outcry. Prominent Italians protested—even Mussolini, along with the Vatican.

"Just three days ago, half were freed. Two were visiting professors at my university and had many contacts among the faculty. They were Poles and well-known communists, of course, which is how they are still among our 'esteemed' faculty. One was the brother of my Russian literature professor." He paused. "They said they knew of three other incidents, scholars less widely known who just disappeared. Up to now, this master plan was just rumors."

Frau was uncharacteristically at a loss for words. Tasa heard her father say what she was thinking.

"God help us if the Germans take over."

Magen David
February 1942

Racing thoughts, heightened by the predawn darkness and quiet, aroused Tasa from a fitful sleep. Frost etched the window alongside her bed. Her mind still foggy, she reminded herself that it was February, that she was in Podkamien and living in the apartment attached to the house of her grandfather. She closed her eyes, feeling the winter winds blowing in the music of Tchaikovsky's *1812 Overture* as she pictured the French attempting to retreat from the Russians in that historic battle, their guns stuck in the freezing ground.

It had been nearly eight months since she'd returned to Podkamien after Hitler's betrayal and attack on the Soviet Union. Eight months since her father and Danik had fled to Brody, barely escaping as the German army marched into eastern Poland and encircled Lvov. Eight months since she had last seen her beloved Frau, during a surreal day spent frantically packing her things to leave Brody with her father and cousin, ending six years under Frau's loving guidance and the safety of what had become her second home. Her hasty and tearful goodbye with Frau blurred into a bittersweet reunion with both Grampa Abram and the Dorfmans, her only relatives still in Podkamien, as she returned to her village for the first time since war had broken out.

Here she was, home again. Yet her mother was gone. And her family's estate was taken over by the Germans or their surrogates, just as it had served the Soviets after her mother was deported to Siberia.

She got up and quickly dressed for the frigid temperature, tightening a scarf around her neck. She reached for the armband all Jews were now required to wear and pulled it over her right sleeve, its yellow MAGEN DAVID a sharp contrast with her black coat. As she stepped outside, she scanned both directions. The main street in Podkamien was deserted, but for a couple of stray cats. She lingered a moment, studying the vacant shell of her grandfather's fabric store, which he had closed before the war. Situated behind and above the store, the residential portion of Grampa Abram's house was long and narrow. A gravel walkway ran along one side, across from what had been Glas Hardware, a locksmith now in its place. Abram's was attached to two, and sometimes three, small apartments, depending on her grandfather's hobby of renovating the space to accommodate renters. Now, two entrances came off the walkway into the private quarters, the one that housed the Dorfmans, and the larger unit where Tasa, her father, and Danik stayed, both opening into a common living area, kitchen, and parlor.

Tasa's early-morning walks were now a habit. She welcomed this time to clear her mind, caught as she was between feeling like a sheltered eighteen-year-old—always with an adult at her side—and someone much older. But these days, roaming freely in Podkamien came with caution. Her childhood village was much changed, as she was, from the days when her father read to her at night and her mother played games with her in an orchard that in spring would come alive when the cherry blossoms burst into full bloom. When she and Mama might lounge in the shade for hours, surrounded by acacias and daylilies, lilacs and lavender. The Podkamien she returned to was a powerless pawn, like so many of the rural enclaves in Poland. The people who remained carried the weight and scars of wartime. With the harsh February winds and snow producing drifts thigh-deep in places that obstructed doorways of houses and shops, the villagers were prisoners not only of the war but also of the very elements.

Tasa retraced the steps she used to take with Mama and, later, Danik to school. She stood in the middle of the long street at the village center and observed the connecting facades—mostly one-story houses facing one another, the forest behind them. Every step she took in Podkamien brought forth thoughts of her mother and their weekday walks into town along the dirt path from home, maybe a half a kilometer from where she now stood. Reaching the edge of the main thoroughfare, she passed the house previously owned by the Riesmanns, where Aunt Ella had hosted festive family Shabbos dinners, where Uncle Judah's law offices had been, where Albert and Danik had grown up. Tasa looked into its gated courtyard, set back a bit from the street, and noticed the black ashes of a bonfire still smoldering.

She inhaled the charcoal-scented air as she passed the small stucco house next door where Uncle Ehud and Aunt Sophia had lived with Dalila and Mela. When she had returned to Podkamien, she had learned Ukrainian peasants killed Uncle Ehud days after her father fled the village, so Aunt Sophia and their children had been deported, grief-stricken, to Siberia with the others. Tasa stopped in front of what had been Chabad Lubovitch Synogogue, now just concrete slabs atop frozen ground, and offered a silent prayer in his memory. She walked farther, only to find the old bookstore was also gone.

By the time she reached Felix's watch store and Kuchar's bakery, a wave of nostalgia swept over her. The jovial watchmaker had always rushed from his work desk to greet her on her way to school. The honey-spice aroma of *piernik* from Anna and Henryk Kuchar's bakery would make her stomach growl, despite the fact she'd already eaten a hearty breakfast. Anna would usher her inside and insist she take a *pierniczki* with her, and she'd happily comply. Munching on the cookie, she'd wind around a crooked cobblestone road until she arrived at her elementary schoolhouse, where she learned alongside the children of farmers and tailors and butchers. Now, both shops had been closed, as were most businesses owned by Jews, shortly after Germany's occupation of Podkamien.

She decided to turn around, back toward her grandfather's house. She walked behind the stretch of houses adjacent to the forest that often sheltered Podkamien's town center from gusting winds. The tall, stick-bare trees stretched upward toward the expanse of overcast sky, the earth beneath her layered by a sheet of ice. A lone dog meandered by, sniffing his way along the path, his legs sliding as he began to run off. He reminded her of Mr. Gnyp's pup, and she thought back to the times Theo had lain at her feet as she practiced her violin, his tail thumping up and down. She stood still for several minutes, until the hammering of woodpeckers and squawking of ravens broke the morning silence. Shielded from the snowdrifts, the ground glistened during the rare moments when the emerging sun escaped from the cover of clouds. Her eyes followed the cluster of evergreens, as she took in a deep breath of crisp, pine-scented air. A sudden gust of wind struck her face as the sound of steps in the distance sent her scurrying toward warmth and safety.

The pale glow of dawn greeted her as she reached the side entrance of Abram's house. She quietly returned to her bedroom, aware of the thin wall partitions resulting from her grandfather's most recent renovation. She threw her coat, hat, and gloves on her bed and pulled out the small stool resting under her desk. Writing in her journal was another morning ritual, staying true to the promise she'd made herself in Brody. She opened the desk drawer and withdrew a small bound tablet and pen. She read through her most recent entry and then began to put her meditations to paper.

February 2, 1942

I can't wait until the thaw of May, when the sun will shine and the pink blossoms will burst forth on the cherry trees! I can smell the whiff of freshly cut hay as I think about Cairo, of riding him bareback. I can still see his black, silky coat as he grazed lazily in our field and hold on to the hope that he is alive and being well treated.

Here in Podkamien you are more present than ever, Mama. Thinking of you, and of springtime, is joyful. I have so many happy memories of the open countryside of my childhood. I remember summer days lounging with you in the orchard. These are the things I miss, Mama, and these are what I try to think about when I'm scared—so much better than focusing on this bitter winter, the chaos of war, and a world that seems so irrational. Now, in our village, the Ukrainian police are doing the Germans' dirty work, fingering and arresting communist sympathizers. Surely we are safe—everyone here knows of our philosophical distance from Soviet ideology. It helps that Uncle Jakov privately treats Ukrainian police officers and Danik translates German documents for the police department. Still, a host of fears often collect in my mind at night, and I have to work hard every morning to empty myself of them. Sometimes I take bread crusts with me on my early-morning walks, and when I crumble them for the birds, I imagine each crumb I drop as another negative thought removed from my cluttered brain.

Anticipating spring, I've been practicing Vivaldi's The Four Seasons, "La Primavera," conjuring up the trills of birds and the birth of all things I might see growing in the fields. I can almost feel the loosening of the ground following the many weeks of winter's melt and spring rains.

My heart feels full with the love I have for you, Mama, and for our family here and in distant places. I'm so happy to be with Papa, Danik, and Grampa Abram, because I've missed them so much these past years. I became so close to Danik when we both lived in Brody. When he was gone, the love I felt for him seemed different somehow.

At that, Tasa paused, uncomfortable in what she had written. She scratched out her last sentence and continued.

When he was gone, I thought about him a lot and am happier now that he is here again. It's nice to get closer with Uncle Jakov and Aunt Sascha, and they've been very good to Grampa

Abram over the past two years. Little Tolek is now twelve and not so little! I do miss Frau Rothstein terribly. Not having you or Frau around has been the most difficult for me. And I desperately miss my best friend, Irina. I pray everyone is safe and

At a sudden, light tapping sound, Tasa turned to catch Danik's head peeking into her bedroom, the door now ajar. His hair was tousled, and he still wore his flannel pajamas.

"I didn't know if you were up. Have you eaten breakfast?" Danik glanced past Tasa at the outerwear on her bed. "Did you go out this morning? It isn't safe, you know."

"I couldn't sleep." Tasa quickly closed her journal, put it in her desk drawer, and moved toward the door. She realized then her need for more private safekeeping for her personal musings. After all, her journal held all her fears and longings. So many feelings, all were confusing her. Already she felt herself too careful as she wrote. "And I needed to get out, Danik. I'm suffocating."

She saw that look of his, a kind of divided expression both admonishing and affectionate. She was touched by his concern, pleased by it as well. "I wore my armband," she murmured, still holding his gaze.

"You act as if the armband will protect you, Tasa. Haven't you seen and heard enough to know that nothing and no one is protected? I need . . . you need to be careful."

She cast her eyes at Danik. His flannel shirt unbuttoned enough to expose his reddish chest hair. His broad shoulders underneath. The intensity of his eyes as they fixed on her. How they stirred something deep inside the pit of her stomach. Tasa willed herself to look away. "Let me get us some breakfast."

Danik ran his hand through his auburn waves, now almost shoulder-length. "I'll help. I can make a pot of tea and cut up some cheese."

"And maybe I'll give you a haircut after breakfast?" Tasa tried to hold back a smile, knowing her cousin's reaction before his words came out.

"You are the *last* person I'd let have a pair of scissors near my head!"

"Shush! You'll wake the others!"

At that, Danik reached over, as if to give her a playful nudge, just as she moved backward, losing her footing, and they fell, together, onto her bed. Their faces inches apart, she held his direct gaze this time, conscious of how clear his hazel eyes were in the morning sunlight now beaming through the window, aware of the scent of his body, savory and familiar. She felt the rapid beating of her heart, and something came loose in her. They weren't touching, yet they were close enough their breaths fused. Danik took in a gulp of air that caught in his throat, his chest quivering through his exhale. She thought about him touching her, then felt torn between her desire and self-imposed restraint.

In truth, the depth of her love for Danik knew no boundaries. How could it? The bond had begun in their childhood. They had grown into young adults together—living under one roof—as their world became increasingly dangerous. Danik understood her. He balanced her. Being together was as natural as the music they played and the conversations they had and the walks they took.

Tasa could pinpoint the night her feelings had rushed to the surface—it had been at their reunion in Brody two years earlier. She knew she was holding herself back, always sidestepping moments of tenderness between them. What was she afraid of? That she misread his overtures? That she couldn't trust her own feelings, thrown together as the two were in war? Or did these circumstances, the constant uncertainty in their lives, make a relationship impossible? All she knew for sure was that her feelings for Danik filled her with a growing tension.

Tasa hoped the color in her face didn't give her away as she pushed herself off the bed. "I'll take you up on that tea, Danik."

The family gathered in the parlor of Abram's apartment, something they did every night after dinner. Its interior space, unchanged since

Tasa had played there as a child, offered privacy, and its wood-burning fireplace provided needed warmth during the long winter months. The sun had disappeared from the horizon several hours earlier, the dimming of the day to dusk taking place while she helped Aunt Sascha prepare their meal from staples that Abram and Danik brought back from the local farmers—tonight they cooked cheese pierogis, boiled potatoes, and served cucumbers with sour cream. Now, Tasa curled up next to her grandfather, reading *Narcissus and Goldmund*, by Herman Hesse. She looked up periodically, her concentration interrupted by the steady ticking of the wooden cuckoo clock, its pendulum swinging evenly like the metronome she sometimes used during violin practice. The "cuckoo" reverberated through the house each hour of every day, as it had for as long as she could remember.

Tasa glanced over at her grandfather, whose eyes were closed; the flames of the fire cast a glow on his creased face and graying beard. He, too, had been reading, but now his wire-rimmed glasses had slid down his nose, the book still opened on his lap. She stared at the dancing flames for a moment, the crackles and sparks of the burning wood feeding her restlessness. Across the parlor, her father was teaching Tolek how to play chess while Uncle Jakov, rubbing his beard, stood behind his son, watching. Aunt Sascha sat in an adjacent lounge chair facing the fireplace, cross-stitching a geometric pattern of black-and-red embroidery floss on a linen tea cloth. Like the sewing classes her mother used to take with Aunt Ella. Tasa wondered if her mother and aunt were allowed to do anything pleasurable during their long days and nights in the Siberian work camp.

She looked over at Danik, who was engrossed in a game of Solitaire. Her stomach was in knots. They hadn't talked about the incident in her bedroom all day. She felt so much and said so little. All of that pent-up emotion put her on edge, made it difficult to concentrate, unlike Danik, who pulled one card after another from the deck, placing each on one column or another. She wanted to read his mind. He seemed so oblivious to the others in the room, so absent of other thoughts.

She put her book aside and walked from the parlor to the kitchen to make a pot of tea. A draft of cold air struck her as she stood next to the room's mullioned window, the muted light of street lamps coming through its sheer lace curtain. She eased herself onto the windowsill, still wide enough for sitting. In the distance, she could hear a cacophony of voices—likely Ukrainians—from the nearby tavern, interrupted by the clang of the cast-iron radiator as its coils began pumping out heat. She sat for the next several minutes, quietly watching the water in the copper cooking pot begin to bubble.

Numb. Maybe that was how she could deal with her life now, with the rush of feelings and thoughts swirling inside her. *Bury it*, she told herself. If only she could bury all her fear from this war and the loss she felt every day without Mama or Frau Rothstein near. Bury her growing desire for Danik, a pull that had become her own internal battle. The steam rose off the water as she heard steps approaching, only to look up and see the source of her anguish. As Danik strode into the kitchen, her eyes met his for an instant before she looked away. She stood up in the half-light, glad he'd interrupted her solitude but suddenly nervous to be alone with him.

"What were you reading in there?" Danik motioned to the parlor.

"A book by Hesse. I'm sure you've read it: *Narcissus and Goldmund*."

"Ah, the individualist and the wandering artist. Are you struggling, like Goldmund, to find yourself?"

Tasa knew Danik's playful questioning masked his serious intent. "Aren't we all just trying to find meaning amid the atrocities?" Her calm and steady voice belied her emotions.

Danik touched Tasa's cheek gently, and she looked up at him, feeling his sadness and fear like her own, her eyes beginning to tear up. Now they were facing each other, motionless. His look spoke volumes of shared understanding, of love, of his own struggles. Her earlier emotions again rising, she drew her head against his shoulder as he put his arms around her and they stood silently for a moment. Then, stepping back, she placed the kettle strainer on the teapot, slowly pouring the boiled water over black tea leaves.

As they returned to the parlor, the chess lesson had ended and

Aunt Sascha was putting away her embroidery. Tasa was not handy with any form of sewing and admired the intricate design her aunt had created. "What are you making, Aunt Sascha?"

"Covers for some of Grampa's wood side tables. They're so old. At least these will hide the scratches and chips."

"That's assuming the German pawns leave us alone and let us stay here." Uncle Jakov's disdain for the Ukrainian police came from his frequent contact with them at the clinic where he worked as a physician. Feeling a rising panic at what his comment suggested, Tasa glanced from her uncle to Danik.

"What kinds of things are you hearing, Uncle?" Danik's work translating documents at the police station made him a good source of political developments and local dangers as well.

"I urge you two—temper your conversation." Grampa Abram's voice was deep but gentle. He shuffled toward the fireplace to poke at a piece of burning wood and motioned toward Tolek, who was skittishly manipulating the chess pieces. Her grandfather, as elder patriarch, simply wanted to keep peace in his household.

"None of us can live in a bubble, Abram. Tolek is no exception." Uncle Jakov was respectful to his father-in-law but often spoke candidly in front of his son. "The world is at war. Poland's in the middle of it. We must be aware of the things going on around us. Especially now that the United States and Great Britain have declared war against Germany."

"I heard some interesting, maybe hopeful, news today." Danik put down his teacup on the nearby side table and leaned forward in his seat. "Last week, the first Japanese warship was sunk by a US submarine. And yesterday, the Americans pulled off their first air offensive on Japanese bases."

Tasa knew the Japanese bombing of Pearl Harbor in early December was a good omen for Poland and its neighbors, since it had moved the United States from its previously neutral position. "What does this mean for Mama and Aunt Ella and the others, now that the Soviets are also fighting the Germans?"

"I think the women are safer than we are here, Tasa." Jakov gestured for Tolek to sit down by him. The fate of Danik's father was an unspoken worry, left unaddressed.

"I heard that Mrs. Glas was deported to Siberia right after her husband fled Podkamien like you did, Papa." Tasa thought about her morning walk past the shop where Glas Hardware used to be. "I wish we could hear from Mama, from Aunt Ella . . ."

"We all do, Tasa, but all correspondence is over now. At least the one letter that came to Podkamien a few months after their deportation was able to get through. It gives us hope." Aunt Sascha lifted the teapot and got up from the armchair to refill their cups. "We know they're staying together, that they're not being mistreated."

"And that the weather is harsh." Tasa was glad to be reminded of that early letter.

"I agree with Uncle Jakov that they may be safer than we are." Danik raised his cup as Sascha poured him more tea. "I've heard some disturbing stories out on the street from Polish refugees who have come here from the West. They told me of large ghettos being formed elsewhere, of Jews being segregated."

"But we are well liked here; the Ukrainian police act as friends to us." Her father remained skeptical of these stories, so convinced was he that the kind treatment by their fellow Poles in Podkamien would somehow protect them.

"Salomon, you are naive," Jakov blurted out. "We have to wear Magen Davids on our arms, for God's sake!"

Sascha, having returned to the parlor, gave her husband a sharp look, then turned to Tasa and Danik. "How about if we hear some pleasant music in our time together, instead of this nasty talk of war?"

"Danik, you have to sing for us!" Tasa was grateful to her aunt, edgy from the weighty tone of the conversation.

"I have just the song, but only if you play the melody while I sing, Tasa. It's something you know well. Get your violin!"

"My dear daughter, you read my thoughts." Abram smiled at Sascha. "There's nothing better we can do tonight than listen to my two gifted grandchildren!" He turned to his youngest grandson. "Tolek, pay attention—you need to practice your violin as much as you work on your chess game."

As Tasa returned to the parlor with her violin, Danik was entertaining the others with his description of the character from Mozart's famous opera, *Die Zauberflote,* that he would assume in their joint performance. "I'm a rather goofy bird catcher named Papageno. And I have a large birdcage on my back that contains all sorts of birds. Are you ready, Tasa?"

She began to tune her violin, playing the A string continuously, carefully listening to it while tightening her tuning peg toward the pitch she was seeking. Then she quickly moved through her D, G, then E strings until she heard the resonating frequency of a perfect fifth. "Ready."

Tasa put her violin to her chin, her bow high as she began the lively introduction to the song, her volume of melodic chords swelling as Danik's vocal entrance neared.

A jolly trapper of birds am I
And tra-la-la is what I cry.
The Birdcatcher is how I'm known,
In every corner, by child or crone.
My snares are laid. My sights are set.
Then I whistle them into my net.
Mine's the life, so gay and free,
For all the birds belong to me!

She drew inspiration from Danik's spirited portrayal of Papageno and his smooth baritone. She felt Danik's joyfulness, as he inhabited his character's reckless frolic, something she hadn't seen in him for several years. She couldn't help but notice how natural his seamless shift in dynamics and sense of rhythm was, despite his lack of practice. When was the last time she had heard him singing? Tasa closed her eyes, smiling at his playful emphasis of the song's rhyming words.

A jolly trapper of birds am I
And tra-la-la is what I cry.
The Birdcatcher is how I'm known,
In every corner, by child or crone.
If only there were traps for girls,
I'd catch a dozen by their curls.
I'd keep them in a cage, you'd see,
For all would then belong to me!
When I'd got them nice and plump,
I'd trade some for a sugar lump,
Then give it to my favorite one
And woo her till her heart was won.

As Danik drew out these last words, she felt him watching her, baiting her, their singing and playing now an act of gleeful communion. The room around her faded into the surrounding darkness, the softened edges of the parlor furniture and her family members hardly discernible.

And if she'd kiss me tenderly
I'd ask her next to marry me.
Then snuggled in my nest we'd lie
And rock and rock to a lullaby.

The lyrics struck Tasa as a personal plea, and for a moment she let herself imagine a peaceful life of love and abandon with Danik. As their song ended, she could sense the rapt attention and pride in Grampa Abram's eyes, in all their eyes, their applause, then much excited talk all at once. Danik grabbed Tasa in a celebratory embrace. This time she held on to him tightly.

The sound of strange vehicles interrupted their gaiety. The mood of the room shifted abruptly, like light and shadow on a windy day of clouds and sun. Danik walked cautiously to the kitchen. Tasa followed, her heart racing. They stood far enough from the window so as not to be seen, Danik slowly peering out from the corner. He motioned to Tasa to follow him back to the parlor.

"The Gestapo squads are making one of their unannounced visits. Uncle Salomon, smother the fire. Aunt Sascha, snuff out any remaining candles. We need to hide." Danik spoke softly but firmly. Tasa had seen the alarm on his face when he'd looked outside. She knew they had to be quick. The squads "visited" without warning at any time of the day or night, a surprise even to the Ukrainian police. At random, they would round up Jews walking in the street and arrest them, along with others previously detained. These captives were never seen again.

Tolek's face reddened, terror blazing in his dark, round eyes. "What's going on? What should we do? Are we going to die?" As his questions were met with silence, he turned to Sascha. "Mama, help me!"

Sascha took her son in her arms, calming his cries, which were more like a young child's than those of a boy of twelve. She guided him along the narrow hallway as the family hurried toward the back of the house, away from the street. Just above them was an attic connecting the lofts of adjacent apartments, and, for a while, neighbors had taken turns watching for strange vehicles from these lookout spots. But most in Podkamien had begun to let their guard down, as the Gestapo squad visits had become more sporadic. Now, the family members headed down the rear stairs.

As the rest of them huddled quietly in the dark space of Abram's basement, Tolek whimpered softly. Tasa reached her hand out toward her father on one side, to Danik on the other. She felt Danik's fingers interlace with hers and sensed his body closer to her then, tamping down her escalating fear, even as she wondered how much longer they all could be safe in Podkamien.

Judenfrei
Autumn 1942

Tasa heard the staccato sets of double taps at the side door, separated by exactly five seconds, the signal they all had agreed to use when anyone left and returned to her grandfather's house. Her hands trembled slightly as she turned the latch. She slowly opened the wooden door, relieved to find her father and Danik carrying several filled burlap knapsacks. "You look flushed. Let me give you a hand." She took one of Danik's bags and lowered it onto the metal counter, unloading milk and eggs, cheese and breads, and a variety of fresh vegetables.

At dawn, Papa and Danik left to get food. It had become increasingly dangerous to leave home, and Tasa always worried when they were away, even though she knew her father was circumspect in his dealings. He was well acquainted with almost every farmer in the region after a long history of relationships established in the years before war. They gave him produce for free, and he returned their favor with gifts when he could.

Sascha, Jakov, and Abram were finishing their tea at the kitchen table. Jakov addressed Salomon, who was lowering the two remaining sacks onto the floor. "Did you have any trouble?"

"We used the back roads; they're too narrow for German vehicles." Her father turned to Sascha. "Gustaw and Fryderyk loved your embroidery, said their wives would be grateful."

Smiling, Sascha got up and began to rinse the potatoes and parsnips at the sink. Tasa joined her, picking out cheese for their breakfast and placing the rest in the icebox. Putting the eggs to boil in a pot of water on the stove, she then turned around to face Danik. "Come, come. You can certainly slice apples, can't you?" She winked at him and turned back around.

Danik walked behind her, planting his hands on her shoulders. He moved her hair aside and began kneading her upper back. "Your muscles are tight."

She became conscious of a stirring deep inside her from his touch, her face suddenly feeling flushed. She tossed her head his way and smiled playfully. "I could use more of that, but we need your hands on the cutting board right now." As Danik brushed against her, the look he returned was filled with a comforting tenderness.

Through the morning, the three worked side by side, colliding with one another in the small space. For Tasa, the festivity brought to mind the kinds of breakfast preparation her mother used to concoct when she was just a young girl, half her current age. But this particular morning, it was Aunt Sascha taking the lead.

Tasa watched Grampa Abram shuffle silently over to the window, gazing for several minutes out at the street. She thought it curious, since street activity had practically halted, but for the periodic surveillance by the Ukrainian police or the unannounced Gestapo squads. "What are you looking at, Grampa?"

He shrugged, continuing to stare outside. It was, in fact, a quiet and peaceful Sunday morning. Maybe her grandfather was admiring the multicolored leaves, their autumn brilliance captured by the rising sun. Finally, Grampa Abram turned toward them and offered a smile just for her.

Then his knees seemed to give out as he crumpled in on himself, his fall on the hard floor a resounding thud.

Tasa froze. Her aunt's screams drew Tolek from his room. As he burst into the kitchen, Uncle Jakov lurched forward, feeling for Abram's pulse. Tasa reached out for the boy and wrapped her arms around him, shielding him from the scene. As if in some kind of stupor, she watched as her father, Jakov, and Danik struggled to lift her grandfather's lifeless body.

In the weeks that followed, the leaves blew off the trees and the scent of rain clung to the air amid the pall of continuous clouds. The early chill of winter brought with it rumors of the Nazis' methodical movement of Jews from the smallest villages in eastern Poland into ghettos established in the bigger towns, about signs placed around the towns and villages deemed *Judenfrei*, about a ghetto for Jews that had formed in Brody. Tasa expanded the scope of her sorrow, fretting incessantly for Frau Rothstein, Joshua Fishel, and Irina and the Zalenski family, as well as her non-Jewish friends back in Brody.

In Podkamien, the curfews were more tightly enforced, the wearing of armbands more visible. Tasa kept her head bowed and avoided eye contact on the rare occasions she ventured outside. During her recent solitary walk along the town's main street, she'd looked up long enough to see a poster inside a nearby store window; her skin prickled as she read its harsh words: *Die Juden Sind Unser Ugluck!* (The Jews Are Our Misfortune!). Even her father began to realize their fate. "Why do the Germans want us in a ghetto together?" he'd asked. "The only reason would be to kill us off." It was then that the visits by the Gestapo squad to Podkamien started occurring more frequently.

Also around this time, Uncle Jakov heard through one of his Ukrainian patients that all remaining Podkamien Jews were to be transported to ghettos, with the intention of having the town become *Judenfrei* no later than December. Every fresh piece of news that her uncle or Danik brought to them from their Ukrainian sources felt like a further assault, layered as it was on top of the grief she harbored over her grandfather's death. She increasingly turned to Danik for comfort, giving in to the solace of his arms when words were inadequate. She fought the sensation of hopelessness but increasingly felt trapped. Their fate seemed sealed.

One afternoon in late November, her father called the family together in the parlor. Sascha poured tea and passed cookie biscuits that he'd brought from his most recent outing. As Tasa looked around at her family, she saw how anxiety etched itself on their faces. She had stared at her own reflection that morning, shocked to see how pale and drawn she appeared.

"I might have a way to give us more time." Her father settled back into his chair. "Work to pave the only road in town is about to begin. I've been talking to some of the Ukrainians in charge."

Jakov put his cup down and turned to Salomon. "What did you give them?"

"Never mind. It's done. They'll use Jews for labor. Those chosen to work will be allowed to remain in Podkamien. Their families as well."

"Is there a guarantee for us?"

"You'll be assigned as the unit doctor. Danik and I will be assigned to the labor unit."

"How long do you think it will take to build the road, Uncle Salomon?"

"I'm suspecting work will continue through the early spring."

Only her father would have been capable of negotiating this deal. All those years he had built up their community—putting his money back into the land, helping to construct windmills, and bettering life for everyone. This wasn't lost on the Ukrainians now dictating their future. "What happens to the Jews not working on the road, Papa?"

"I'm afraid they'll be forced to move to the ghetto in Brody."

Outside, the sky was dark—black, immense, invisible. Only the unbroken sheets of early December snow falling through the yellow light of the street lamps blocked the horizon. As Tasa peered out the kitchen window, she kept picturing the morning her grandfather died, wondering what had gone through his mind as he gazed at this same view. Caught in a trance, she could hear the third movement of Chopin's Piano Sonata no. 2, "Funeral March," the slow and constant pace of the piano chords, its sound repetitive, somber, and colorless. The piece kept running over and over in her mind, grave and serious like a weighty tome, pressing on, closing in, mirroring the sense of numbness and detachment she'd experienced when her grandfather collapsed in front of her.

She took a glass from the shelf and poured herself some water. The coolness of the liquid in her mouth shut off the solemn music in her head. She wanted to remember other things about Grampa Abram, those special moments she shared with him. As if it were yesterday, she could recall the day he had first introduced her to her own miniature violin. She had been not quite six then. And the concerts she had attended with him, how he'd spurred her curiosity about each piece of music and its composer. Thinking back to her first solo public recital in Brody, she recalled playing the valuable violin he had given her for her fourteenth birthday—the violin she still played today. She could almost see his dark, smiling eyes at the end of her performance, beaming with pride. How she had wanted to please him.

Tears filled her eyes as she walked from the kitchen to her bedroom, almost running into Danik in the hall outside her door. It was late, and she was surprised he was still up.

"You're crying."

They stood motionless in the half-light of the hallway, silent, looking at each other, close enough to touch. Danik took her face in his hands, lifting her chin toward his face, and her eyes followed. His single gaze expressed what no words could.

The quiet of their interaction always settled her down. But whenever he moved closer to her, she felt that shock of longing that she pushed away time and again. Tonight she turned toward her room and motioned him to follow her, closing the door behind them. He touched her shoulder tentatively at first, then pulled her around to face him. She locked eyes with him again, slid back a step to gaze at him fully. Tears now streamed down her cheeks, naturally, silently. She didn't try to hold them back. As if in a dream, she could see what he, too, was seeing.

Like contained water held behind a dam for too long and suddenly released, she found herself filled with an acute and urgent longing she could no longer control. It swept through her body, leaving a pulsing sensation deep in her belly. He pulled her against him, lifting her onto her toes, kissing her tentatively at first, their mouths searching, then pressing deeper, his warmth firing through her and emptying her mind of all sorrow. His chest against hers, his heart beating into her, every part of their bodies touching.

He scooped her up then and gently laid her on her bed. He began unbuttoning her shirt, fumbling at first, until she helped him. She closed her eyes, aroused, as he moved his hands across her breasts and belly and down from there. She pushed aside any thoughts or judgment of what they were about to do. Wasn't their love the only thing that felt right anymore? She nudged his shirt over his head, unzipped his trousers, felt his bare skin on hers as he slowly lowered himself down and entered her, climbing deeper until she felt a loosening within her like a knot being cut, and a sharp pain.

"Are you all right? I don't want to hurt you."

She shook her head. "It's okay. I want this."

He held her tighter then, rolling to one side as they remained as one, locked together in comfort and consolation. "I love you, Tasa," he said, his words barely a whisper.

She gasped for more air as their bodies moved faster, gliding together, their breathing deep and synchronized. Then her mind soared to a higher place, where she felt a part of the wind and the sky. Slowly exhaling, she opened her eyes to his, and a thought flashed through her mind for an instant. What had they done? But she didn't care. In that moment, their touch and locked gaze were the only two things that mattered.

They stirred quietly in the darkness in a mutual state of half sleep, drifting in and out of consciousness. Several hours had passed, and the light of the moon gave the room a peaceful glow. Tasa slowly opened her eyes and watched Danik's chest rise and fall. She thought how easily he slept, as though he would always be safe. She mused again about the peaceful life of love and abandon she could have with him, willing herself to stay with this feeling, not to let her mind spin to the dark reality that surrounded them. She noiselessly moved closer to him, careful not to let her hair, now spilling over her shoulders, brush against his cheek as she lightly touched her lips to his. He smiled first, then opened his eyes. They lay still, watching each other for several minutes before either spoke.

Danik broke the silence. "What are you thinking?" He caressed her hair, then traced her lips with his fingertips.

"Happiness. A bliss I haven't felt in a very long time." She closed her eyes before she continued. "Guilty that I feel this way. What about you?"

He lifted himself onto one elbow, his face hovering just above hers. "I'm thinking . . . that I've been in love with you for quite some time." She sensed an odd tug in his voice, perhaps a question he hadn't posed. And that her answer mattered.

"Danik." Her eyes never left his. "I've never stopped thinking about you since you left for Lwow. My feelings confused me. It felt wrong. Like maybe it was irresponsible for us to get involved. You know, with everything so uncertain now. Unforeseeable."

She rolled onto her side, their faces nearly touching. "But my love for you is all that ever seemed real—all that is real now. I don't feel guilty about what we did tonight. That doesn't seem wrong, though our family might judge it so. It's the world that seems immoral to me."

He was quiet for a few minutes, holding her eyes in his. "We have nothing to apologize for. We're in love with each other. It's wartime." He paused. "But what *about* the others—your father?"

"It would be nice to allow some time—some private time that's just between us. For a while, at least. Without other people's views and reactions—without them interfering in what is special. And new." Tasa wished she had Irina, or Frau Rothstein, to talk to. Not her mother. Not for this. "And we need to be careful in other ways."

Danik's face became pensive, his lips pursed. "You're right, and we will be careful. This was unexpected, I hadn't thought . . ." His expression softened then. "I don't think much ahead. Maybe that's what keeps me from feeling loss . . . and being hopeless. Besides our love, Tasa, all we have, for certain, is today."

"So, you never imagine your life after all this?"

"With the war going on . . . no, I don't." Danik pulled her tighter against him.

Tasa warmed in his embrace but felt a familiar pang, an empty space inside her that she always sought to fill. She wanted this moment to last a lifetime. "That's why we need to hold on to something of certainty." There was something she needed to express to Danik, but so many feelings were churning in her head, like the sea in rough winds. "Earlier tonight, I was thinking a lot about Grampa Abram, and I couldn't help but think about how our mothers don't know."

"Better they don't. Better they didn't have to see what happened so they don't have to carry that picture like Aunt Sascha does now."

"Do you think about your mother and father a lot?" She studied his face. "I'm constantly thinking about Mama. It actually helps me feel close to her."

Danik sat up and drew her up with him. "That's one of the many things I love about you, Tasa. You have ways to work all this out."

She realized it was true. She thought back to the devastating news of her mother's deportation to Siberia. The note. The depth of her melancholy. "When I first learned that Mama was gone, it was Frau Rothstein who helped me get through my grief." She searched for the words that would make it clear to him. "She told me to find a place of safekeeping for my sadness, somewhere hidden from the world. That it would get coaxed out over time, by a song or a memory, like it did tonight. But that's a good thing. Frau said tending to our grief was important so it could go back inside us again. So we can move forward."

"How did that work for you tonight?"

Tasa hesitated, her eyes seeing something beyond their surroundings. "I realized Grampa Abram is part of me. Through my life, I continue his life." Her gaze returned to Danik. "We're all formed by others—our family, our friends, our teachers . . . our lovers. And they make us who we are. I understand that now."

Darkness and Light
March–April 1943

It felt like a long time ago when Papa had burst in on them and they fled to the Gnyps', to this bunker. Their desperate, exhausting trek through the forest transported them much farther than seemed possible in a single night. Tasa had spent the past few hours lying on her cot in perfect, stunned silence, a further distortion of time as she slipped in and out of wakefulness, struggling to absorb her initial shock at where they were now—underground, the war battling somewhere above them. The minutes inched along while she considered their new reality: six of them living in a partitioned shelter. Absent her music. Absent any privacy with Danik.

She and Danik had been intimate for only four months, and yet it struck her that they had always been together this way. She recalled how she could blush at the sight of him, long for him when they were separated, turn to him when she was afraid. How she could finish his sentences, know his thoughts. How connected they were when they performed, her violin and his voice—just as their bodies had been when Papa discovered them.

Tasa closed her eyes and listened to the blankness of the night. It actually wasn't night—perhaps approaching sunrise—but it felt that way. After their harrowing journey, after they put away their scant belongings, after her father extinguished the flame in the kerosene lamps, the six of them collapsed into unconsciousness. Was she the only one who hadn't stayed sleeping? Down here, the darkness hid them—even from each other. But the absence of sound was its own noise, magnifying even subtle movements. Tasa could make out her father's slow breathing, though he slept at the far end of the bunker. She could catch the creaking of cots as bodies shifted in fitful slumber.

She reminded herself she had her father, she had Danik, she had the Dorfmans. And the Gnyps, thank God. Suddenly gratitude for their incomprehensible sacrifice overwhelmed her self-pity. The family was now safe. She willed herself back to sleep to join the others, insentient around her.

Everyone soon adjusted to life in the bunker. The Gnyps brought them food. When Josef said it was safe, they ventured outside. He lent them books and other items to more easily pass the days when they were confined to the underground shelter. Today, as she had done so often in the past month of hiding, Tasa awoke well before daybreak, squinting at the old timepiece she kept under her pillow. She sought illumination in this predawn darkness, was watchful by listening, conscious by drawing from the past. But hers was a restless consciousness, the images she recalled unsettling.

Like the mental picture she had of her father from the previous evening. He was sitting in one of several clustered chairs in their cave-like communal living space. She noticed him staring at nothing in particular, lost in thought, unaware of being observed. He had on a ratty jersey held up by the kind of suspenders Uncle Judah used to wear. His graying stubble and crusty skin made him look to her much older than his fifty years. He carried the worry for all of them, she knew, and she loved him for that. In that moment, so preoccupied and introspective, he reminded her of Grampa Abram. How she missed her grandfather, even as she was comforted that he hadn't lived to experience the fate they now faced. How she worried for her father. Worried for all of them.

She told herself they were relatively safe for the moment, despite the sounds of gunshots nearing as combat raged—the Soviets and Germans battling for control. As she lay alone with her thoughts, she felt the drift and pull of memory, back to their fateful escape in the middle of the night, her father stumbling upon her and Danik in the same sort of dead hour in which she now found herself. She had approached her father two days into their hiding. She knew the unspoken between them hung heavy in the air like a fog and had sensed her father's expectation for her to come forward.

"Papa, I don't want you to judge me badly. You must understand the depth of my love for Danik. And these are not normal times."

Her father had been sitting on his cot away from the others. "While I never expected to find the two of you sleeping together in your bed, I suspected where your relationship was heading. I imagine your aunt and uncle had some clue as well."

"We never intended to sneak around, Papa. We just wanted to make sure . . . to live with the change by ourselves before we shared it with the family, given our confined space. Now even more so." Tasa had felt an unburdening, grateful for the closeness she had with her father and the ease he always brought to their conversations.

"Are you taking precautions?"

She nodded, feeling color rising in her face.

"Have you two talked about a future together?"

"Papa, we don't know if we have a future, period." She remembered how it had hurt for her to admit and verbalize their reality, as she told him: "We live for today."

Just as the memory of that night evaporated into the stuffy air of the bunker, Tasa felt a hand against her leg and reflexively jerked.

"It's me."

When she heard Danik's voice, her nerves calmed. She felt him searching for the edge of her cot in the darkness and grasped what was his arm, drawing him close, her voice a soft whisper. "How long have you been up?"

"I never went to sleep." As he pressed up against her, she absorbed his warmth and they held on to one another. He ran his fingers through her hair, loose and falling against the pillow. His hands caressed her back.

"I was too agitated from yesterday."

"I know." Tasa understood Danik's alarm. Josef had brought them a newspaper with a chilling report on the possible fate of Polish prisoners taken by Soviets—prisoners taken the same time his father was arrested. "The article described rumors, Danik. Without facts, it's easy to imagine the worst. We mustn't lose hope."

As they lay facing each other, she touched Danik's cheek, brushing her fingers across his face and eyes, his lips, then down his neck and along his shoulders, where she felt a muscle knot that she gently massaged, as he often did for her. The night was still, and her eyes, only partially adjusted to the dark, could barely make out his face. "You know, when I finally fall asleep, I dream I'm in Podkamien—I mean, the Podkamien of our childhood. And I'm comforted."

She felt his cold feet rub against her calf as she continued. "I dream about you and our families back then. They all come alive. We are whole in my dreams. Then I wake up and find myself in this bunker and I immediately get a sickening feeling thinking about . . . about everyone who isn't with us." Tasa propped herself on her elbow, leaning the side of her face into her hand. "But I tell myself I'm lucky to have my father here. And I think about what you and I have together."

Danik pulled Tasa up to him, burying his face in her neck. "Our love reminds me that I'm still human, that I'm not alone. But it's getting harder and harder for me to balance the atrocities of this war in my head. You help me, Tasa. You remind me to focus on what's inside us.

"But there's something about these rumors by the Polish railroad workers I can't get out of my mind. Why would mere hearsay continue to be reported? And the specificity of the reports—all pointing to a mass grave in Katyn Forest." Danik lifted his head as he spoke his next words, his voice breaking. "I haven't heard from my father in more than three years, haven't seen him since the war began. I have a terrible premonition about this." He sank his face into the pillow, and she felt his muffled sobs through her hand as it rested between his shoulders.

For a while, Tasa was silent. She knew there was nothing she could say or do, and inside feared the worst for Uncle Judah. She kept that feeling to herself. "So much is out of our hands now. I try to push these thoughts away, as you probably do, but they're always present, aren't they? Like our mothers. But we know enough to hope they're in a safer place than we are." She couldn't help calling to mind other grave concerns. "What about Frau and the others in Brody? I keep turning over so many scenarios in my head. Tangled thoughts, none good."

Danik carefully repositioned himself in the narrow bed. "I'm afraid it's not much different than the situation with my father. We have no way of knowing. I welcome getting news from the world outside, but it's always bad. And the details from the underground papers are the stuff of nightmares. Germans shooting Jews who leave their ghettos? Concentration camps where conditions are worse than prisons? It's paralyzing to think about."

"I keep thinking backward, to peaceful times. I . . . I need to." Their faces were so close, Tasa felt their whispers crossing from one into the other. "Maybe I escape too much into the past."

"You do what helps you get through this ordeal." Danik stroked her hair as he sighed. "Where is the meaning of our lives, if not in our memories? The times we were challenged and grew from those troubles. When we loved and were loved. It's up to us to remember all those who helped us be who we are, to keep them alive—you've taught me that."

Almost imperceptibly, dawn began to seep through the slits in the ceiling, the underside of the stable floor directly above. In the murky light, Tasa knew their private time was over. She still yearned for physical intimacy with Danik, but that wasn't possible now. Not with the six of them living in such close quarters. She gave him a parting kiss before he tiptoed back to his separate sleeping area.

The next morning when Jaga brought down several rolls for their breakfast, Tasa asked if she might come into their house later that morning.

"I don't want to intrude, but I'm wondering if it would be all right for me to practice my violin." Tasa saw uncertainty line Jaga's face and added, "Only if it's absolutely safe. You know I don't want to take any risks. It's just that I'm . . . I'm craving my music. It's hard to explain. It just . . ." Tasa paused for a second, then blurted, "It nourishes me somehow."

Jaga gave Tasa a hug. "I think this is a calm time now. So maybe you can become nourished." She grinned and quickly added, "I'll go ask Josef."

By noon, Josef lifted the ceiling panel and suggested Tasa wear her warm jacket. The early April air was chilly, and low clouds hung in the sky. He accompanied her into the back room of his house. Theo's tail wagged back and forth as he greeted her, burrowing his nose against her leg.

"I'll leave you both here for, what, a few hours?" Josef looked down at Theo. "You behave."

Tasa nodded gratefully. After Josef left, she began to tune up her violin, the strings way off pitch. Theo shook his head back and forth as if he didn't like what he heard. Tasa broke into a belly laugh, putting her bow down to ruffle the dog's matted coat. "Okay, Theo, I'm getting there. Be patient!"

She realized how she'd missed the dog. Theo had to be about ten now but still had the spirit of a puppy. She remembered how he loved to listen to her play. "I have a few more songs up my sleeve, Theo. Just wait."

She finished her tuning and decided to play the lively segment from Mozart's opera that she and Danik had performed when they were living in Grampa Abram's house. She put the violin to her chin, the melodic chords filling the silent space. Theo thumped his tail up and down just like he used to, escalating into happy howls as the piece rose to a crescendo.

She put her instrument down and sat cross-legged on the floor with him, tapping her hands against the hard wood. He slid his front paws down, his butt up in the air, shaking it from side to side. He stretched his head toward her expectantly. His long, shaggy hair was a muddy white with sandy patches; some of his coat hung over his large brown eyes. He was a medium-size dog, small enough that she could pull him to her lap and wrap her arms all the way around his belly. "I love you, Theo," she whispered, her heart unfolding.

Spring finally arrived at the end of April. It was a day when Josef told them it was safe to venture outside. The German front line again had moved several miles to the east; that boded poorly for the Soviets. Tasa found it ironic to be rooting for the communists in this war, but that meant the fighting was much farther away. They were free for that moment.

As she climbed the stepladder into the barn and walked into the open, the brightness stung, so accustomed were her eyes to the dim light of the kerosene lamps of the bunker. Squinting, she held her face toward the sun, its light shining even through her closed lids, its warmth absorbing into her skin. Aware of a shadow, she then felt Danik's lips on hers and she kissed him back, remembering the endless days they'd spent in her orchard in Podkamien.

She grabbed his hand. "Come!" And she pulled him with her as they ran to the wooden plank, then stood to admire the undulating creek, now filled from the melting of the winter's snow and ice. "We've been hiding for only six weeks, but it feels like a lifetime without the sunshine, doesn't it?"

Danik nodded, donning a slight grin, despite his increased melancholy since they had gone into hiding.

"Smell the air, Danik! It's delicious, isn't it?" She studied his face, his jaw sharply defined, masculine. His eyes were expressive and penetrating when they looked at her, greenish in the outside light. She squeezed his hand and leaned her head against his shoulder. In the quiet she could hear shots like echoes far in the distance.

She looked back toward the barn and saw how hesitant the others appeared, barely stepping outside the stables. Tolek stood behind his father, looking awkward, uncomfortable. He hadn't had his growth spurt and was still shorter than she was. Her aunt stared at the ground, subdued, and Tasa realized Sascha had been that way since Grampa Abram died. Her father and Jakov glanced around, almost tentatively, as though acknowledging the moment as the temporary respite it was. Just then, Theo squeezed past the front door, left ajar, and ran up to Tolek, the mood of the boy and his parents immediately lifting.

It occurred to her then that she'd be twenty years old in less than two weeks. Twenty. Living underground, with the war raging somewhere nearby. Her mother absent, impossibly far away. Her grandfather dead. Worry a constant for her father, for Danik. Unable to play her violin except for rare interludes. Yet, despite all this, she still felt happiness. Happiness in the sunshine.

She looked back at Danik, determined to allow herself the pleasure of this morning. She concentrated on the heat of the sun, lifting her face upward. It felt so good. She needed to savor as much of it as she could, take it down to the bunker with her for the endless days when their only light came from a lantern or candle, or the slits from the ceiling.

The sky suddenly turned overcast. Tasa frowned. She thought Danik was just beginning to relax. The others hadn't even allowed themselves this brief enjoyment. After lingering a bit longer with Danik at the creek, the two moved up to join her father, who by then was sitting in a rocking chair on the porch. Josef followed them back into the bunker, bringing several decks of playing cards and books.

That evening, the heavy April downpour finally stopped its vibrating patter, leaving Tasa inside the melody of the second movement of Beethoven's *Spring* Sonata as she waited for her father to discard during their game of Gin Rummy. It was a sonata she'd mastered at age fourteen, playing the violin with Frau Rothstein accompanying her on the piano. She imagined herself, bow held high, gliding it across the strings, her other hand fingering the notes. Feeling the joyfulness, the bucolic and romantic side of nature alongside a dynamic tension, just like her experience a few hours earlier.

They were content after the dinner Jaga and Stefania Gnyp brought them, occupying themselves much like they did every night—Tasa playing Gin Rummy or Crazy Eights with her father, Danik playing Tolek in a game of Go Fish, Sascha doing some form of needlework, and Jakov, sitting close to one of the four lanterns, reading the latest reports Josef brought to their attention. Several candles were flickering, the wax having melted down the wick.

"Gin!" Tasa had beaten her father three of their last four games.

He displayed his cards—a king, a jack, and an ace—with great disappointment, giving up forty-six points. "You win the match, Tasa. You have your two hundred." He started shuffling the deck. "Anyone want to play the loser?"

Danik raised his head. "Tasa, did you see the books Josef brought over?" Then he turned to Tolek. "I think you're ready for Gin Rummy." He rose out of his chair after lightly patting the boy on the head. "Uncle Salomon, I think you have a partner in Tolek if you're willing to offer some moderate instruction. Then maybe he'll challenge you to chess."

Tasa and Danik walked away from the other four to the basket of books, several tattered and all more than gently used. Tasa assumed they belonged to Jaga, who'd attended university in the '20s. Danik began to finger through the pile. "Josef has quite the collection. *Pan Tadeusz*, by Adam Mickiewicz. I read that in Lwow just before all things Polish were expunged. This epic poem was his masterpiece. It tells the story of two feuding noble families." Danik continued to pick through various poetry collections. "Here's a rare one—Anna

Akhmatova. It was difficult to sneak her stuff into the university, even though she'd been Russia's leading female literary voice. She wrote a lot about the difficulties of living and writing in the shadow of Stalin, and it got her into trouble." He pulled out a thin booklet, its cover torn, and began paging through it, finally stopping on one poem. "Here, listen to this. It's called 'Everything.'"

Danik lowered himself onto the hard, earthy floor and sat cross-legged, then drew Tasa down next to him. He began to read slowly, pausing after each word or phrase for emphasis.

Everything is plundered, betrayed, sold,
Death's great black wing scrapes the air,
Misery gnaws to the bone.
Why then do we not despair?

By day, from the surrounding woods,
cherries blow summer into town;
at night the deep transparent skies
glitter with new galaxies.

And the miraculous comes so close
to the ruined, dirty houses—
something not known to anyone at all,
but wild in our breast for centuries.

Tasa placed her hands on the floor behind her, shifting some of her weight onto them. The poem stirred something inside her. Its depiction of misery butting up against the world's miracles took her breath away. Poetry affected her, in many ways, just like music did. Reading poems to each other reminded her of when she and Danik played music together—those were the times she felt most alive. Tasa put her head against Danik's shoulder. They sat quietly, conscious of the intermittent voices of her father and Tolek playing cards, of Sascha speaking softly to Jakov.

"Do you want me to find more in here?" Danik motioned to the basket, and Tasa nodded. He shifted forward and waded through the collection, lifting out a book with a bright red cover. "Another book about the bitter reality of war—Isaac Babel's *Red Cavalry*. And look at this! Pushkin's *Eugene Onegin*! We studied this back at Brody Catholic. Didn't you as well?"

"Yes, Pushkin's wonderful." Tasa smiled. "I had a run-in with one of our new instructors when Brody Catholic became a Soviet state school—seems a lifetime ago now. I was looking forward to nineteenth-century Russian literature, and this puppet, Vetrov, was all about Stalin's socialist realism. No Pushkin or Chekhov, just Maxim Gorky and Fyodor Gladkov." She paused for a second and grinned. "You know, Danik, I always wanted to see you sing Onegin's part in Tchaikovsky's opera. After all, it calls for a baritone and his character is a lazy man who likes to go to parties and socialize. You'd be perfect."

The two started laughing. Danik caught hold of Tasa's arm and brought her toward him, planting a wet kiss on her neck. She glanced over to make sure they weren't in full view of the others, especially Tolek, then took Danik's face in her hands and slowly skimmed her lips across his forehead and down to his mouth, offering him a prolonged kiss before she moved away. She reached into the basket. "Look at all these Pushkin poems, Danik. Let me read one . . . Here's a favorite of mine: 'Wondrous Moment.' Sit here beside me."

Danik leaned against her, his chin resting on her shoulder to view the words. She read it through silently, feeling its poignancy, so steeped was it in love and dreams and memories. Finally, Danik took the Pushkin booklet from her and skimmed through it. "And here's my favorite, for you: 'The Night.'"

My voice for you is languid, low, and light,
Troubling the silence of the dark, late night.
A sullen candle at the pillow's verge
Glows; and my verses murmurously merge
And gush; the brooks of love flow full of you

And in the darkness that your eyes shine through
To smile at me, there are the sounds I hear:
I'm yours . . . I'm yours . . . my dear . . . my only dear.

As he spoke his last words, their eyes met. All she desired was to wrap her arms around him and let time stop.

Laughter coming from the family's shared space broke in on the moment as Tolek called out, "Danik, Tasa, come join us. Uncle Salomon is about to offer his favorite Hitler joke." Jakov folded his newspaper. Sascha rolled her eyes, as if saying certain matters were out of her control.

Tasa sat next to her father just as he stood up. His smile was wide and moved through his eyes and mouth, through his whole face, a sort of youthful exuberance she used to see in him when she was a child.

"So, Hitler visits a lunatic asylum, where the patients all dutifully perform the German greeting." Her father paused for dramatic effect. "Suddenly, Hitler sees one man whose arm is not raised. 'Why don't you greet me the same way as everyone else?' he hisses at the man. And the man answers: 'My Führer, I'm an orderly. I'm not crazy!'"

As Danik began snickering, Tolek asked, "What will the Gestapo do to us if they find us with these jokes?"

"The better question is what they will do to us if they find us, period." Danik nudged Tolek's shoulder lightly.

A tapping noise arose from the secret-panel entrance, their glee turning to alarm in a split second. As the ceiling panel moved, Josef Gnyp's large, ruddy face appeared and Tasa let out a breath of relief. The reality of their danger was never far from their consciousness.

"I'm sorry to scare you. But the radio has broadcast an alert all day saying there'd be a significant announcement now coming from Berlin. Let's see if we can get a clear signal." Josef had a grim look on his face and was clutching the receiver. Salomon moved aside the deck of cards before he lifted the table toward the entrance. German law forbade Poles to own radios, but Josef already had far more at risk. He turned the knob until it clicked, pulled up the antenna, adjusted the tuner, and then turned up the volume as they waited for the Berlin Radio broadcast to begin.

The seven surrounded the brown, wooden rectangular box. Tasa had a feeling of anxiety in her chest as she stared at the mesh indentation from which the sound emitted.

It has been confirmed. German military forces in Katyn Forest, near the villages of Katyn and Gnezdovo, have uncovered a ditch . . . twenty-eight meters long and sixteen meters wide, in which the bodies of three thousand Polish officers were piled up in twelve layers.

In clipped German, the announcer continued his report, the grating static on the airwaves increasing as the shrill tone in his voice grew louder.

This was a mass execution and was carried out in April and May of 1940 by the People's Commissariat for Internal Affairs, also known as the NKVD or Soviet secret police. Thousands more were also found dead—those Polish nationals imprisoned in Kalinin and Kharkiv prisons and elsewhere. While most were police officers, those executed also included intelligence agents, gendarmes, landowners, saboteurs, factory owners, lawyers, officials, and priests, all captured by the Red Army during the Soviet invasion of Poland.

No one said a word. Danik's face was white, his posture expressing resignation, his eyes revealing something else, something Tasa couldn't discern. Something far away, outside his rational being. She reached for him. An unspeakable acknowledgment of this finality froze in the air as Josef clicked off the radio.

Gestapo Overhead
January 1944

Tasa woke before dawn. Without Danik beside her, she was restless. This morning, like so many others during the past year, she lay there for hours, unable to contain the disturbing thoughts racing through her mind. She felt a chill in the air that went beyond the raw morning and knew its double-edged source: being in love with Danik, while taking on his melancholy and pain.

Distant booms jolted her awake. The approach of fast-moving footsteps felt heavier all at once; she sensed them right above her. Seconds later, the pounding at the bunker's hidden ceiling panel cut short her next breath.

Josef jumped down into their private shelter, landing loudly on both his feet before she could move the ladder into place.

"I saw soldiers on horseback! Quickly everyone, come! We haven't much time!" Josef's voice was high and tight; lines of worry unsettled his face. Her father had already joined him, lantern in hand, as they listened to the gravity inflected in every word Josef spoke. "The German front, it's dangerously close now. They're approaching our property!"

Tasa saw terror in the eyes staring through the dim light. "I expect them to come directly to my house. Jaga knows to invite them inside, offer them tea and biscuits." He instructed them to distance themselves from the entrance, to remain quiet, to await further directions from him.

Turning to leave, Josef promised to pile a thick layer of hay on the stable's floor, fully concealing the single opening that could expose them all. Just then, Jaga's head appeared at the opening, fear etching her delicate face, tears in her eyes. Her arms were filled with loaves of bread.

Josef plucked the bread from her, then turned back to face them. "Please, do as I say and we'll be okay."

His last words were muffled. He was gone moments after he arrived.

Immediately, they began to hustle, dragging Tasa and Danik's sleeping cots and sparse belongings away from the entry area and pushing the others farther toward the back of the bunker and into two groupings, one for the Dorfmans, the other for Tasa, Danik, and Salomon.

Tolek began to hyperventilate, finally unable to be that brave soldier her father kept reinforcing. Sascha's face drained of color, and she seemed unsteady on her feet until Jakov grabbed her and pulled her to him.

Danik stepped forward and took one of the paper bags Jaga had brought them, removing the loaf inside. "Here, breathe into this." He held his arm around Tolek's bony shoulder, cupping his hands around the bag to form a narrow opening.

Tasa felt some of her tension release, her fear blurring into her ache of love. She remembered Danik's recent words: *If you give up, I'll lose my faith in everything.* She was determined to be strong for him—for all of them—and turned then to her father. "Papa, we can get through this."

Her father rubbed his thick gray stubble, closing his eyes for a moment. "I hope so." Then, quietly, to her: "Maybe you can help with Tolek."

Tasa nodded, glancing first at Danik, then at her young cousin inflating and deflating the bag. His breathing seemed under control. She walked up to Tolek and stood eye to eye, conscious of his slight, gawky frame and the lingering fright in his reddened face. She knew he presented the greatest threat to their safety, and she needed to figure a way to steady him. She lowered herself onto the nearest cot, patting the space beside her. The others moved away, giving them the appearance of privacy.

An idea popped into her head. "Tolek, I see how serious you are during your chess games, how closely you listen to your papa. Why do you like the game so much?"

Tolek glanced at Tasa, his eyes wide and quizzical. "I don't know, exactly. It's like a puzzle, and it's fun to figure out how to use all the different pieces to get to the end game."

"How do you get to the end game?"

"Well . . . it's all about how you position yourself on the board, how you take control of the center. You know, with the different pieces."

"So, all the pieces have a different role on the board?"

"Yeah. Like the knight—it looks like a horse's head. It's the only piece that can leap over the others, two steps one way, one step the other. Like this." Tolek used his index finger and thumb to make an "L" shape. "Way different from the pawn. Or the rook and bishop, which can move across many spaces. I can get the chessboard and pieces and show you."

"Let's do that later, Tolek." Tasa noticed how the boy began to sit forward on the cot, how his posture had opened up and he made eye contact with her. "I'm intrigued by this idea about how you get all the pieces to move together, to get to that end game."

She let Tolek go on about the game's strategy. His eyes were focused, and he spoke with growing confidence. "You're always thinking about what your next move might be."

"So, what I'm learning from you, Tolek, is that all these chess pieces have important roles to play, that you don't want to sacrifice your pieces, and that when you follow the right tactics and plan, you win the game. Maybe I've stated this too simply?"

Tolek grinned. "No, you get the game."

"I'm thinking that all of us being down here in the bunker is like a chess game." At that, Tolek gave her another puzzled look. "Just hear me out. What end game do we want right now?"

Tolek paused. "For the Nazis not to find us."

"Exactly. And we can all be players on our own chessboard. I personally would like to think of myself as the rook. And you . . ." Tasa paused to think. "You could be a pawn. Don't pawns determine the whole structure of the board?"

Tolek nodded in agreement as Tasa continued. "So it's all about following the right plan, having the right moves. That means whispering like we are now, keeping back to this end of the bunker. And leaning on whoever can help us be brave, so we stick to our plan."

Tasa stood up, took a few steps away from the cot, the chess game swirling in her mind with the fear. She turned back to face Tolek, locking eyes with him.

Tolek seemed thoughtful, pausing a moment before he spoke. "So, Uncle Salomon is the knight and Danik is the bishop and Papa and Mama are the king and queen."

She leaned down to tousle his hair, keeping eye contact. Tolek's face softened as he rose up and reached out to her. Tasa wrapped her arms around him. As she held him tightly, rocking ever so slightly back and forth, she closed her eyes, hoping for a vision about *their* end game. But she saw only darkness.

After several hours passed, Tasa crept toward the front of the bunker, wrapped in her blanket. As she lowered herself to the floor, she heard voices in the distance, gradually getting louder. She could make out Josef's broken German. Then just the clipped voices of two or three soldiers. She felt the weight of them moving about overhead—her ceiling, their floor—steady marching steps, a rhythmic pacing, perhaps. She pictured their dark uniforms, their caps pulled down low over their foreheads. She felt the chill that always settled in her head, the familiar tingling like needles all over her scalp. She bit down on a corner of the blanket to keep her teeth from chattering. She tried to slow her breathing, quiet her heartbeat, as she lay motionless inside her covering. Over the next few moments, pronounced steps became indistinct and guttural voices grew muted, until there was nothing.

When she was sure they were alone again, she moved noiselessly to the back, to Danik, who was sitting up in his cot, leaning with a book into the dimmed light of a lantern.

"What are you reading?" She eased herself down next to him.

"Stanislaw Witkiewicz. *Insatiability.* Do you know it?"

Tasa was familiar with the novel, a controversial one in Poland when it came out in 1930 and among the many rare books in Frau Rothstein's library. Part fantasy, futuristic into the next century, the book's plot seemed to predict many of the kinds of battles and oppression that currently ruled their lives. She was concerned that Danik was delving into this book now.

"Listen to this passage. I swear it's as if the man was clairvoyant. 'Life was rocking back and forth on a crest like a seesaw. On one side one could see sunny valleys of normality and great numbers of delightful little nooks to curl up in; on the other, there loomed the murky gorges and chasms of madness, smoking with thick gases and glowing with molten lava—a valley inferno, a kingdom of eternal tortures and insufferable pangs of conscience.'"

"Danik, this is morbid. Why read this now? Let's find some poetry, or something less . . . less disturbing!" She put her hands on each side of his face and stared directly into his eyes, trying to melt away the quiet rage she faced.

He held her gaze before his eyes seemed to recede, filled with a resignation of sorts, a blank defeatism. "I find myself lying in bed in a peaceful form of depression."

"Is that supposed to mean you're feeling calmer or suffering less?" Tasa knew Danik wanted to clear his mind, pass the time. He lay back on his bed, curled under his blanket, patting the space next to him, a slight upturn to his mouth. She knew he was trying. For her. As she drew closer, she felt a muddle of sorrow and joy, tension and desire, rising inside. She lifted his shirt and slowly rubbed his back, settling her own frayed nerves, her thoughts retreating to just a month earlier, to Christmas Eve.

That particular morning, Josef had come to the bunker, Jaga and Stefania at his side, excited to personally invite the family into their home to share in their celebratory Wigilia feast. The Gnyps had covered all their windows with black cloth so as not to call attention to the light or activity, even though fighting that late December morning was farther away. Jaga invited Tasa and Sascha to help her and Stefania in the kitchen with delicacies saved just for this occasion, coupled with what they'd grown from their land and what Josef had bartered on his recent visit to town. Tasa recalled how the four women prepared multiple courses—carp fillets served with a spicy horseradish sauce, mushroom soup, sauerkraut, apple-walnut filled pierogi, noodles with honey and poppy seeds, and poppy-seed rolls. She again pictured how the pierogi had overtaken Jaga's kitchen that festive day. How she'd rolled the loose dough of flour, eggs, and water until it was very thin, just like she'd learned while baking raspberry walnut rugelach with Frau Rothstein in Brody.

But it was the dinner traditions that Tasa held in her memory. Like when Josef broke off small pieces of an unleavened wafer and gave them to his wife and daughter and passed one to Tasa, her father, and the others, wishing them much health, happiness, and the Lord's bountiful blessings. Josef had called the wafer *oplatek* and said it was a symbol of forgiveness between two people meant to remind them of the importance of Christmas, God, and family. Salomon then broke off a piece of braided challah and passed it among them. That Christmas Eve fell on a Friday night, also the Jewish Sabbath, and this hadn't been lost on Jaga, who had prepared the ceremonial bread for them. Papa had explained to the Gnyps that challah was symbolic of the manna that fell from the heavens to feed the Israelites when they were in the desert for forty years after their exodus from Egypt. He'd recited the blessing for the bread: "*Barukh attah Adonai Elohenu melekh haolem, hamotzi lechem min haaretz.*" Jaga had said that the braids in the challah looked like arms intertwined, and Tasa suggested they could represent love, like the overwhelming love she'd felt for the Gnyps that night.

Or the overpowering love that now surged through her for Danik, who had fallen asleep as Tasa was daydreaming. She looked up and saw that her father, who was sitting in the cot adjacent to them, had been watching her silently rubbing Danik's back. Her eyes met his, and a rush of childhood memories washed over her. Like the feel of his unshaven whiskers that brushed her cheek each morning, or how he held her small hand as they walked to Podkamien's town center for food or clothing. She thought of the photograph she found one early morning in her attic, taken just before her parents were married and now tucked safely inside her knapsack: her father's dark, square mustache matching his thick hair, his square jawline, and the prominent cleft in his chin; how erect he stood, dressed in a tailored suit and tie—a stark contrast with the uniforms he must have worn several years earlier.

Quietly, she turned to face her father directly. "Papa, I remember the stories you used to tell me about the Great War. Do you ever think about that now?"

He had a faraway look in his eyes. "It seems so long ago. When I fought back then, I didn't understand the consequences and causes of that battle. I was living it, was inside it. I didn't see the war in the context we now understand."

A pained expression darkened his face. He took in a gulp of air. It was as though he wanted to share more but thought better of it.

"Papa, what is it?"

He leaned forward and put his hands on Tasa's shoulders. "I couldn't see this war coming, even though all the signs were there. This failure I turn over in my mind every day."

Tasa noticed the muscles around her father's mouth tighten as he continued. "You don't want to believe you are hated as a people, hated enough to be hunted. I couldn't imagine that such evil truly existed or that it could spread like a disease."

"You can't blame yourself, Papa. You wanted only to keep our family together."

"My emotions got in the way. I see now how myopic I was, how I denied what many others saw, what they warned me about. But this hatred of us as Jews, this persecution and mistreatment, were not what I was seeing, not what I experienced as I came into contact with our neighbors every day. Not until it was as obvious as the tanks rolling and the Germans marching into our town."

Her father's eyes suddenly widened, and there was a certainty in his whispered words. "In a way, the kindness of people like Josef—a kindness that, God willing, might save us—kept me from seeing the evil rising and spreading around us. I guess I wore blinders in both of these wars, seeing only what was right in front of me." He looked at Tasa, his eyes sad and defeated now.

"But in this one, I had much more to think about than myself. Much more was at stake."

Tasa saw only her father's silhouette in the bunker's darkness, his shoulders drawn forward, the weight of decades pushing against him.

It had been nearly a week—six and a half days, to be exact—since Josef Gnyp had first warned them of the approaching Gestapo officers. Tasa had been counting the passage of time since that morning, guided by the tiny slits of outside light entering and disappearing from the bunker. Their days were spent in relative darkness, but for those slits and a few lanterns they used for reading. They lived only on bread, now stale, and water.

She fought to keep her own state of mind far above the desperation she often felt, and absorbed, from the others. Their claustrophobic quarters intensified the weariness they all carried. Tasa tried to draw from her rich prewar memories—the swath of Podkamień's open countryside to combat their endless confinement, the buttery aromas of Frau Rothstein's *babka* to counteract the shelter's musty smell, the freedom and energy of days spent playing her violin to negate the oppression of silence. She would transport herself to happier moments, like the last time her extended family had been together: on a sweltering summer day when they had gathered in the new home Papa had built them. She could re-create the gaiety of her duet with Danik, imagine tiptoeing later that night into the orchard that stood alongside her front porch. Feel the warm breeze across her face, smell the familiar fragrance of geraniums and red poppies, see the silver moon reflected in Papa's pond. But when these daydreams dispersed, she was left craving the presence of her mother, suffering the deep pangs of her hunger, or feeling a visceral need for music.

Her steps sluggish, Tasa walked to the unoccupied part of their bunker. Feeling a cold stiffness in her bones, she hugged the blanket around her as she stood against the front wall directly under the concealed ceiling panel. Diffuse light beamed down, and the quiet above her now felt almost soothing.

Suddenly she heard a soft pattering of taps that got louder, like footsteps but not those of a full-weighted adult. Then a scratching. It was immediately above, right at the ceiling panel. A familiar, high-pitched whining. Theo was pawing at the hay piled over their hiding place! She froze, panic crawling under her skin and into her nerve endings. She slid silently to the floor, her blanket engulfing her.

"No, no, Theo," she whispered, almost to herself. "Please. Stop. Please!" The dog's scratching and growling grew louder. He'd found them, and they were about to be exposed. They would all die. The Gnyps as well.

Tasa's heart was pounding into her ears, a deafening noise broken suddenly by heavy footsteps. A piercing yelp. Rustling of hay. Then silence. The steps receded.

She didn't dare move, straining to learn what was happening above her through the sounds.

Nothing.

Minutes passed. She took deep breaths—in and out, in and out. She wished she had a paper bag to breathe into. She tried to steady herself, but thoughts fluttered in her head like trapped birds. Was their hiding place still secure? What had happened to Theo? Whose steps had she heard? Was it Josef? Was he safe? How had he gotten Theo to stop his scratching?

More deep breathing. More time passing. She felt numb, floating outside her body, her limbs rubbery, the silence deafening. She told herself that Josef must have discovered his dog and stopped him in time. Otherwise, their secret shelter would have been uncovered, the panel opened, guns directing them to come forward.

Heavy pounding, as if the earth were vibrating. She shuddered. Conscious now, she sensed Nazi soldiers were moving above her, their muffled voices in clipped and guttural German.

As the voices amplified, Tasa realized she was holding her breath and began a slow exhalation, trying to release the tension in her body. She thought about her childhood, the times her mother put her to bed at night, hushing and calming her by humming a melody. But the booming voices of the Gestapo men overhead and the image of Theo, dead, shattered this image. Unable to quiet her thumping heart, she worried it would expose her. The morbid and grating opening bars of Chopin's Nocturne no. 7 pulsed through her mind, and she strained to bring forth the full range of its dark melody. She inhabited the music, so matched with her own agitation, its restless and vehement power actually calming her, overpowering the sound of the Germans as the piece's climax melted first into a pleading melody that descended into melancholy, then into what she imagined as dancing streams converging under the umbrella of sunshine.

She became aware of the soldiers' movement away from the stable, the resonance of their voices weakening. Listening closely, barely breathing, she caught the sound of a horse's whinny and a man's exertion, followed by a weight being dropped. A saddle? She sensed the presence of a single Nazi fighter standing directly atop the ceiling panel and, in her heightened state, imagined he was not a man at all but an animal. A predator. Perhaps a bear or, more frightening, a wolf. She tried to keep her emotions in check, but her exhaustion intensified her fear and panic. Noises in her head kept her from thinking clearly, but then those reverberations began to organize into something else. A familiar tune. Her mind tried to locate it.

Of course! It was *Peter and the Wolf*. Her orchestra had performed it in Brody only two years after it premiered in Moscow. Tasa now thought back to Professor Fishel's lesson. She could hear the carefree melody of violins, their high notes meandering forth as Peter opened the gate from his home, a staccato array of sounds bringing to her mind the young boy frolicking and jumping in an open meadow. She saw the bird he met in that meadow, the chirping and singing of flutes, the music swirling just like the bird flying in circles of delight. As Peter continued his playful journey, the slow, lower tones of an oboe revealed a duck, its quacking amid the bird's chirping—the oboes and flutes and violins now in a cacophonous dialogue. The sly and loping movement of a cat entered the scene through the nasal sounds of a lone clarinet. Each new instrument began talking to the others: meandering violins, chirping flutes, quacking oboes, the creeping clarinet. Discovering Peter's wanderings, his grandfather—in the form of repetitive, snoring bassoons—told the boy the meadow was a dangerous place. If a wolf should come out of the forest, then what would he do?

Suddenly, the ominous bellowing of the French horns came forth—magnifying, marching. A wolf prowling in wait, drums rolling in the background. The weight and burden of the growling horns, almost like the rumble of thunder, began to dissipate into the frolic and gaiety of the strings as Peter captured the wolf and freed the animals.

Playful meanderings, a marching wolf, a frolicking Peter all blurred together with the music in her mind. The Nazi standing above her was no longer an animal but a man, like her father and uncles. She imagined the soldier before this war, wearing street clothes. Just a husband and father who took pride in wholesome pleasures like a son's first step or a daughter's early words. A man who may have wanted nothing more than to watch his children grow up, live and thrive in a peaceful world. She began to wonder then what had happened to bring about the metamorphosis of this man into a hunter

157

of Jews. What changed for him? What scared him—scared an entire country—into judging and persecuting people with different beliefs? Did he ever question himself? Or did he have no choice but to follow orders for his own survival?

Her mind continued to wander. The music and news coming from the family's radio in Podkamien fused into Frau Rothstein's radio, then Josef Gnyp's. Tasa lost herself within vivid images of Grampa Abram and Uncle Judah. Of Cairo's black mane. Of her mother and Frau Rothstein. She drifted in and out of consciousness. Her angst dulled; she sensed stillness above. Then hefty footsteps, at first close, becoming softer and weaker. Retreating. Then silence.

Tasa heard a light tapping on her bedroom door and wondered why Frau was waking her for school on a Sunday. She caught the baking smells of fresh bread, and intense hunger pangs shook her out of a fog. She felt a gentle tugging at her shoulder, heard her name being called. She struggled to open her eyes in the pitch-black surroundings, even though her eyelids were heavy. A dim light revealed Jaga Gnyp in front of her, holding a tray with a still-warm loaf of rye bread, a wedge of cheese, and a bowl of honey.

Tasa almost jumped, emerging quickly into full wakefulness, confused by Jaga's presence, not knowing how much time had passed.

"The Soviets have again pushed back the Nazis. Our visitors left in the middle of the night. It's early morning now, Tasa. We are all safe. But you must eat, all of you. I'll bring more food, but this will get you started."

Tasa gave Jaga a weak smile as she watched her set the tray down on the floor and immediately asked, "Where's Theo?" But she caught sight of the dog's tail wagging through the narrow portal just as Jaga climbed back up the stepladder and out the ceiling opening. Tasa lifted the tray and walked, unsteadily, to the back of the bunker to join the others and share their first taste of fresh food in a week.

Her father and Danik were just stirring, as was Uncle Jakov. She used all her strength to speak and didn't have to prod to get their attention. "We have food again; the soldiers left, and we have survived!" In a state of stupor, Jakov woke Sascha.

Salomon's steps shuffled across the floor, his face showing signs of strain as he pushed a small table into what had been their common space. Danik, with labored movements, slid chairs up to the table. Uncle Jakov, his hands shaking, lit two lanterns. Aunt Sascha donned a sweater over her frayed flannel shirt, rustling Tolek out of a deep sleep, and the two joined the others.

Josef tapped at the entry and lowered himself into their shelter. A smile of relief on his face, he held another tray of food—this one with apples and hard-boiled eggs, another wedge of cheese, a jar of jam, and two more loaves of dark bread. "I'd invite you to the house, but we must be careful for a few days as we see how far west the front has moved. The Soviets have finally made progress."

"We must express our deep thanks for this food. And to you, Josef!"

Her father recited a Hebrew blessing. A chorus of *amen*s filled the room. Then silence, except for the chewing of food. Tasa had never tasted bread and cheese as intensely as she did at that moment, her hunger growing with each bite. She looked at the faces around the small table and shuddered to reflect on the past week's threat to their lives. Swallowing her last bite, she was about to speak, but a laugh and a sob, all at once, caught in her throat. All they had had to do without, increasingly, over the past four years was of no consequence. She was very clear about what mattered, and it was right in front of her.

A Country Apart
March 1944

Tasa strained to make out the conversation between her father and Josef Gnyp. She felt sorry for Stefania, who sat alone on the small couch separating the two men, their words darting back and forth over her head. Drying her hands on a towel, Tasa walked from Jaga's kitchen to the parlor to join the others.

"I went into Litovyshche yesterday. Only Soviet tanks and soldiers occupy the village. And no combat." Josef eased back into his walnut rocking chair. "The Russians have held back the Germans for nearly a month. I was told the towns around Podkamien are also liberated at this point."

"There's only one way to find out for sure, and that's to go there." Her father took a cup of tea from the tray Jaga offered after their dinner. Jaga set the tray on the oval side table and sat down next to her daughter. It was a near-normal evening, Tasa and her family now able to live openly at the Gnyps' with little risk. "We won't relocate to our village unless the Soviet control of this portion of eastern Poland is certain."

"Of course." Josef fixed his eyes on Salomon as he continued. "I can get you out past our property and well into the forest the morning after next, if you'd like. You and Danik should go. Let Jakov stay with the others until you send word."

Tasa, still standing, felt a growing uneasiness as she listened to the exchange. "Papa, Josef, this is so . . . sudden. How can it be safe?" She struggled to keep her voice even. "What I mean is, the boundaries can change again. Back and forth, back and forth. The battle seems to have no end."

Danik patted the empty space next to him as he looked up at Tasa. "Josef has solid intelligence now that he's safe to enter Litovyshche. We haven't seen this stability before. And the farther we can situate ourselves from the German line, the better. I think his suggestion is reasonable."

Calm as Danik sounded, she was unable to rein in her distress. She knew their plan was sensible but couldn't keep from fretting over any separation from Danik or her father, however brief. Her eyes quickly swept the faces around her. She was struck by how pale they looked— a year without sunlight—and the way fear painted itself on them, like the lines drawn onto Papa's forehead. Her gaze ended on Danik before she lowered her eyes and sank into the down-filled love seat. "I want more than anything for us to be back home, to let the Gnyps return to their lives. But I'm scared."

Her father leaned forward in his armchair. "I share your worry, Tasa, but I don't know what else to do. Our only alternative is to wait indefinitely." He looked to the others. Across from him, Tolek sat snugly between his parents on a davenport. "Are you all okay with this plan?"

A conspicuous tightening began to settle in the room, until Tolek spoke up. "There's one thing I don't understand, Uncle Salomon." Tasa felt a surge of pride, thinking how far Tolek had come, gratified at how he had comported himself during the most harrowing moments of their hiding. How often he had reached out to her before panic seized him fully. "If the war isn't over, how can Podkamien be liberated?"

"Papa, I think I can answer that for Tolek." Tasa held Tolek's eyes as she spoke directly to him. "War is a process, a back-and-forth battle that we've watched firsthand, right?" He gave a slight nod. "So it proceeds like a game . . . like your chess game."

"But chess ends in checkmate."

"Yes, but isn't there a point in the game when the board becomes clearly controlled by one side or the other? And don't the pieces captured by the dominant player usually remain his, before final checkmate of the king?"

Tasa saw the gleam of understanding in Tolek's eyes and felt her own clarity at that moment. Podkamien was a captured pawn, but it was now captured by the "good" guys. Their jeopardy was, in fact, minimized, as Josef had concluded.

Sascha's voice interrupted Tasa's thoughts. "You've brought this relic out of hiding tonight." She pointed to the leather case leaning against the fireplace. "Let's hear music, Tasa. The Gnyps have rarely been treated to your talent."

Tasa stood and moved toward her violin. Bending to open it, she ran a finger across a veil of dust that had accumulated on the black holder, resting her eyes on her beloved instrument as if for the first time. A rush of memories flooded through her. Grampa Abram. Frau Rothstein. Joshua Fishel. Her school orchestra and recitals. Performing with Danik at family gatherings. Beethoven, Paganini, Tchaikovsky, Chopin—all the masters whose lives and work she had absorbed and made her own.

Josef moved his rocker closer to Jaga and Stefania to leave a space for Tasa. Holding up her violin, she felt shy, tentative, at first. It had been a year since she'd had a practice session with Theo as her audience; the many months that followed had been too risky for violin playing. She delighted in the delicate feel of the instrument's neck and hourglass shape and ran her hand along the ebony fingerboard as she considered what she might play this evening, what melody might transport all of them into an expansive dream of peace and freedom. She sought to share a magnum opus, her gift to the Gnyps, even though she knew nothing she could offer would ever repay them for their love and selflessness.

She drew out a few notes with her bow, using these minutes of tuning to decide on her selection. She chose the second movement, the adagio, of Louis Spohr's Violin Concerto no. 9, whose soul and charm stirred her whenever she played it. She then raised her violin to her chin, easing the bow against the strings to enter the piece's lyrical opening. Immediately she became immersed in the music, building the delicate high trills, carefully cascading down several octaves, then guiding the melody forcefully upward again and again. It was as though the composition had stayed in her mind during this absence, as if waiting to be given a voice. Closing her eyes, Tasa inhabited the song's soft, dreamy sadness, breathing soul into her play, swaying with the flights of fancy and fire entering the melody. Her bowing firm, she expressed the music's pure and precise tone. Inside she felt a spirit and elegance, the song leaping and soaring, the freedom of movement in its full range of resonance. Then its final note—quiet and peaceful.

As she opened her eyes, their faces swam back into focus—a softening of lines that suggested an absence of fear. Their bodies loose in their seats. No one spoke. Tranquility seemed to waft throughout the room like a warm summer breeze.

$$\int \iota$$

Her father and Danik left for Podkamien with Josef as planned. Josef returned the same evening, optimistic that the village was solidly in the hands of the Soviets. Tasa busied herself as she waited to get word with further instructions. She played chess with Tolek (who checkmated her twice), read poetry, and wrote in her journal (mostly about Danik). She showed Jaga how to bake rugelach and Stefania how to arrange her blond hair into a stylish bun appropriate for a girl of seventeen.

After they'd passed the time for three days, the sound of gunfire from the west put Tasa on edge and made the Gnyp home again off-limits.

The next evening, right as she finished taking a bath in the tin trough at the rear of the bunker, Josef came to tell her and the Dorfmans that the Germans had again taken over the village just beyond Litovyshche.

"How can that be? I thought we were safe!" Tasa stopped short of reminding him of her earlier warning about fluid boundaries.

"Some predicted that setback, so it doesn't come as a complete surprise. The fact that my property is closer to the German line is the very reason your father wanted to get everyone back to Podkamien." Josef paused, as if allowing her to take in this information.

"I've received word that Podkamien remains secure. The Germans completely withdrew from your village, and it's firmly under Soviet control. You're so close to freedom now, Tasa. I need to get you back with your father tonight! Then I will bring the others." Josef's voice was assertive, his eyes pleading. "Ready yourself with essentials; I can get the rest of your things to you when things are calmer. I'll be back for you in an hour."

The reality of the situation suddenly seized her. She was now in German territory, her father and Danik under the Soviets. A country apart. She went to pour a glass of water from the nearby pitcher, feeling her hands shaking. She noticed a thin layer of ice had formed a crystal ceiling for the liquid below. In nervous haste, she combed her wet hair, then divided it into three even sections as she sorted through what lay ahead. The night was frigid. She and Josef had nearly ten kilometers ahead of them. She pulled the first knot tightly, crossing each subsequent strand first under, then over, the other as she called to mind what Danik had told her in calmer times as she learned to swim in the nearby lake: *fight your fear*. She continued to tighten the braid until it rested like a rope across her right collarbone and down her chest. As she ran her fingertips along the length of her plait, the image of a lifeline came to her.

Later, she exchanged hurried hugs with Aunt Sascha and Uncle Jakov, lingering a moment as she squeezed Tolek against her and whispered in his ear, "Take care of your parents. We'll all be together again soon." Jaga and Stefania met Tasa as she emerged from the barn for a final embrace. Seeing Josef's gray woolen cap drawn tightly over his ears, she pulled her *ushanka* farther over her still-wet head. She had brought only her violin with her, its hard case hidden inside a large satchel strapped across her shoulder.

They crossed the wooden bridge leading away from the cottage. As the creaking planks blurred into the sound of distant gunfire, Tasa lost her footing and grabbed Josef's arm. When he turned to her in the dim light of the moon, she caught his full, angular face, his clear blue eyes filled with gentleness, like her father's, and she thought back to herself as a young girl skipping down the stairs one winter morning, only to be greeted with that same reassuring expression. Josef's body was firm and straight, like Papa's had been before the war. He spoke to her softly, confidently, easing her fear, exhaling clouds of frosty air with each word. "We need to pick up our pace, Tasa."

They continued toward the Soviets, toward the liberated Podkamien, and away from the Germans. The harsh winds hissing at their backs propelled them forward as trees tossed and bent. Dense, low clouds appeared as a veil along the horizon. Tasa turned around to see a strange glow in the distance where she imagined the Germans were stationed. The air smelled like rain, but there were patches of snow on the expanse of field they crossed, spots of frozen ground that in warmer months were rich black soil that grew wheat. As she looked up at the swollen heavens, snow began to fill the air, descending like waves of tiny white butterflies.

Suddenly, she heard a whine and shrill. "We have to stay low!" Josef grabbed her, pushing her down into the ground, just as the *pooooooo* sound neared and rockets swished over their heads. Motionless, momentary silence surrounding them, Tasa could smell Josef; he was so close to her: warm, smoky, tinged with the earth around them. She felt the soggy cold against her face. A thundering boom shook the ground as the Katyusha rocket exploded toward its German target far in the distance behind them.

The warlike third movement of Sibelius's Violin Concerto entered her consciousness, the showy and melodic passage evoking for her the expanse of a battlefield—the very theater of war she now sought to escape. She became a cog within this grand machine, the music so powerful it pulled her inside, beginning with its march-like percussion. The violins, so bold with staccato double-stops, rapid runs across strings, then jumping octaves, swept her along full arpeggios.

She felt her strength swelling as she merged into a steady layering of horns, first soft, the sound then building into a forceful, blaring and booming orchestral tutti.

Josef's terse commands broke into her musical trance. "Okay, let's move!"

He seemed to know exactly when to stop and when to advance, and Tasa now shot ahead without hesitation, keeping her satchel tight against her hip. There was little time to consider fear as they began running, crossing an area still under attack and approaching the snow-covered forest, bullets flying over their heads. Her heart was pounding, synced, it seemed, with a series of short, detached gunshots in the distance. As they ran toward the Russians, faster and faster, she gulped in cold air until her chest filled and felt dry and raw. A tightness broke in her lungs; her sides ached. Her head began to feel disengaged from her body.

They continued to race forward as fighting and fires erupted behind them. "Look at the tank, Josef!" They were in another holding pattern when Tasa pointed back into the distance at a dark Soviet vehicle moving westward. They heard a smattering of distant fire, and then suddenly there was quiet, not even the rustle of trees in the wind. As they approached Podkamien, the fury of combat subsided. Several soldiers came toward them when they emerged at the other end of the forest.

"*Kto tam?*"

Shivering from cold, she was overwhelmed by relief to hear, in Russian, a request for identification.

"*Polska!*"

It was close to midnight when Tasa and Josef reached her grandfather's house. She was light-headed and her back ached as they knocked loudly on the side door. Her father's heavy eyes quickly widened when he saw their faces. "My Tasa! Josef! You're safe! I was so worried!" His voice trembled; his tight embrace was prolonged and protective. He hugged Josef, expressing his gratitude and relief in silent sobs. She had never seen her father cry before.

When Danik took her into his arms, she inhaled his warmth, his savory smell, and listened to his beating heart against her ear. She lifted her head and looked up at him, the dim parlor light illuminating his face, the glint of red in his short-trimmed beard. She smiled reflexively, then dropped her head down and began to melt into his body, feeling suddenly drained and spent. She could scarcely hold herself up, aware of her own weightiness in Danik's arms as he held her more tightly. Even as Danik led her to bed, she might already have been sleeping.

As the four walked outside the next morning, Tasa savored the brilliant blue sky, the glistening sun, and the crispness of the air before spring's arrival. She also relished a new feeling of freedom. It was evident in the activity on Podkamien's main street, despite the presence of Soviet soldiers. How different her reaction from just five years earlier, when she had equated their appearance in Brody with oppression and threat. She observed a lone dog across the street as his black-eyed stares turned to howls, reaching for Danik's hand as they approached the dirt path that would lead them to her parents' property and the house that Josef had helped her father build when the threat of war hadn't figured into their thinking.

The Germans had abandoned their house, a Soviet soldier told her father, and this time it had been left empty. She caught the red roof first, surprised by the sudden, hollow ache in her chest. The expanse of their estate, now in full view, took her breath away. She quickened her steps with Danik so they could be closer to her father and Josef. She caught their conversation midsentence: " . . . some twenty drawings. You always envisioned how the house would sit on the property, what you would see from every window." Josef sounded pensive. "I was proud to help you build this house. You loved this land as much as any Pole. It was part of your hopefulness for our country's future, something few men were feeling then."

She wasn't ready to enter the house. Whatever they found inside, it wouldn't be her mother. She left the others and ran to the barn, but it was vacant, as she expected. Still, she could almost see Cairo there, the sleek blackness of his coat, how he'd nuzzle hay from her hand.

She heard footsteps and Danik appeared, compassion in his eyes. "Come." He extended his hand toward her. "Your father and Josef are going inside."

The state of the house was a shock to her senses, the furniture weathered and dust-encased, the foyer space dark despite the late-morning light. She walked up the curved mahogany stairwell to her old room, so sparsely furnished now she felt numb, rather than nostalgic. She approached the bay window and looked down. Several linden trees remained, the sunlight cast across their trunks. The trees would be blooming soon, the air filling with the scent of lemon and honey. She eased back from the window and walked across the room, pausing momentarily at her original nightstand. Some wisp of a memory prompted her to open the bedside table's top drawer. And there, right where she had left it before soldiers had commandeered the house, was the single golden zloty, the very first coin her mother had hidden for her in the old garden.

She pocketed the now-obsolete coin and crossed the hall to her parents' bedroom. There, the silk bedcover was tattered, her mother's dressing table converted into a work desk. Opening the closet, Tasa felt her throat catch at the sight of a Nazi uniform hanging next to some of her mother's dresses, a few pairs of her shoes still in boxes on the closet floor. She closed the door and turned just as her father approached.

"We'll continue to stay in Grampa Abram's house, won't we, Papa?" Tasa knew their visit was as much for Josef's benefit as it was her father's way of putting closure to his former life as a landowner.

They walked Josef back to town and over to the entrance of the forest, where he would begin his trek home. When it was her turn to say good-bye, she held on to Josef a bit longer, unable to express in words the gratitude she felt to him for saving their lives. They admonished him to travel safely and he returned with a promise to get the Dorfmans to safety as combat to the west stabilized.

After her father retired to bed that night, Danik came to Tasa's room, their first private time since they had last left Podkamien to hide at the Gnyps'. The tension of the past week heightened her longing to hold Danik close, to feel his body next to hers. As he lifted her covers and eased himself against her, his touch along her spine awoke a dormant desire within her. She turned to face him, her mouth on his, their usual whispers and slow touching lost to an urgent need that could be satisfied only at once, silently and intensely, until he withdrew as they both climaxed.

For several minutes, they exchanged not a word. Tasa could hear the wind gusting outside; her eyes grew heavy. Danik curved himself around her back. His fingertips began softly caressing her neck, across one shoulder, then the other. She scooted higher into the envelope of his embrace, feeling him harden again against her. This time their lovemaking began slowly, with Danik's hands moving down her thighs and calves, massaging her feet before he inched back upward, his touch arousing her until she couldn't hold back any longer. She rolled over, brushing her lips against his neck, his ears, his mouth, then lifted her head to lock eyes with him as she guided him inside her.

Afterward, Danik curled around her and they slept for several hours until he began rubbing her back, stirring her out of a peaceful dream. She uttered a sigh and turned to face him, still in a half sleep, until she heard his urgent whisper. "Tasa, I need to talk to you about something that's been on my mind."

His tone roused her to wakefulness. "What is it?" She propped herself up, her eyes just beginning to discern his face in the darkness.

"I've been doing a lot of thinking." He kept his eyes downcast as he spoke. "It seems all I've had time to do during this war is think. Since I learned Papa died, and then when the Germans nearly found us . . . when I thought we'd never make it . . ." Seeing more clearly now, Tasa noticed his facial muscles tightening. "But we survived. And now the war is turning and . . . and I need to be part of it."

"What . . . what are you saying? That you want to fight in this war?" At first incredulous, she felt a growing agitation anticipating Danik's next words.

"I want to make a difference. If I join the Soviet army, I can play a role in ending this war and—"

"Your father was killed at the hands of the Soviets, Danik! How can you fight alongside them?"

"The Russians are our liberators now, Tasa, and Poles are fighting with them against our common enemy. A Soviet victory is a Polish victory." He swallowed hard and paused. "But there's something else, too. I must find my mother . . . and your mother, and the others. There are severe travel restrictions now, but not if I'm traveling as a Soviet soldier."

Tasa raised her head, trying to read his eyes. She had seen how much his father's death had affected him. How deeply he felt the absence of both of his parents, just as she longed for her own mother. She knew he wanted to take control of his life, and now he finally had the opportunity to act. All this, she mulled over in her head. Then that ache returned, piercing in its ferocity—an ache that took in all of Danik, all of her love for him, all of his pain and grief, and the void she'd felt throughout her life in his absence, first when he left for Brody, then for Lwow. Even now, she felt how fiercely she had missed him after less than a week apart.

"I've been talking to a few Soviet soldiers here since I got back. The Soviets are recruiting Poles into the People's Army of Poland. There's a winter offensive going on just north of the Dniester River near Drohobych, and the forces of the First Ukrainian Front are expected here in the next few weeks. I could join up with the army then."

"But you are no communist, Danik. It seems so wrong somehow."

"We live in an imperfect world, Tasa, where good and evil coexist. I'm on the side that needs to win this war, and I can either stand on the sidelines and hope it all turns out right, or be part of the action."

Keepsakes
Spring 1944

As Danik had predicted, Kamenets-Podolsky, near the Dniester River, was captured by mid-April and more Soviet forces arrived in Podkamien. Danik's talk of enlistment escalated, as did the arguments between him and Tasa. For weeks she'd been trying to change his mind, but her pleas for him to abandon his plan were having little impact. Despite her failure to sway him, she couldn't help from bringing it up again. It was late, her father had already gone to bed, and she and Danik remained in the parlor, absorbing the warmth of the fire's last embers.

"No one is forcing you to enlist."

"How many times do I have to explain my reasoning to you, Tasa?"

"Sometimes I don't think you're considering *me* at all—considering us—in this decision." She could hear a shrillness in her voice, her love for Danik now masked by rising panic.

"This isn't about you or us versus the war. Versus finding our mothers or reaching peace. I've tried to make you understand this." Sighing loudly, Danik swept away the strands of hair that had fallen onto his forehead.

"I understand the significance of your decision, and I admire your courage, Danik. But there's no guarantee you'll reach our mothers. And you won't bring your father back." She saw pain flicker across Danik's eyes and immediately regretted her last comment.

"You've always been the hopeful one of us, Tasa. A soldier who signs up for duty represents our greatest hope. I expect more from you—to encourage me. *Not* to give up." He stood, leaving her alone on the couch, as he lifted the wrought-iron poker to move the smoldering wood in the fireplace.

"I'm not giving up. I'm just being realistic." She couldn't seem to change the tone of their conversation or keep her emotions from spiraling out of control, and she knew he was turning away from her in anger. "Can't there be other ways you can play a role in this war without joining the front line?"

"My decision's been made." He turned back to face her. "Maybe you're being a little selfish?"

She felt his words like a slap, before the hurt radiated throughout her body. "If loving you too much is being selfish, if not wanting to lose you is being selfish, wanting to be with you for the rest of my life . . ." At that, she broke down in sobs.

Danik scooped her into his arms and held her, not speaking for several moments until her crying spasms began to subside. His next words came out softly, calmly. "Tasa, Tasa. I hate when we fight like this. I love you more than anything. You are my life." He tightened his arms around her and began to rock her. "Hell, if this damn war were over, we'd begin that life together right now." He drew a handkerchief from his pocket and wiped the tears from her face, then kissed her long and hard. She felt a swell in her chest, so full of love and longing. She was desperate to hold on to Danik, to protect him from himself, even as she realized the futility of her efforts.

That next Monday was Tasa's twenty-first birthday. Danik did everything to make the evening special, including procuring a fine bottle of wine, preparing a dinner by candlelight out in the parlor, and making sure her father left them alone.

As they sat quietly, he took her hands in his, then bent across the table and kissed her on the lips—a prolonged, serious kiss. Afterward, he held her eyes with his. "I know recently you've been unhappy with me, Tasa. But my commitment to you is unwavering." He paused, taking a deep breath. "I want to marry you. Spend my life with you. Have children with you." His voice implored her. "I want to have the future you see for us."

On the one hand, her answer took only an instant's thought. Yes, of course. In her mind they were already married. She had fallen in love with him long before they became intimate, their bond built over so many years and experiences. On the other hand, the war was ever present. Everything around Danik's commitment to join the effort threw her into a fragile emotional state. She was still unable to come to terms with his decision, her thoughts muddled from all she'd already suffered and fears she couldn't keep out of her mind. And yet the ideal of a future for them was what he offered. She reminded herself of his need for her to be strong. *If you give up, I'll lose my faith in everything.*

So she answered the only way she knew how. "I will always be here for you, Danik. I know no other way. My love for you has no bounds."

A shyness sat between them now. Tasa knew some of this came from what she withheld—worries she no longer shared with him aloud—and the uncertainty they both felt inside, despite their brave professions. Gazing at the flickers of candlelight in his eyes, she could almost make out her own reflection. She hoped the fear that stuck to her like sweat wasn't visible to him. She needed to become an unshakable spirit for Danik so he could depart with a clear head and heart. She closed her eyes, willing the certainty of their fate together, envisioning that future for them.

"In a way, we already are married, Danik. That is, if commitment is what defines a marriage." Tasa smiled, reflecting on their journey as lovers—two virgins who would certainly have taken a different path had not war pulled them apart, then drawn them together at such a young age.

"Yes, we are, in many ways." Danik suddenly stared off into space, and she could tell he was turning something over in his mind. "We could get married before I leave, couldn't we? I mean, have some kind of civil ceremony now and then a proper one later—once the war ends. Once our mothers are back and our families are together again. Or am I being crazy?"

She couldn't help but smile as his idea spurred her to consider, then discard it. The risk and haste involved in pursuing some kind of makeshift ritual felt wrong in her gut. And the reality of finding an officiant to perform the ceremony diminished the sacredness of their commitment. "We don't need some kind of validation or approval just because we've been intimate outside of marriage. In the eyes of the One above, *we* haven't done anything wrong, Danik. Many others have, considering the mess the world is in now."

"I'm not looking for vindication. I'm wanting to take what we have, what we are to each other, and give it permanence. Vows to each other of the immortality of our love . . ."

His last words hung in the air, the glow of the candle illuminating the space around them. Tasa felt his pronouncement as a revelation of sorts, a letting go of all kinds of burdens she carried. A relief. Private vows. Perhaps a symbolic ceremony to make their love immutable. Carved in stone. They rose from their chairs and rushed toward each other. He reached for her and pulled her to him, his lips pressing against hers with fresh urgency as mixed emotions shot through her: yearning and desire and a deepening ache.

She took a small step back from him and held his face in her hands, an image forming in her mind. "Danik, we can have our own private union. I have something I want you to have that has been as constant as you have been in my life. We can exchange personal tokens and vows of our love for each other. Our own secret promise. Before you leave." And she thought, *To seal our fate to be together. Always.*

She planted a kiss on his forehead and gestured him toward the couch. "Sit. I want to play something for you . . . for us." At that, she turned and hastened into her bedroom. Plucking her violin from its case, she felt a surge of irrepressible love stream through her body, grounding her in this moment.

Danik had added a log to the hearth in her brief absence and was ministering to the wood to rekindle the flame as she returned to the parlor. He smiled broadly and his eyes brightened as he watched her adjust the pegs of her instrument, drawing several notes out with her bow. "This is noteworthy. My own private concert."

She watched him lower himself onto the couch, conscious of the pleasure conveyed in his eyes as he looked at her. She gazed at him intently as she placed her violin up to her chin and sat her bow against the strings. In a downward motion, she launched into Beethoven's Violin Romance no. 2 in F Major.

The melody began slowly at first, yearning in its tender tone as it drifted and became, for her, an emotional narrative. She closed her eyes, lost inside its delicate mood as she drew out each note, lengthening its affect, the sound lingering in the air, her body stretching upward as the pitch ascended. She drew in her own breaths with every pause, her breathing and body movement synchronized with the music's trills, leaps, and turns. She was uninhibited and free, the grace of the notes rising and falling in slight shifts as she reached for the sweetness of a single bird in song. Carrying the thread back, then forward, like distinct waves in the wind, she rose with their dramatic surges, retreated with the descending scales and arpeggios. As she built the lyrical layers toward the climax, the final trills resolved into one high-pitched voice and she imagined a peace, electrifying in its stillness. Slowing her breathing at the final measure, she opened her eyes to see Danik's face, radiant in the firelight.

Later, their lovemaking was unhurried and they held on to each other well into the night. Staring into each other's eyes as if in a trance, they exchanged private words filled with every truth they could summon to bind one to the other, memories to carry them through their separation and beyond. Tasa, sharing the story of her mother's childhood game, gave Danik her cherished golden zloty, the coin a symbol of all the discoveries of her life. So many she had experienced with Danik, so much she still wanted to discover with him. Danik gave Tasa a silver locket with a chain to wear around her neck. It was the gift his father had given him before he had left with her for Brody and then Lwow, the last time either of them had seen Judah Riesmann. The pendant opened onto a tiny photograph of Danik and his father from more peaceful days.

By the next week, Danik was on a truck with other Polish recruits, officially a Soviet soldier. Tasa and her father accompanied him to the main Soviet office to see him off. His parting kiss lingered on her lips as she stood and, fingering the silver at her throat, watched the truck fade, then disappear, into the distance.

Following Danik's departure, Tasa tried to occupy herself productively. She put her energies and attention toward her father. She cooked dinner every night, and they took early-evening walks through the village once the troops moved out of Podkamien, heading north and west. The days began to blur together. The longer she was apart from Danik, the more she had to struggle to shake off her despondency and self-pity. Strangely, she couldn't bring herself to play her violin.

One evening right after they sat down to eat, her father offered a suggestion. "Why don't you volunteer at the clinic?" During one of their walks, they'd passed the health center where Jakov Dorfman used to work and learned it was seeking more staff.

"I don't have any experience . . . or aptitude for that sort of thing." Tasa picked at her food and pushed the potatoes around on her plate, a habit she'd acquired at a young age whenever conversation unsettled her.

"I'm sure there are nonmedical tasks, Tasa. And it would get you out of the house, doing something of purpose." He stood to take his dish to the sink and looked down at her plateful of food.

The two visited the clinic the next day and learned of yet another planned offensive, which was to begin in June, bringing additional Soviet troops to Podkamien.

"We could use Miss Rosinski's help, sir. We expect the clinic will be getting much busier in the coming months."

The Soviet soldier in charge at the clinic couldn't have been five years older than she was. His uniform was pressed, his short brown hair combed neatly with a side part. And he was competent, certainly not like the soldiers she had come across in Brody.

"But you might want to think this over. You and other Podkamien residents will be encouraged to leave in a few weeks. Those who stay will remain under our control and protection. But it may get rough." The young soldier at first spoke directly to Salomon, then looked back at Tasa. "As I said, though, we could use help here . . . if you choose to stay."

Later that evening, Tasa and her father discussed their options.

"I'm tired of this nomadic existence. I don't know where it's truly safe anymore." Her father looked worried—about another decision that, Tasa knew, could place them in jeopardy.

She also didn't want to leave Podkamien and made the choice easy for her father. "Shouldn't we stay where Mama might try to send word to us, and where Danik can also write to me?"

Many of their neighbors did abandon the village as the fighting approached. Tasa and her father received word that Uncle Jakov, Aunt Sascha, and Tolek had left the Gnyps' and relocated to Krzemieniec, about thirty kilometers northeast of Podkamien. Feeling isolated, Tasa signed up to work at the clinic three days a week, but it was mostly filing records for the doctors. Through May, the only patients coming through the clinic were village locals—the elderly with acute illnesses, children requiring stitches or the setting of broken limbs. The doctors taught her basic first aid, and she became useful in calming down both hysterical children and their anxious parents. Some afternoons she complained of being bored. "Wait until the next offensive begins. We'll be plenty busy," one Soviet physician told her.

Instead of occupying her mind and easing her melancholy, Tasa's time at the clinic and the anticipation of battle—of tending to injured soldiers and the associated danger she knew Danik faced as a soldier on the front line—heightened her anxiety, and she finally turned back to her violin almost obsessively. Danik had been gone a month, and so far there was no word from him. She told herself she was being unrealistic but couldn't stop herself from visiting the Soviet postal office during any lull in the clinic activity.

As May turned to June, Tasa again made that trek, feeling weary and hopeless. The mail office was a one-room cubicle in the village center—so tiny it accommodated three bins of mail, one attendant standing at a narrow counter, and a single customer. She often had to wait outside, in line, for up to an hour just to inquire whether she'd received a letter. For the attendant, hers was a familiar face by now.

"Miss Rosinski, there's no letter for you. Frankly, there haven't been many coming through here the last few weeks, certainly none postmarked from this past month." She could tell the man felt sorry for her. He'd been a sympathetic listener when she told him of Danik's enlistment. "Look, if you write a letter, we'll try to see that it reaches him."

Later that day, she took out her pen and wrote her first letter since Danik had left.

Dearest Danik,

These past weeks, without a word, have been long and lonely. I've been escaping much more into my violin, shutting out the world and numbing my feelings. Who would've thought a pursuit as noble as music could become such an anesthetic in my life? Paganini is my sole diversion to keep from fretting over all that I don't know—like where you are or when you'll return. I mostly muddle about. Papa says my melancholy was to be expected.

I can't help replaying my reactions to your decision to enlist. My choice of words at times was thoughtless and emotional, and I regret that now, but you understand the depth of my feelings. Despite my misgivings, you know how much I admire your courage in wanting to play a role in ending this crushing war and trying to reach your mother—our mothers. Selfishly, as you've pointed out, I'm still angry at your decision. And my fear for you has not subsided. On the contrary.

I now work at the clinic and hear rumors of a Soviet offensive to be launched later this month. Such secrecy surrounding the war, not being able to know what you're going through or if this letter will reach you—it has worn me down. In your absence, I realize more than ever how you've been the balance in my life and the one closest to my heart—so much more than family. You know that now, Danik.

I keep thinking about the Podkamien of our childhoods. Those carefree days when our world was small and secure. When we had our whole family around us. Looking back, it's hard to believe all we've been through.

When I get myself agitated—and you know how I can do that—I think about the many champions along this road we've traveled together and I become overwhelmed by gratitude. Our parents, of course. But also Frau Rothstein and Professor Fishel. Who knows what's become of them, or our Brody friends? And how can we ever forget the valiant Gnyp family?

But you, dearest Danik, you are my greatest hero! What a special son you are to your mother to risk your life to make contact with her. I pray for your safety every day, for this horrible war to end, for us to have our mothers back. And to have you return to Podkamien, or wherever we can be together again.

I love you with all my being,

Tasa

Answered Prayers
February–April 1945

Tasa was lost inside her thoughts as the horse and carriage advanced unhurriedly toward the farmland outside Podkamien. This morning they were paying a sympathy call to Gustaw Pawlak, whose wife had died of a virulent form of pneumonia that didn't respond to the medicine Tasa was able to obtain from the clinic. The sun shone high against a cobalt sky, and the winds were calm despite early February's frigid temperature.

She and her father were free to roam around and beyond Podkamien now that the Soviet troops had left the village. It had been a long and lonely winter. The summer offensive had spilled into another sustained attack, and they had quickly learned to live with war in their midst. Tasa at the clinic. Every night alone at Grampa's house with Papa. Empty streets. The sounds of rockets so frequent, she stopped noticing. During lulls in the combat, her father borrowed this same horse and wagon to obtain fresh food from nearby farmers, like Gustaw.

Tasa couldn't help associating this ride with that last trip to Brody she had taken with Danik through the humid heat of August. The memory warmed her at first, until the emotional weight of that journey, just before the war broke out—before she and Danik went their separate ways—congealed in her mind. Today's trip to the Pawlaks' carried a different kind of poignancy, one for that family's loss and her own. It had been eight months since Danik's enlistment, her only connection with him through infrequent letters. His expressions of love were transparent and affirming, alongside the many ways he veiled the dangers he faced. But she knew the truth. Through her work at the clinic, she witnessed firsthand the consequences of battle.

The last group of wounded soldiers coming through the Podkamien clinic presented the harshest picture of the war's toll she'd yet seen. So many deaths. Injuries leaving men unrecognizable. At first, the sight of the mutilation drove her to the back room, retching and heaving until she had nothing left. But she swiftly built up an emotional armor. She had to. The casualties were mounting. One young man, no more than twenty, arrived in a half-conscious state, shot through his spine, his moans conveying extreme pain. The doctors immediately administered morphine and operated to save his life. She sat by his side for hours after he came out of surgery, listening to his delirious and fragmented outbursts—horrific images of war, as well as more comforting visions of people and places that she sensed were home to him.

As Tasa and her father rode farther from the village, the expanse of the wide-open countryside became interspersed with worn farmhouses, adjacent to run-down red barns and fenced-in plots with horses, cows, and sheep. After less than an hour, they approached the Pawlaks' property. Her father pulled up on the reins, then tightened his grip as he eased the wagon to a halt in front of a dilapidated house, the brown stain on the wood siding abraded by years of harsh weather. He jumped down from the carriage and held his hand out to her. The creak of the wagon and the smack of Tasa's impact on the frozen ground brought Gustaw onto his porch, his three daughters close behind.

The youngest, Lidia, was around six, her amber eyes round and puffy. She grasped Gustaw's leg, her long, tow-colored hair unkempt, falling below her shoulders. Ivona, brown-haired and thin, looked to be about thirteen. Juliana, the oldest, seemed the age of Tasa when her mother had been deported to Siberia. Dark circles under her rheumy eyes and her blank expression revealed the girl's sorrow. Juliana's hands rested protectively on Lidia's shoulders.

"Come in! I'll get some water for the horse while you join us inside and warm yourselves." Gustaw ushered Salomon and Tasa through the doorway into a sparsely furnished, cramped parlor, a crackling fire at its center.

Tasa fumbled inside her coat pocket and pulled out a piece of dark chocolate left over from what Josef had given her almost a year earlier, "for energy," he had told her during their desperate flight from the Germans. The bar, having been kept in the icebox and then pocketed in the dead of winter, was frozen solid. She broke the block into several pieces and offered one to each girl. Lidia shyly came forward, Tasa earning a hug from the child as she handed her the treat. Gustaw watched the gesture, smiling appreciatively. She eased herself onto the couch and patted the spot next to her for the child to sit. As Tasa turned her head to the right, she recognized the intricately embroidered cover atop the adjacent side table, and then looked over to her father.

"We're so sorry for your loss, Gustaw. Joanna was a good woman and always welcomed me to your home, as you did. We might have starved if not for you and Fryderyk supplying my family with food during the days when other Poles turned us away."

"You always insisted on paying us back, Sal. For us, it was a tithing. Regardless, Joanna deeply appreciated Sascha's artful needlework and, as you can see, loved to display it in our home." Gustaw's voice caught then, and he took a moment to collect himself before he continued. "How are Sascha and her family?"

"They're fine. They didn't want to be amid any more fighting in Podkamien and have relocated to Krzemieniec for now."

"Have you heard anything about Halina?"

Tasa spoke up. "I received a letter from Danik that had some news about Mama. It was two months ago—actually, the last letter of his that's come . . ." This admission stated aloud overwhelmed her, and she swallowed hard, feeling her father's eyes on her.

He continued for her, his voice quiet. "You know, Danik had hoped he might reach his mother, Halina, Sophia, and her girls by joining the Soviet troops. As it turned out, all he could do was trace their whereabouts."

"But this is good, yes?"

Salomon nodded. "His information was valuable but limited. The Soviets classified each deportation separately. That grouping defined its location, even the living circumstances. Danik learned that the women and children had first been assigned to a labor camp in southern Siberia, where they lived from February nineteen forty until the Soviets released them in late forty-one. Many of the deportees left their original destinations once the Soviets joined the Allies, especially those in the north, where the conditions were harsh. But those Poles wanting to rejoin family here had to find other places to live, waiting out the war." He looked from Gustaw to his daughters, but Gustaw gestured for him to continue.

"It seems the women may have traveled south, within Russia, to a milder climate. Danik's information also pointed to his mother's traveling with one other woman, and he believed that to be Halina."

"Did Danik share anything further, anything about the war?"

By this point, Tasa had located a comb and was braiding Lidia's hair in pigtails as Ivona and Juliana looked on intently. She tightened the ropy mane as she spoke. "Last summer Danik was part of the Lvov-Sanomierz offensive, where German troops were forced from the Ukraine and eastern Poland. By the end of August, both Lvov and Brody were liberated, thanks to this effort. I'm not sure you're aware . . . Danik and I studied in Brody and . . ." Tasa struggled to control her voice, stifling a sob as she drew in a deep breath. "By the time Danik's troop arrived there, he learned that all the Jews assigned to the Brody ghetto had been sent to concentration camps elsewhere, many to Auschwitz, near Krakow. There was no word of many who had become like family to us during those years."

As the families caught up on each other's lives, the solemn mood of the visit lifted and their stay extended well into the afternoon. Tasa observed Gustaw's plainspoken manner and the ease with which he and her father shared their experiences, despite the fact that one was a Jew, the other a Catholic, just like their relationship with the Gnyps and her friendship with Ania back in Brody. After eating a light snack of cheeses and breads with the Pawlaks, her father readied the horse and carriage for their departure. Gustaw loaded the wagon with fresh produce, and Tasa promised she'd return the following week to spend time with the girls.

Two days after they returned, Tasa was at the house, nursing a scratchy throat. Happy to have a day off from the clinic, she used the quiet time to practice her violin, something she hadn't done enough of over the past few months. It was late morning, sunshine streaming through her window, despite the bitter cold outside. The images of winter filled her head with song: the fourth of Vivaldi's concertos, *The Four Seasons,* and its allegro non molto first movement. She could visualize the frozen landscape as she entered the piece's repetitive rhythm, could feel the biting, stinging winds as she reached the high string notes, the melody's intensity building. The rapid tempo, quick, pulsing notes moving up and down the range of the fingerboard, the agitated tone and back-and-forth repetition—all in an escalating volume—conjured the picture of someone running across the snow and stamping his icy feet. Inside this blustery scene, she became invigorated, pushing herself until the last measure.

As the music still vibrated in her ears, the slamming of a door broke her spell, followed by hurried footsteps already reaching the hallway to her bedroom.

"Tasa! I've a letter! From Kazakhstan. From your mother!"

She nearly dropped her violin. "Oh my God! Papa, what does it say?"

His face was red, his breathing ragged. "I didn't open it. Ran like hell so we could read it together."

Tasa reached for the envelope, her hands shaking. Tears filling her eyes forced her to blink several times to make out the postmark: *January 15, 1945.* "That's more than a month ago!" She looked again. *Shymkent, South Kazakhstan.* She studied the handwriting. "It's Mama's, isn't it?"

Her father nodded excitedly. "You open it."

Tasa's fingers trembled as she ripped into the envelope. She unfolded the two full pages of parchment in what felt like slow motion, eyes focused on the salutation and the letter's first sentence. She looked up at her father, smiled, cleared her throat, and began to read aloud.

Dearest Salomon and Tasa,

I pray this letter reaches you, that you are alive.

I've been told that correspondence can now get to eastern Poland, that much of it is liberated, Podkamien as well! I am hearing that the end of war is near.

How long we have been apart! I don't know if any of my letters have reached you; I assume not, so I'll briefly share the following. When we first arrived in southern Siberia, Sophia, Ella, the girls, and I were not separated—fortunately—and we lived together in a labor camp outside of Chelyabinsk, just east of the Ural Mountains on the border of Europe and Asia. As life has likely been for you, it was terribly rough here, the worst in the beginning months—the harsh weather, manual labor, lack of hygiene. It was a miracle we survived the malnutrition and conditions. I worried about Sophia, so distraught in her grief for Ehud. But a kind man in our settlement from Lwow, Louis Krantz, who had lost his wife and children, took us under his wing, made sure we had enough food, attended to Dalila and Mela. Over time, Sophia fell in love with him.

We were officially free as soon as Russia joined the Allies, but had nowhere to go as long as Germany controlled the war and Poland was a battlefield. Sophia, Louis, and the girls left immediately, but I couldn't. I developed rheumatic fever toward the end of our exile. Ella, who has harbored her own fear around Judah's fate, has been my angel, nursing me until I was able to travel. By late '41, we took a train going south—everyone did— to anywhere the weather would be milder and, for me, where there might be medical care. We ended up in Shymkent, in central Asia, where the winters are warmer and the summers are hot and relatively dry. Here, I was able to regain my health.

We've lived here for the past three and a half years among Jews and Muslims, Poles and Russians, praying every day that you're safe and that the war will end. After my first letter from Siberia, I knew it was useless to write. Since I've been here in Shymkent, I've sent letters to Podkamien, but many told me I was wasting my time.

I've received news in bits and pieces, some rumors as well. Some say no Jews are left in the villages of eastern Poland, but how can they know that? My belief in your survival has kept me alive. I'm afraid to ask about Papa Abram. Is there any word about Judah? And how have Danik, Jakov, Sascha, and Tolek fared? Ella worries with me and sends her love. These are not normal times, and we are both braced for the worst.

Please write me as soon as you receive this, and I will take the next train to be with you again.
All my love,
Halina

Tasa's reaction to what she read was an emotional whirl: elation at knowing her mother was alive, horror at what she had endured, loss in the fresh reminder of how long she'd been missing her. "After all these years of keeping Mama in my heart . . ."

She looked at her father, and his tears matched hers, a sob catching in his throat. "Your mama lives! Thank God!"

Tasa thought about that first note she had received from her mother. How assured Mama was that *she'd* be safe, only worried about *their* protection. How, in the midst of the chaos of her deportation and the soldiers' commands, she could think to send a message to her daughter: *All you have, dearest Tasa, is your mind and your heart.*

"What will we tell her? So much has happened." Tasa was suddenly struck by how very far away her mother had been living all those years, how far away from them she had been even then. She hadn't even known that Lwow was no longer a Polish city.

Tasa and her father talked through the options of what to include and what to leave out in the letter they composed. They considered the repercussions particularly for Ella—if she were to arrive in Podkamien only to hear that her father and husband were dead, her younger son in combat alongside Soviets and Poles. They decided to keep their message brief but forthcoming about the consequences of war on their family. They sent their letter later that day, and Tasa was already impatient about the time it would take for its arrival, anxious for her mother's travels back to Podkamien.

The smell of spring hung in the air as the days grew longer. A glistening layer of dew lay above still-frozen ground. The chirps of robins and sparrows interrupted Tasa's thoughts as she returned to her village from her now-weekly visit with the Pawlak girls. She decided to again check whether any mail had arrived for her and walked toward the postal office. The officer in charge began to sift through a growing pile of letters. Her heart skipped a beat as the man pulled a letter out of the pack and handed it over. "Today must be your lucky day."

She could see the address was in Danik's handwriting and was comforted temporarily in his safety until she read the postmark of March 1, a full month earlier. Silently bemoaning the crawling pace of mail correspondence in wartime, she hastily thanked the officer, turned, and quickened her steps toward home, where she could experience Danik's letter privately.

She could hear the pounding of her heart as she began prying open the envelope, careful not to tear the letter itself.

My dearest Tasa,

I received your last two letters today, and I read them over and over.

I miss you so much and share your frustration at our separation and the difficulty of our wartime connection. Know that I close my eyes every night and dream I can hold you, and that I count the days for this war to end so we can begin our lives together.

I apologize for the lag in my communication, but there was no postal service anywhere near us for months. And I wish I could have found out more about our mothers. There were three deportations in '40—February, when our mothers were taken, and April and June. The irony was that for many Poles, despite the brutal conditions they had to endure, this capture saved them from German camps. Given my itinerant situation, I couldn't get any further information about where our mothers, aunts, and cousins went once they left southern Siberia. Have you heard anything?

Shortly after the new year, we traveled from the Vistula River to the Oder River, seventy kilometers from Berlin. We secured Krakow on January 19. It was a deadly assault—a nightmare—with many lives lost, many more maimed.

We moved westward toward Silesia in early February to protect yet another military drive that's moving toward Berlin. We're in a holding pattern right now, but another offensive for my troop is to begin soon—within a couple of weeks—with the goal of pushing the Wehrmacht out of Silesia. I'm part of the First Ukrainian Front under Marshal Ivan Koniev, who's become a Soviet hero—one of his commands liberated Auschwitz in late January. We've heard all sorts of stories of what they found there, but I can't bring myself to write of them here.

It's been ten months since I've left, but it feels like a lifetime. I was thinking how I'm only twenty-four but feel much older. Everything is so hard. It's terribly cold. There are days when I'm tired of taking orders. And I still don't know how I'm supposed to feel about the blood that's been spilled. It's difficult to see all the suffering—all the images burned in my mind—and not think about death. I don't want to die.

War has a way of distinguishing between things that matter and things that don't. I can't pretend that all is well, even though I can see we are close to the end of this war. At this point, I'm fighting not for justice or freedom, but for my life and another day in the world, so I can be back with you.

There's no question that the possibility of death strengthens the depth of our love. I want to emerge from the bleak and desolate midnight of this war. I ache to be in your arms again. With thoughts only of you,
Danik

Tasa was light-headed when she finished the letter. She realized she'd been holding her breath. She went back and read it over, disturbed by the fear and fatigue permeating his sentiments. His expressions of love were heartfelt, but she couldn't take pleasure in those assurances when something much more despairing came through his thoughts. There was a fatalism in his spirit that she'd never heard before. And she was powerless to help him. Even if she wrote him right that minute, he might not read her words for weeks or more. And this letter, she remembered, had been penned a month earlier.

That instant, her love and yearning for Danik were tinged with a renewed anger at him for enlisting, for putting his life, and their future, in jeopardy. After all, he hadn't had to enlist. He was well intentioned but stubborn and unrealistic about trying to reach his mother as a Soviet soldier. What was he thinking? What was she thinking?

She suddenly felt small and self-centered. How could she judge him now? He wasn't thinking of himself when he joined the war effort. Nor was he thinking about their relationship. That was what had provoked her selfish and emotive reaction. Wasn't that the issue—that they ultimately looked at things differently? That was the attraction

. . . and the tension. She read the letter again. No, she couldn't let her anger protect her from the growing ache that filled her chest. She loved this man unequivocally. Their separation and his danger frightened her, left her without defenses or answers.

The early morning's dark, baleful sky morphed into a relentless rain that finally ended as Tasa strolled from the house to the clinic. She now worked only one or two days a week, the patient load having been greatly reduced as fighting moved farther west, close to the Polish–German border. A pervasive mist and the soggy ground were all that remained from the earlier storm, along with her dull state of torpor, a lethargy she increasingly felt with so little to do. Marking time. She was about to turn twenty-two, and here she was—with no purpose, no sense of future, and so much out of her control. She spent her days on hold—waiting for her mother, waiting for Danik, waiting for the war to end, waiting to begin her life.

As she entered the health center, her gloom must have been clear to the squat and balding middle-aged doctor in charge. He opened his drawer, fumbling inside, until he pulled out a hard piece of candy. "Here, Tasa. Strawberry, your favorite flavor."

She appreciated his gesture and sat down in the chair beside his desk. "Thanks, Dr. Bacha." She opened the wrapper and popped the candy into her mouth. "Hmm. It's good. Now you may find me raiding your stash." She slouched down in the seat and gazed out the window in front of her. She noticed pedestrian traffic picking up outside as the sun finally emerged through some remaining clouds. She thought she discerned the shape of a rainbow and leaned forward for a closer look.

"What are you seeing out there, Tasa? Seems you've got quite a bit on your mind today."

"Yes, I'm distracted, I suppose." Tasa rose from her chair. "What do you have for me to do?"

"Well, you can see it's quite slow right now, which is good, yes? No sickness, no injuries. So I thought we might get our files in order."

She took another glance at the street, partly because of her reluctance to spend the afternoon dealing with paperwork. Something caught her attention, and she moved toward the window. Dr. Bacha started to speak, but Tasa gestured for him to wait. A middle-aged woman walked past the clinic and paused, looking up at the sky. She wore a brown overcoat and was carrying a jute tweed suitcase. Her navy-black hair, streaked with gray, was contained neatly in a bun and her posture erect. Something about her felt familiar. Tasa blinked, and, in that instant, she knew. She leaped over a trash basket and flung open the door.

"Mama?"

The woman turned her head and cried out, dropping her suitcase as she rushed toward Tasa. Tears streamed down both of their faces as they embraced. Tasa's sobs unleashed years of wanting. Her whole body shaking, she entwined herself around her mother, unable to let go and forgetting, for those minutes, that they stood in the middle of the street.

"Oh, Mama, I've waited so long for this day!" Her words came out detached from one another, broken up by the deep gulps of air she took in to calm herself. "I always felt your presence, but I wanted you near so badly . . ."

"We have too much lost time we must recover. And such enormous loss for everyone. Papa's letter was heartbreaking, and yet I know there's so much more." Her mother stood back, cupping her hands around Tasa's face. "Oh, my lovely Tasa. You've grown into a beautiful woman!" Her mother's face crumpled as she began to cry again.

Tasa could see the past five years had changed her mother: toil and worry marking her face, her cheeks hollowed, her hair now faintly streaked with gray, her body thinner. Tasa lifted the suitcase with one hand and hooked her other arm through her mother's as they started walking toward what had been her grandfather's house. She looked back at Dr. Bacha, who had witnessed the homecoming and now stood outside the clinic. He waved to her, his expression kind and understanding.

The afternoon was spent around the kitchen table. Her father's reunion with her mother was as fervent as Tasa's had been. They learned that it had taken three weeks for Halina to get to Podkamien and that she had left immediately upon getting their letter.

"Ella became hysterical when she learned about Judah and Grampa's deaths at once, and of Danik's enlistment. I tried to calm her, but she was desperate to reach Albert in Palestine, rather than return with me to Podkamien." Her mother stared down at her hands as she spoke, her voice cracking. "After all, I had you to come back to. She had no one.

"She decided to go to Romania with some Polish Jews we'd been living among. She was sure that was her way to Palestine. She felt certain that Danik would join them, as she hoped all of us would, once the war ended."

Her mother went on to describe the horrible night in February five years earlier, her comments directed at first to Salomon. "After I sent you away from Podkamien—and not a moment too soon—I had Ella, Sophia, and the girls stay with me. The Russian soldiers came in the middle of the night, banging at the door, with guns pointed at us. Still, they were generous about letting us take food and supplies, bedding and warm clothes, that literally saved us from the bitter winters in Siberia." She paused, her eyes unfocused, before she seemed to recall a new detail. "I had the clarity of mind during that horrible night to write a note for Julia to bring to you, Tasa, and to hang onto a photo of the two of you. That kept me going." Silent tears fell down her cheeks.

Tasa felt the pain of Julia's visit like a fresh stab.

The three grasped one another's hands without speaking. Finally, her father rose and walked toward the stove. "I'm going to boil water so we can have tea. Please, Halina, keep talking. Tell us more."

Her mother closed her eyes and drew in a deep breath. "We were locked into cattle cars with about fifty or sixty people in each car. We traveled for three weeks in the middle of winter—without knowing a destination, without relief from crowding and the smells of body odor, sickness, and sometimes death—packed so tightly that if you had died, you couldn't have fallen down."

Tasa shivered as she took in her mother's words.

"As the train neared and then crossed the Ural Mountains from Europe, I felt a growing alienation from everything familiar. It was the depth of winter then, and we traveled through deep snowdrifts into the dark forests of Siberia."

Tasa's head was spinning, but she wanted to know everything. "What was it like in the labor camps?"

"We lived in barracks constructed from logs cut in the forests. We stuffed moss in the cracks to insulate us from the bitter cold. There was no electricity or running water, but each room had a tiny wood-burning stove. Food was rationed. Each day we received a piece of bread and a bowl of watery cabbage soup, sometimes soup made of fish heads boiled in clear water. But, you have to remember, we managed to stay together. Many families were split up.

"And we all worked. There was a Russian saying—*u nas kto nerabtaet tot I ne kusaet*—that translated as: 'here, if you don't work, you don't eat.' We did what we could—women often worked in the sawmills; the children picked mushrooms and berries in the forests; the men were tasked with clearing forests, felling trees, and hauling timber, or they had to dig frozen earth to lay track for a railway. We had the good fortune of being placed among hearty peasants and workers who shared food rations with us. We learned to do what we had to do to get by."

"When did you get sick?" Her father, who had remained quiet, brought a hot pot of tea and began pouring a cup for each of them.

"Toward the second winter there, I developed rheumatic fever. Louis, whom I wrote you about, helped smuggle in penicillin for me. I began to get better, but when the Soviets released us, I still wasn't strong enough to handle the long train journey. Ella stayed back with me, while Louis, Sophia, and the girls left immediately. Their intent was to try to reach Palestine—since they had no family to return to in Poland. At that point, both Ella and I had reasons to get back to Podkamien."

"You always had an inner strength, Halina. That's what I love about you, and you passed that on to Tasa." Her father took Halina's hand in his. "We've all been through so much."

Halina gazed into Salomon's eyes. "Now, tell me everything—everything. I need to know."

"I will. But let's go into the parlor. Tasa, cut some fruit and cheese and warm some more water. I'll start a fire."

After the three settled together on the couch, her father carefully shared the events that began the day he fled Podkamien early in 1940. He included all the touch points he'd briefly outlined in his letter, offering particulars—as Tasa helped to fill in the gaps. His time hiding in Lvov. Their hasty return to Podkamien once the Soviets joined the Allies. Their year living in Abram's house with the Dorfmans and Danik. Abram's collapse and death. The year of hiding at the Gnyps'. The discovery of the Katyn massacre and confirmation of Judah's death. And, finally, details about Danik's enlistment.

Her mother was incredulous over Danik's decision. "What was in that boy's head?"

Salomon shared that Danik had enlisted partly in order to get word of, or reach, his mother, Halina, and the others. "Danik actually located all of you in southern Siberia. He wrote us this many months ago. But he couldn't follow your whereabouts once you moved into Kazakhstan."

"There's one more thing, Mama." Tasa looked over at her father, who nodded for her to continue. "This is a good thing . . . amid all that you've just heard." She took a deep breath and smiled, trying to hide the worry she harbored. "Danik and I have fallen in love and will be married when he returns from the war." Tasa fixed on her mother's face, trying to detect her true reaction, instead noticing her mother's eyes were the color of molasses, the flames of the fire catching their warmth and shine.

Halina paused, taking in this new detail that had not been alluded to in their letter. "Danik and you were always close." For a brief instant, she seemed to be in another place, her eyes glazing over. "Your friendship developed first, the way your father's and mine began." Halina locked eyes with Salomon, the sort of private exchange that used to confuse and annoy Tasa when she was a child but that she now understood almost more fully than she could bear.

"I've always loved Danik. I imagine he's grown into a wonderful young man for you to have fallen in love with him, Tasa." Halina took in a deep breath. "I pray for his safe return."

Kol Nidrei
May 1945

Tasa stood next to her mother at the kitchen counter, peeling and slicing carrots for a salad as Halina jiggled a frying pan filled with onions sizzling in butter, nearly caramelized. The smells blended with the slow-cooking beef that had been roasting in the oven for the past two hours, stirring Tasa's hunger pangs. She'd watched Mama marinate the beef in olive oil, along with the juice of lemons and several herbs. And she joined her in kneading a fresh challah, the buttery aroma of the baking bread wafting in waves as it had in Frau Rothstein's kitchen all those years earlier. The day felt near blissful, her emotions as bountiful as the food they were about to eat. It was as if she needed to pinch herself to believe that her mother was really standing here in the kitchen, that they were a family again.

She noticed the slight flush now rising in her mother's cheeks, different from her pale and drawn appearance on the first day she had arrived back in Podkamien. There was so much Tasa wanted to express to her mother, but the enormity of her feelings often stopped her. A quiet minute passed as she relived that wintry day in Brody when she was sixteen and had gotten word that her mother was being deported to Siberia. She spontaneously shivered at the memory, cold and palpable after five long years. All that time in between to retrieve. Could it ever be recovered, really?

She tried to comprehend the isolated and impoverished existence her mother had described over the past weeks. But rather than bring her mother closer, those grim details painted someone else, someone different from the idea Tasa carried in her mental knapsack. Her mother was no longer this absent figure to whom, in her journal, she addressed her deepest hopes and dreams. Her mother was alive and she was here now, having lived through experiences vastly disparate from those of Tasa and her father.

It was impossible to conceive how Mama had made it back home. Hard to fathom that most of her family had survived the obscenity of this war, one that *was* winding down. Tasa reminded herself Danik *would* be returning soon. She pushed away the fatalism in his last letter—penned two full months ago—and thought about his triumphant return. He was a fighter, after all, and desperately wanted to be back in her arms. She began to fill her mind with mental pictures of Danik and let herself imagine, as she had so often in the past, the life she could lead with him. A family. A future. That heightened sense of what it meant to be alive. The source of pleasure she felt when the family was together. The joy of performing simple domestic tasks, like now, alongside her mother.

"So . . . what are my two favorite women huddling over tonight?" Salomon walked into the kitchen, interrupting her ruminations. "The house is awash in mouthwatering aromas. I thought I'd make myself useful and set the table." He glanced from Halina to Tasa and back to Halina, fixing his eyes on her.

Tasa looked up and smiled. Her father's affectionate gaze at her mother reminded her of earlier days, of a time when their combined presence could quell her childhood fears and bring clarity to all her small confusions. Tonight that sense of security offered only a partial blanket, not enough to swathe the adult thoughts swirling inside her head like a brisk north wind. Even her mother's homecoming couldn't calm the hollow ache she suffered in Danik's absence, an ache that became sharper as she observed the depth of love between her parents.

During dinner, her mother shared rumors she'd heard during her three-week train ride from Shymkent. By the time she reached the

Volgograd train stop a week before she arrived in Podkamien, she saw Soviet soldiers in groups, their mood optimistic, their talk centering on the weakness of the German army. Her mother said she overheard several officers gloating over a failed German offensive in Hungary near the Danube River in early March and that Soviets were able to cross from Hungary into Austria. By the time she reached Kharkiv several days later, she learned Vienna had been liberated.

When they finished, Tasa washed the dishes and put on water to boil for their tea. Her parents had retreated to the parlor and, like old times, turned on the radio. As she brought the tea out, Chopin's Polonaise in A-flat Major, dubbed *Military* Polonaise, was playing. How ironic to hear this now. She recalled when she was in Brody in '39, during the German invasion of Poland, Polskie Radio broadcast this piece every day as a nationalistic protest and to rally the Polish people. She set the tray down on the low table in front of the couch, just as an abrupt hissing noise cut into the music, followed by what sounded like the ringing of church bells and then the voice of a British announcer.

> *We are interrupting our program to bring you a news flash. The German radio has just announced that Hitler is dead! I'll repeat that. The German radio has just announced that Hitler is dead. General Weidling has finally surrendered, and the war is now over!*

"Oh my God! Can this be true?" Her father leaned closer to the radio. Tasa, still standing, saw her own frozen reaction in the eyes of her parents, no one speaking as the words offered them a new visual image.

> *Hitler was last seen on his birthday, the twentieth of April, decorating Hitler Youth members while the city of Berlin was crumbling.*

Halina put her arm around Salomon and motioned Tasa to sit down. Tasa didn't want to move, didn't want to displace a single, charged molecule from the suddenly electric air.

The radio announcer confirmed that three Soviet fronts, including forces of Marshal Koniev's First Ukrainian, had succeeded in encircling Berlin, shelling the center of the city, then advancing inside, where close-quarters combat raged.

And heavy Russian casualties have been reported.

Tasa's excitement turned to alarm. That was Danik's unit.

Her mother's words sounded faraway, muffled. "You look like you've seen a ghost . . . Come sit."

A cacophony of dissonant sounds rang in Tasa's ears. Her heart pounded; a queasiness spread until it hit her gut. She felt her legs give out. The room went black.

Just six days after the shocking radio report, a jubilant crowd filled the main street in Podkamien. Tasa stood beside her parents, watching the cheering of fellow Poles and Soviets gathered in the village center. Several brought their short-wave radios, and people shared bits of news from around the world. Public exultation had spread from Great Britain to America; reports described mobs in London's Trafalgar Square and Times Square in New York City.

Still, Tasa felt removed from the elation. Her anxiety had remained high each day that went by without word from Danik. She could see how her frame of mind had shifted since Danik left. Before, she had drawn her strength from him, had been as steady as he was by her side. The range of emotions she'd felt over the past year—especially this last week—had been exhausting. She agreed to join her parents, in hopes of snapping out of her funk, but once they arrived she felt only conspicuous among the celebrants. Several farmers her father knew were among those reveling in the Allied victory. There was much talk focused on the German surrender and Hitler's death, opinions and facts exchanged in rapid succession that came to her in bits and pieces.

"Fighting went street to street . . . Civilians in the center of Berlin when the Russians got there . . . Lasted for days."

"Hitler's guy Goebbels . . . Chancellor for a day. Said he wouldn't surrender, and he didn't . . . Took his life as well . . ."

"When we stormed the Reichstag, Hitler took his life."

"No—it wasn't until the Red Army controlled Germany's Parliament that Hitler knew it was over." Tasa recognized the voice of Gustaw Pawlak and listened more closely as he continued. "One report said two soldiers raised a Soviet flag on the building's roof. They'd sewn it out of tablecloths."

It was Lidia's pigtails that she spotted first. Lidia was holding Ivona's hand as they stood just outside the health clinic. Dr. Bacha was giving them candies. Tasa smiled. Her eyes scanned the crowd for Juliana but stopped short when the postal office came into her view.

She nudged her father. "Find Mama. I'm walking over to the post office to check whether there's any mail."

Tasa pushed her way through the crowd, tightness radiating from her neck and shoulders as she neared the tiny mail cubicle. She took a deep breath to calm her nerves, then swung open the door.

The attendant seemed to expect her. "Miss Rosinski, a letter for you just came in this morning's batch!" The Soviet clerk began shuffling nervously through a basket of envelopes.

Tasa fixed her eyes on him, then on the letter he yanked from the pile. "I know you've been eager for news about Mister Riesmann. I was about to close the office and try to find you in this crowd."

"What do you have?" She heard Papa's voice, suddenly at her side. Her parents must have followed her across the square. She was relieved not to be alone, continuing to stare at the letter he grasped between his fingers.

"It's a special delivery for Miss Rosinski. From Soviet authorities, sir."

She turned, detecting a shift in her father's expression, a tightening of his facial muscles. Her mother, who had been listening to the exchange, put her hand lightly on Tasa's shoulder.

"It wouldn't be unusual for the army to send its appreciation to the family of soldiers who helped fight the enemy. You know, sir, ensuring that victory for us."

"Thank you, young man." Her father took the letter and locked eyes with Tasa. "Let's take this home to read in private."

She instinctively turned from the office and began walking with her parents into the crowd, her mind oddly disengaged from the movement of her body. The correspondence *could* be, as the clerk had suggested, almost a form letter, a tribute to Danik among all the courageous soldiers. But it *had* been a week without contact. Or was she being impatient, unrealistic, to expect word from him? What if he was mending in a clinic outside of Berlin? Images of fallen soldiers appeared to her, unwelcome and without warning. She tried to push them away, tried to turn off the noise of her thoughts.

The sounds of the villagers' voices grew more distant until they merged into the clip of her rhythmic steps on the paved road, dulled as she trod with her parents on the gravel path near their house. As the sky blackened with clouds, the delicate notes opening Beethoven's *Moonlight* Sonata played inside her mind. But rather than moonlight shining on a lake, the music evoked for her the most humane and compassionate funeral march, its first movement—adagio sostenuto—steady and rhythmic, soft and melancholic. Frau Rothstein often played this piece late at night. So to Tasa, it conveyed a nocturnal scene, a deep, unearthly voice whispering in the distance, the lowest bass notes calming and steadfast, the higher tones painting a solemn but empathetic melody. Illuminating and hopeful, singular at moments, the notes wandered and climbed and stepped up and over one another, then eased downward until they joined a pair of rich final chords that dissipated, just as breath disappeared into the air or dust might scatter across the earth.

As her father read the letter, the words contained in it—that Danik fought valiantly to the end, that he lost his life just days before Germany's surrender—didn't register. Danik was too alive in her mind for her to conceive of his death. His absence felt like their first separation in childhood, when he was in Brody and she was in Podkamien.

Or akin to their time apart when he moved on to what was once Lwow and she was finishing high school.

When her father got to the letter's ending—*Daniel Riesmann's selfless effort contributed to the Allied victory*—his blank gaze transformed into one of anguish, tears spilling down his cheeks. "The boy was only twenty-four years old. I was there at his birth."

Her mother covered her mouth to muffle her sobs.

Yet Tasa remained in a stupor, stoically watching her parents as though from some distant place. She noticed the rain outside but felt nothing. Empty. Vacuous. She held her gaze toward the window for several minutes, dimly aware of her parents' choked whispers. The rain grew hard and unrelenting, like the deep throb that settled underneath her chest. A pain started to spread through her body, and the spasm left her breathless and shaking.

She heard her own voice, disembodied. "Danik *can't* be dead."

After all, they were bound to each other. They'd made a secret promise, sealed their fate to be together always, hadn't they? She'd given Danik her cherished golden coin as a symbol of all she still wanted to discover with him. Now the zloty was lost with Danik in the rubble of a fallen Berlin. She touched the small pendant hanging from her neck, felt the smooth silver, cold between her fingers. She snapped open the tiny ornamental case. Saw what she needed then.

Her heart beat faster as she studied Danik's face in the locket, recalling the intensity of his hazel eyes, picturing how clear they were in the sunlight, how fervent they were when they fixed on her. How she could feel his eyes watching her, and how they stirred something deep inside her. His single gaze could express what no words could. She could see her own sadness and fear in his eyes, could see what he, too, was seeing.

She clicked the locket shut, and Danik's image vanished like a wisp of cloud in the open sky.

Tasa took solitary walks around the village the next few days, lacking a destination or purpose. She was tense and craved movement. After Danik's death, it was as if the whole world had died. She saw her surroundings as shadows, a world in black and white, the signs of spring lost on her. The crowded marketplace, its faces and voices, felt lifeless. She filled the hollow space inside her with thoughts of Danik, persevering in her memories despite the sensation they produced—as though someone were standing on her chest. She'd see his reflection in a window. Feel his arms around her. She imagined his fingers brushing against her cheeks. His smell came to her on the breeze. She was searching for him, not wanting to believe he was gone forever.

One morning, her stroll took her to what remained of the tiny Podkamien cemetery. She walked over the brown, uneven ground, aware of her muffled footsteps as she passed several angled headstones. She recognized surnames of families she'd known in the village and spoke them aloud—Kuchar, Kowalski, Glas, Nowaki, Pawlak— the trailing echo of her voice sentient amid the lifeless graveyard. She stopped in front of one marker, tilting her head to read its carved-out words, then realizing it was a cenotaph erected in honor of a fallen World War I soldier. So quiet now, she could hear her own thoughts. This headstone was all that remained of someone's beloved. Gone now. She kneeled and brushed her palm across the stone, feeling its cold, coarse surface. She touched the soft soil that held it in place, pulling her into this earthly life. She bent her head, closed her eyes, and offered a silent prayer.

Ringing church bells resonated then, and Tasa felt the sensation of the sun's heat beating down on the back of her shoulders. She looked toward the sky and watched a pair of white-tailed eagles—their broad, fingered wings spread widely, their yellow bills distinctive against mousy-colored feathers, their calls sounding like a duet.

There were more and more sounds of life around her each day, despite her desire to shut them out. She wanted to remain with Danik, but the world kept dragging her away from him. She'd hear the patter of rain against the windows and roof as downpours came and went.

The light of another day would be followed by another sunset. When she'd wake in the morning, there'd be an instant when her life felt normal. Then she'd remember. And the grief would come rushing back. At night, she'd sit in the parlor for hours in the dark. The steady ticking of the wooden cuckoo clock broke into her consciousness hour after hour, reverberating through the silence.

Soon, her thoughts gave voice to melodies. Music offered an architecture around her heartache. She inhabited sorrow-filled compositions—like the adagio movement of Brahms's Sonata for Violin and Piano in G Major and the andante second movement of Tchaikovsky's Violin Concerto in D. In her music, she allowed herself to enter a barren cave, what she imagined to be the cave of death. Of Danik's death. Perhaps Danik had become such a part of her that she fell into this dank, dark place to be with him and couldn't find her way out. Or didn't desire to.

Not yet.

But her parents began discussing a funeral ceremony for Danik. They talked about the need to bring closure to all of them and to honor Danik's memory. She agreed. Her father spent those days seeing that a cenotaph be erected and placed in the village cemetery. Without a rabbi nearby, he said he'd lead their private service. Tasa chose to bring her violin to play Max Bruch's *Kol Nidrei*, op. 47. The title translated to *All Vows*, and she recalled a teaching in Judaism: that promises are sacred, not to be broken.

It was an overcast Sunday morning. The streets in Podkamien were empty. Her father dressed in a charcoal suit, her mother in a dark dress, an ivory brooch fastened at the neckline. Tasa chose the dress she had worn on her twenty-first birthday, more than a year earlier, when she and Danik had exchanged their personal tokens and expressed their vows of love for each other.

Arm in arm, the three walked slowly along the street. The lack of a casket or formal procession allowed her to disengage her mind from the finality of the ceremony to come. She caught her breath when she saw the handsome limestone monument her father had erected in Danik's honor, his work an act of love. She understood how much pain he, too, was suffering. After all, Danik had become like a son to him ever since the war had begun and they had all lived together. As she read the epitaph—To our beloved Danik, who will live in our hearts forever—her throat caught and she looked at her parents' faces, saw the pain set in their eyes. She leaned her head against her father's chest as her mother stroked her hair.

When it was time, she stood for a minute, her violin in one hand, her bow in the other. She raised her instrument to her chin and lifted her bow, playing a few notes, adjusting the pegs. She paused to clear the air, closed her eyes, as she often did before she began playing. The first notes were halting and low, plunging deeper into a haunting tune that shuddered and wept. A pleading melody ensued, Tasa's body instinctively moving back and forth as though releasing the mournful notes from her own heart, expressions of a love forever lost. As she drew out the deepest of notes and boldest of chords, from lightly melodic to sharp and unyielding, and the song asserted its melancholic voice, she felt her tears fall, unrestrained, down her cheeks. Her bow sliced the air and strings along a range of emotive tones, louder and stronger, unrelenting in their narrative promise, exhorting the eternity of her love and the enormity of her loss.

The sound of the last note, tender and soft, brought images of Danik to Tasa then—his reddish mop of hair, the frustration expressed in his furrowed brow, the way his deep-set eyes could hold fear and sadness and express love and vulnerability all at once, his magnetic smile capable of capturing everyone's affection. She loved Danik now where there was no space or time. The sun emerged from a veil of clouds in slow motion, enlarging the expanse of a brilliant blue sky. Tasa felt the kiss of a breeze against her face, sunshine warming her body.

June arrived, and the rains subsided. Tasa and her mother were preparing breakfast one morning as her father arrived back from the village center—a paper in his hand, urgency in his voice. "Halina, Tasa, this memorandum from the Polish Provisional Government of National Unity suggests the *equal* treatment of Jews in regard to emigration. It's essentially encouraging the exodus of Jews." He put down the paper, a pensive look on his face. "As a family, we must have a serious conversation about leaving Podkamien. We will not live under a communist government. This time, I won't ignore the facts in front of me."

Tasa had completely isolated herself from political news in the past month. Her father's pronouncement felt like a chokehold, and she struggled to respond. "Papa, Podkamien is the last piece of my life with Danik that I have to hold on to! Why must we move now?"

"Do you understand Podkamien is not part of Poland anymore? Stalin's pushed for the Curzon Line to be the postwar Polish–Soviet border. This part of Poland has always been in play. This time's no different." Her father paused, as if to collect himself. "And there are economic reasons—oil fields up north the Soviets want. Look, Stalin has the power with the Allies. Months ago, there were serious discussions among the Allied leaders, anticipating the end of the war." He shook his head, his expression taut. "The annexation of eastern Poland to the Soviets is a *fait accompli*, and many Poles are making plans to emigrate west."

Her mother chimed in. "The Ukrainians are happy. As Poles leave, they can be assured to be the majority. Tasa, we're practically the only Jews left in Podkamien. Many Jews in this part of the country have emigrated already." She turned to Salomon. "Sal, tell Tasa what you've heard from the Dorfmans, what they're planning to do."

"Jakov wrote that they ultimately want to emigrate to America. They plan to situate themselves in Munich, where there's an American consulate, and from there can get an affidavit from Uncle Levi, who lives somewhere in the middle of the United States—in Ohio.

"I'd like us to consider emigrating to the United States as well and want to write to Uncle Walter to sponsor us. We could have a fresh start in a place of opportunity, instead of oppression. But that's ahead of us. Short-term, and I mean quickly, we need to get into what is still Poland while it's still legal for us to cross the border. We'll soon be asked to declare ourselves as Soviet citizens, and that will never be an option for us."

Salomon ran his hands over his day-old bristles. "We can temporarily move to Krakow. It's the nearest large Polish city, about four hundred kilometers from here. But I want to leave Poland as soon as possible and go to Vienna. Like Germany, Austria is being divided among the Allies into occupation zones. I'm familiar with Vienna, and we can be comfortable there." He fixed his eyes on Tasa. "I've put aside some money to take with us, and I've heard the American Jewish agencies are being very generous toward those of us who have survived this atrocity."

Tasa's mind was spinning. Leaving Poland forever was unsettling and filled her with a diffuse sadness. But nothing was keeping her here anymore, and her father's plan made sense. She reached out to squeeze her father's arm as she thought about how they could again be among some of their remaining family: Uncle Walter and Aunt Polona and the cousins she'd never met. She could finally reunite with Aunt Norah and Uncle Levi and the Dorfmans. Despite the weight of grief she still carried, she felt a kernel of joy. Or maybe it was hope.

Part Three

All that we love deeply becomes a part of us.

—Helen Keller

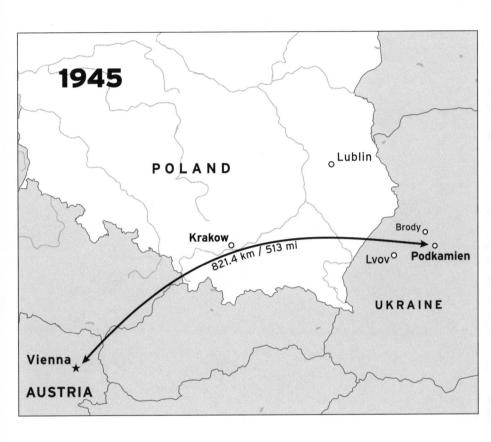

1945

POLAND

Lublin

Krakow
821.4 km / 513 mi

Brody
Lvov Podkamien

UKRAINE

Vienna

AUSTRIA

Staatenlos
1946–1947

"**H**err Rosinski!"

Salomon approached the uniformed man at the counter. Tasa and her mother stepped forward and stood behind him. The official finished reviewing her father's papers and theirs, handed the documents back to Salomon, and offered them a curt "Happy New Year."

Tired after two days of travel, Tasa adjusted her knapsack and violin case, then eyed a nearby wooden bench and the sign above it: Début, Zone Française. She was about to lower herself onto an empty seat, when her father—weighted down by a single large suitcase containing the entirety of their possessions—gestured to her and her mother to follow him, then walked outside the Wien Sudbahnhof Station and whistled at a boxy black cab. As they loaded their bags into the car, he pulled out a piece of paper with an address.

"Pfluggasse one, just off of Alserbachstrasse, please. In Alsergrund. The ninth district."

The driver looked to be in his early thirties, his brown, uncombed hair matching his rumpled shirt and trousers. "It's just a couple kilometers away." He slammed the lid of the trunk. "Where you coming from?"

"Krakow."

"I figured Poland from your accent. Most from there come through the south station, since the Westbahnhof was destroyed last year."

The cab took off northeast. Tasa looked past the bleakness of winter and the intermittent piles of rubble between buildings to see the vibrant and sophisticated city her parents had talked about with such affection. They'd reminisced about Vienna's elegant architecture and storied history over the past several months while readying for this move, until Tasa, too, could hardly wait to encounter the place that had kindled her parents' romance.

"The former house and office of Sigmund Freud is close to where we'll live." Her father gazed out the cab's window, an intent expression on his face, as they drove along streets lined by one prodigious building after another. "Freud was in Vienna until his flight to England during the Anschluss in thirty-eight." His look turned dreamy. "Vienna had everything."

"My favorite composers are attached to this city." Tasa couldn't hide her rising enthusiasm, a departure from her benumbed affect of the past eight months. She recalled all the contextual details Frau Rothstein had taught her. "Franz Schubert was born here. Mozart lived in Vienna for two years. Beethoven lived and died here—"

"Tasa, Halina, we're approaching Alserbachstrasse, a main thoroughfare into our district." Tasa caught sight of another large signpost and recognized the American flag above English words she struggled to translate: ENTERING AMERICAN ZONE. Her father nodded as they passed the demarcation point. Tasa heard the driver tell her father that Alserbachstrasse was the southernmost border of district nine. Amid a creeping fatigue from the long trip, she felt her attention wane and she mindlessly watched the streets and buildings slip past her window, hearing bits of conversation and names that meant little to her—Innere Stadt, Rathaus, Josefsplatz. "It's one of the finest public squares in Vienna," she heard her father say. She saw him squeeze her mother's hand and observed a glimmer of youthful happiness in her parents' eyes.

The driver turned his head slightly toward the backseat, enough for Tasa to observe his angular jawline, as he spoke directly to her. "The foothills of the Vienna Woods reach into Alsergrund, actually surround the entire city on three sides." His Austrian German dialect sounded different to her now that she was listening more attentively. "In the Middle Ages, the woodlands were used for vineyards, but there are many enchanting stories coming from these forests." Tasa began to get a second wind, interested to hear more, but now stared at the back of the driver's head as he zigzagged the vehicle through a curve in the road. "You'll like it where you're living. Lots of people your age."

Despite the late hour, Tasa spotted a pack of young people walking briskly along the street. As their cab passed slowly, she watched three of them enter a café, the placard above the door marked in large script letters: WEINHAUS. Her father asked about the lab coats they were wearing, and the driver told them the city's largest general hospital— the site of the Medical University of Vienna—was nearby.

"They had a pavilion where patients of the Jewish faith could pray. It was pretty much destroyed during Kristallnacht." The driver slowed his cab at an intersection as a vagrant crossed in front of them. "I take it you plan to emigrate to America?"

Her father began answering the driver's query, a story she knew too well. After all, they were now among the many displaced persons who would call Vienna home. For a while, at least. DPs—she'd heard the term. Victims of history and location, they were *staatenlos*—without a country—and awaiting visas in order to enter the United States. Papa said it could take a year and likely more. They really weren't much different from the itinerant gypsies Professor Fishel had talked about back in middle school. She'd been a nomad, like them, since the age of twelve. Was her family's emigration to America to be any different? Would they and the others trying to gain citizenship be seen as outsiders, never really belonging?

The cab pulled up to the Mondial Appartement Hotel. It was situated alongside a row of similar mid-rise buildings on a narrow street several steps from the main thoroughfare of Alserbachstrasse. Feathery snowflakes had begun to fall just minutes earlier, dusting the sidewalk along the curb. The driver put his vehicle in park and stepped outside, white powder carpeting the path to the building's double doorway by the time he finished raising the trunk and swung their large suitcase onto the wet concrete. Her father took out his wallet and handed the man two schillings and a ten-groschen tip.

In the nearly four wintry months since their arrival in Vienna, Tasa hadn't set foot on the balcony. For the first time, she opened the ceiling-high windows of their apartment and walked onto the spacious terrace, glancing at the two empty stone urns in each corner and making a mental note to stop by the floral shop for some red azaleas. The sun, already low in the sky, felt warm as it hit her cheek; the street below teemed with people—businessmen and women, military officers, laborers, university students—as if in celebration of spring.

She scanned the massive limestone structures five and six stories tall that lined her street and beyond it, all in a spectrum of nineteenth-century architectural styles: Greek classical and baroque, Gothic and neo-Renaissance. Sculpted shapes in a sequence of sections in relief, ornate friezes containing many plaster figures in active poses, splashes of colored marble—there were almost too many forms to take in from where she stood eye level with busy rooftops of gables and dormers and chimney pots.

As she closed her eyes, the raw pain of Danik's absence reemerged without warning. *Happiness in the sunshine.* With him, she'd welcomed spring's appearance three years earlier, a brief interlude from the darkness of their bunker when the German front had temporarily moved east. The image of that afternoon and her emotions that day flooded back: The sun's brightness stinging her eyes. Danik's lips on hers. His winsome grin. She remembered thinking how odd it was that she could feel joy when the war was raging, while they were in hiding, with her mother somewhere far away and her beloved grandfather dead. Now she knew. It was because Danik had been there with her. They drew from each other's strengths; hers was to hold on to moments of sunshine, often fleeting, as they had been then. Even now, she could hear the sounds of guns in the distance interrupting their laughter.

Cars honking, the clopping of horse hooves pulling carriages along the cobblestone road and the squeal of metal trolley poles powering shiny red streetcars brought Tasa back to the present—on the fifth and top floor of their transitional home just two kilometers northwest of the center of Vienna, known as Innere Stadt or District One. Central Vienna was the International Zone and under the control of all four Allied powers that divided the city. She thought it laughable that each country rotated its military police, one month at a time, to patrol this crossover area, all speaking German, the language that induced the greatest fear in Tasa and, she imagined, all those survivors in Vienna awaiting emigration.

The setting sun brightened the faded sandstone facades, reminding her that she still had errands to do. She turned around and hurriedly moved through the high-ceilinged living room, her footsteps echoing on the parquet floor. She'd gotten to feel comfortable in the big city, her frequent walks now along streets swarming with people. She remembered when the town of Brody had seemed immense to her, coming from her village of three thousand. Luckily, she had had six months in Krakow to prepare for Vienna. Krakow had a hundred times the population of Podkamien yet less than a fifth of the occupants here—facts she found hard to conceive. She welcomed the crowds and the fast urban pace, especially today, when Danik's absence became a fresh wound.

She took the back stairwell down to the lobby, a simple vestibule noteworthy for its Murano glass chandelier. She looked forward to having this time alone to explore and had encouraged her parents to go out—this afternoon, they'd gone to an American office in Josefstadt to take care of paperwork concerning their visa application. After all, she had reminded them just that morning, she would be twenty-three next week.

Leaving the building, she heard a multitude of languages as she passed several residents on their way inside. As she turned onto

Alserbachstrasse, every building was now at least partially restored; the cleansing of the district had begun soon after she and her parents had gotten there. She recalled how the highest piles of wreckage were removed first, the most blighted streets filled daily with workers. Boarded-up storefronts in the American zone, as if overnight, were replaced with ice cream parlors—now one on every street—or open-air cafés and shiny boutiques. Just last month, she had discovered a new bookstore around the corner from their apartment and had been delighted to find her favorite Russian authors, as well as a variety of language-instruction books. She'd picked up one for advanced English and always took it with her on walks like these.

She strode alongside a middle-aged couple—the man in a light-weight coat and black fedora, the woman in a tailored, burnt-orange suit and matching hat—lingering in front of an Italian *ritrovo*, reading the menu posted by the door. Several of the retail shops were closing for the day. She ambled by a corner bar, Gosser Bier marked above the open door, through which she could see university students drinking from dark bottles.

The street was jammed with cabs, carriages, trams, and even the occasional bicyclist. She noticed the movement of footsteps along the sidewalk had slowed. People were perusing menus displayed on what looked like music stands. Despite the cool April temperature, the outdoor cafés were filled with men drinking out of half-full tumblers. Tasa caught pieces of a conversation in German and glanced toward the speaker just as a middle-aged man held a silver lighter to his companion's cigarette.

She paused in front of Restaurant Feuervogel. She could hear violins playing Slavic music and smelled the rye malt and molasses wafting into the street, reminding her at once of Polish breakfasts and her favorite Russian black bread. As she peered through the window, she first caught her own reflection—the silhouette of a young woman with long, dark hair. She could be anyone from anywhere, and she paused for a moment longer as she considered her current status—anonymous and detached.

Looking past her own image, Tasa caught sight of white tablecloths, dark cabinets—perhaps cherry. And velvet brocade curtains, inner archways, and high ceilings. Several American officers sat at the bar. She was drawn to this place. At the same time, she had to fight the prickly impulse that kept her distant. This instant, she felt the tug of tension loosen and stepped inside.

She passed a table where a waiter was serving caviar sandwiches and showily dousing vodka into cups of sweet coffee liqueur. Another, where a pair of stylishly dressed women conversed over wiener schnitzel and spaetzle. She was seated at a table set for two with a thin crystal vase and single magenta rose at its center. The host removed the extra porcelain table setting when she told him she was alone.

She ordered a Russian ale, Kvass, and within moments a crisply clad waiter poured her a glass. As she nursed her beer, she watched a young couple, their heads almost touching, whispering back and forth. That hollow ache returned. Before she had time to dwell on sorrowful thoughts, a smiling, curly-haired waiter stood above her.

"I'm pleased to be serving you this evening, miss. Do you speak English?"

He enunciated his words. And it was American English. Good practice for the next phase of her life. She nodded, conscious of her heavy accent. "Yes, I do."

"Whatever you order, leave room for *plombir* ice cream. The Russians make it rich and creamy."

Tasa smiled and reached for the menu. After she ordered, she stared into space, the honey-clove taste of the beer reminding her of another time—at Dudek's Tavern, a pitcher of Zywiec and teenage friends plotting pranks aimed, ironically, at the Soviets.

Throughout the spring and summer, Tasa continued to stay within the boundaries of the American zone but ventured farther and more frequently to explore her surroundings. Still emotionally fragile, she was initially more comfortable spending time alone and found spots where she could be among people while separate from them. She often walked as far as the Mozart Apartment Hotel, adjacent to the Danube Canal. The building hosted American officers and had an authentic Viennese restaurant off its lobby with seasoned violinists always playing tableside. She strolled the nearby parks, frequented a local branch of the University of Vienna library, surrounded by people her own age. She registered for fall term at the end of the summer, signing up for classes in English, biology, and music pedagogy.

Then, in early October, her father surprised her and her mother with tickets to a performance of *Die Zauberflote* by the Vienna State Opera and Vienna Philharmonic. A self-satisfied smile on his face, Papa fanned out three tickets. "When Schottel over at the visa office learned you were a violinist, he got hold of good seats for tonight's program."

"Where's the concert, Papa?" Tasa couldn't hide her excitement.

"It's at the Theater an der Wien, not far from the old Westbahnhof station. Closer yet to Innere Stadt and many sights you haven't yet seen, Tasa."

A few hours later, they were on the number 5 streetcar traveling along Mariahilfer Strasse. The sun was in its final descent, the air cool, as they walked several blocks from the end station. Tasa turned her head to admire the handsome figures of her parents by her side: her father in his one suit, a charcoal herringbone, his tie matching the gray-blue sky at dusk, her mother sporting a deep-brown dress that matched her eyes, her hair rolled in a soft bun. Her father chattered on about the Theater an der Wien—how it now served as the temporary home of the Staatsoper; how it was more spacious than any in Vienna, the brainchild of Mozart's librettist and collaborator on *The Magic Flute*.

They arrived at the entrance as her father finished his tutorial. The delicate stone figures adorning the portal—Papageno and the Three Boys—took her breath away, just as she heard him say, "It's called Papageno Gate." She spiraled backward in time without catching herself. A playful duet. Danik's uninhibited portrayal of the reckless Papageno. The moment she knew she loved him.

"Are you coming in? Are you okay, Tasa?"

Her mother's voice whisked her out of her reverie. She hadn't realized she was standing stock-still. She felt her heart race, her face flushing. "I . . . I'm fine. Let's go in."

The theater was completely sold out. Tasa had never been in a performance hall as grand—there could have been a couple thousand people there. She took in all the lavish surroundings. The red velvet seats and heavy curtains. The gold detail framing the stage and defining each level of the side balconies. She craned her head to scrutinize the people seated in the top row.

As the theater's lights dimmed, she found herself enveloped within a fairy-tale world. Mozart's masterpiece was sung and spoken, with instruments leading and guiding actors, both virtuoso and comic. She began to lose herself in the opera's spirited narrative and the tension between good and evil, hope and despair, joy and sorrow, knowledge and ignorance. She understood why Danik loved its message so much—it was the story of the education of mankind, after all, progressing from chaos through religious superstition to a rational enlightenment.

Her thoughts of Danik bubbled to the surface, tears streaming down her cheeks, as she transferred Papageno's lyrics into Danik's joyful portrayal, not even five years earlier, of the lovestruck bird-catcher longing for a wife or lover: *And if she'd kiss me tenderly, I'd ask her next to marry me.* Near the end, as Papageno sang in desperation of his love for Papagena, dreaming of their future and the many children they would have together, expressing his willingness to die without her, the stab of loss left Tasa hollow. If only the ringing of a magic glockenspiel could bring Danik back to her, could carry *her* through life's trials. Despite her irrational wish, she understood the meaning of Mozart's allegory—the blurring of virtues, the complex duality between appearance and inner truth, the human desire for love and struggle to attain wisdom. As she joined in the audience's thunderous applause, she felt her own inner strength surging. After all, courage and heart and joy always rested within her like the music itself. It was just a matter of hearing its wisdom.

She shuffled amid the throngs of people leaving the theater, still in an altered mood, the music and lyrics continuing to play in her head. The loud conversations in several languages brought her out of her trance, and before exiting the majestic setting she took in a final scan to commit it to memory. She wanted to stay in the magic of that performance and appreciated the minutes after they left when her parents were lost in their own thoughts, the noise of the city rushing past all of them.

"Let's walk a bit. I want you to see some prominent hotels along the Opernring." They passed the Sacher Hotel, British officers entering and leaving the opulent lobby. Next door, the Staatsoper was undergoing reconstruction, her father reminded them, its auditorium and stage having been destroyed by flames during the war. He pointed to the large park ahead, explaining that Vienna's public garden was so expansive it extended southeast into the third district.

Tasa glanced past Stadtpark. "Look! A giant Ferris wheel!"

"That's the Wiener Riesenrad. It's the tallest Ferris wheel in the world. Much of it was destroyed in the war, but they rebuilt what they could."

"When your father and I were here, the Riesenrad had thirty gondolas. We used to ride it every Sunday when we'd go to the Prater—the amusement park." Tasa silently counted fifteen red gondolas as her mother continued. "We'd walk through the park and all around Leopoldstadt. It was a lovely neighborhood then." Mama paused, her eyes becoming unfocused, as though her mind were elsewhere.

"A few months ago, your mother and I ventured over to Leopoldstadt, just to see it again. This area used to have many Jews. Its nickname was Island of Matzo because of all the synagogues and symbols of Judaism there—mezuzahs attached to the doorposts of many houses. All of this, gone now." Her father stopped and stared out at the iconic revolving wheel. "We found the park desolate, full of weeds. Smashed tanks were still parked and in full view, like iron statues."

A Russian soldier walked by, a cap on his head and a rifle over his shoulder. They were just outside the second district, now part of the Soviet zone. Tasa watched the officer angle toward the Prater. They retraced their steps, following her father, who seemed to know where he was going, turning at one street after another.

Within minutes, they reached a beautiful public square. Her father told her it was called Josefsplatz, named after Emperor Joseph II. A full-size equestrian statue and monument of the emperor stood at the square's center, enclosed on three sides by sections of a grand baroque palace. "This is Hofburg. It housed some of the most powerful people in European and Austrian history."

Tasa had learned in school about the Habsburg dynasty and its nearly seven-century rule of the Austro-Hungarian Empire.

"And see the building over there?" Her father pointed to a disconnected structure to the left. He said it was the former imperial stable, which had once housed nine hundred Lipizzaner horses. She felt a sudden pang for her family's simple stables, the air of the countryside, and her lost childhood. She closed her eyes, envisioning Cairo.

It might have been a similarly mild October evening, many years earlier. Cairo was grazing in the meadow near the small lake on their Podkamien property, pulling up mouthfuls of crisp grass, the setting sun reflecting off his silky black coat. She had walked up to him, combing her fingers down his coarse mane, his swishing tail his only acknowledgment, and had waited patiently as he had his fill. When he finally raised his head, the two were eye to eye. She rubbed her hand across his velvety nose for several minutes. In return, he nuzzled her neck, and at that moment, they were one. Then, almost abruptly, he took off in a gallop toward the barn—the same barn that, after the war, she'd found vacant.

She felt her mother's arm around her. Halina pointed to a pastry shop and suggested they go inside. They were quickly seated at a dainty marble-topped table enclosed by three parlor chairs. Tasa stared through an interior window just beyond them where several pastry chefs were at work. They were uniformly clothed in white pastry jackets marked by a double row of dark buttons, their heads sporting white chef's hats flopped to one side.

She studied one young chef as he molded marzipan into animal shapes, placing each atop a round brownie. Tasa's eyes widened further as she began reading the menu selections: *kaiserschmarrn*, which she knew was a fried, caramelized pancake topped with powdered sugar. Apple strudel. Hungarian plum dumplings. But the *grillparzer-torte* captured her fancy.

Funny to name a dessert after a dignified poet and dramatist, Tasa thought. She'd learned about one of Franz Grillparzer's greatest dramas, *Der Traum, ein Leben* (*The Dream, a Life*) during her last year of upper school. Her professor used the example of this work as one of the first of his dramas that didn't end tragically. As she'd struggled with all that was taking place around her at that time, Grillparzer's lesson had stuck: the only true happiness is contentment with one's lot and inner peace. An unlikely notion, she thought, to have in a Viennese pastry shop.

Tasa began to enjoy her time in Vienna. She spent the academic year engaged in her coursework and even made a few friends at the university. Those moments when she felt ambushed by grief were less and less frequent. The city had started to feel almost like home. So now she wasn't sure how to take the news her father had brought to them yesterday.

Salomon had nearly tripped over the foyer rug in his eagerness to proffer the announcement that their visas had been approved. They had a date for departure to America in just one week—the first of July. This was the outcome they'd been awaiting, and it had arrived within the expected eighteen-month interval her father had prepared them for. But despite his excitement, she'd reacted with edgy ambivalence. "Why do we have to leave, Papa? Can't I enroll full-time in the university here? I was just getting acclimated to the city!" She had whined like a spoiled child.

Tasa stayed in bed longer this morning, replaying yesterday's scene in her mind. Unable to fall back to sleep, she threw aside her sheets, swung out of bed, and stepped onto her weathered Oriental rug. The summer's heat filled her room, making her feel sticky. Pulling back her curtains, she looked down at an absence of street traffic. Of course, it was Sunday. She quickly got dressed to do what she'd always done— except in their days in the bunker—when she needed to think or to settle herself down. She was ashamed of her earlier outburst and knew it was pointless. But she had grown to love Vienna. This walk would give her a chance to give the city a proper farewell. After all, it was where she'd begun to heal. And now it would be one more link in a chain of places that she was leaving.

The sun was peeking through the early-morning clouds, and she could imagine its beams glinting off the mouth of the Wien River, visualize the multicolored flowering vista blanketing the English-style landscape of Stadtpark. Slowly turning the knob of her bedroom door, she tiptoed across the foyer, careful not to wake her parents. She was excited to greet Vienna's silent streets and began her solitary walk from Alsergrund, stopping alongside the resplendent city hall, the building's hundred-meter spire resembling a cathedral bell tower. But instead of church bells, she heard the echo of cooing pigeons flapping their wings within the silence of the Rathausplatz.

She strolled toward the more imposing Parliament building, taking in its panoply of Greek-inspired columns, reliefs, and sculptures, her eyes resting on a statue of the Greek goddess Athena standing atop a tall pedestal. Four figures lay at Athena's feet, and on the sides Cupids rode dolphins. Tasa couldn't take her eyes off the goddess of wisdom, dressed in armor, her head covered in a gilded helmet. Everything about this statue conveyed strength and courage and inspiration. Tasa took in a deep breath, trying to draw in these same attributes. She headed farther along the horseshoe-shaped boulevard, quickening her steps as she reached Stadtpark.

At first, she saw only the silhouette of Johann Strauss Jr., but as she approached, the composer's form came into clearer focus. The bronze figure stood under a limestone arch and was framed by a marble relief. She walked right up to the statue, its details bringing to life for her the man known as the Waltz King—his full, wavy hair; his thick mustache, which curled upward. He held the violin to his chin, his bow high, touching the strings of his instrument as if he were about to play.

Tasa recalled her initial entry into Vienna, how the driver's comments stirred her imagination about the nearby forests—the Vienna Woods—that she knew had inspired Beethoven's later symphonies, several Schubert sonatas, even *The Magic Flute* itself. She leaned against the edge of the stone structure as the long introduction to "*G'schicten aus dem Wienerwald*" began playing in her mind, evoking the wooded eastern foothills of the Alps. This rustic tone poem, its sounds of birds in song and the flowing water of rivers, conjured images of the countryside.

She could hear the distinctive plucking of a zither, drawing her further into that world of peasants living in a wooded playground, its clear and high-pitched twangs gentle at first, then moving faster. Just as with the wedding dances she'd watched long ago with her grandfather—as *klezmorim* played their violins—she could visualize the peasants' gaiety and whirling movements. Their wide and wild steps became shorter and more elegant as the folk music crossed to city life—from stamping to gliding, from hopping to sliding. In her daydream, the familiar waltz narrative blurred into the zither's twang, before the crashing cymbals and snare drumroll broke the spell. She backed away from the statue and took in a final view of the landscape around her. She noticed a few people now walking along the footpaths and began her trek back to the apartment. She followed the Wien River as it moved through Stadtpark, envisioning its passage into the Danube Canal. With that picture, she felt her distractions fall away and she grasped the reality. A ship would soon be waiting. She would need to find her path, again.

Passage
July 1947

On the seventeenth day of her journey through the turbulent waters of the Atlantic, Tasa awoke abruptly just before dawn, her stomach in somersaults. Trying to maintain her balance, she hastily pulled on a shirt and pants, then raced up to the deck to breathe fresh air. There she met with most of the boat's three hundred passengers—from Poland and Austria, as well as Italy, Hungary, Czechoslovakia, Germany, France, and Russia—similarly nauseated by the surging seas. Nearly five meters of waves crashed against the ship's bow and exploded above the deck railing. She stood back from the side, inhaled the briny sea air, and focused on the horizon, as a swath of coral light began to lift the darkness above the sea.

While she held the scene in her gaze, she imagined her new life in America, a collage she tried to piece together from Uncle Walter's letters. She and her parents hoped to have their own house soon, perhaps on a street named for a great body of water—like Atlantic Avenue—or titled after one of the many states within the United States. Her uncle had explained how Atlantic City's streets were labeled—those parallel to the shoreline were named after oceans or seas. So, she speculated, she could live on Mediterranean Avenue, for the sea they'd crossed from Trieste to get to the ocean. Or, and she smiled when she thought of this, she might live on North Carolina or Illinois Avenue, and, as Uncle Walter had suggested in his most recent letter, she could quickly learn the geography of her new country just by walking around the city and reading the street signs.

She pictured her new neighborhood, tree-lined, with houses in close proximity, as if they were in the center of Podkamien, filled with Americans and immigrants like her. Uncle Walter, Aunt Polona, and her cousins Stella and Caleb would live nearby. She had to remind herself she'd never met them and still thought of Stella and Caleb as children, then remembered that Stella was twenty-two, only two years younger than she. And Caleb was nineteen. Tasa hoped they'd have frequent family dinners—all of them together—like the large gatherings she remembered before the war. She closed her eyes and could almost smell the pot roast and baking challah. After supper, she'd play her violin and, later, they'd listen to music on the radio. Classical, of course—the masters—but perhaps some modern music as well. The news reports would talk not of war but of important matters citizens needed to comprehend so they could participate in their democracy— in a country where freedom was paramount.

Uncle Walter spoke about politics in his correspondence. He gave high marks to the country's president, Harry Truman, and described the nation's efforts to help refugees and restore Europe in the war's aftermath. He wrote a lot about the American pastime of baseball. She had to ask her father to explain this game to her so she could understand such a popular American activity. In his last letter, her uncle had called it "big news" that a young Negro had just joined a major-league baseball team in New York, the city where they would soon disembark. Uncle Walter also said a lot of people were angry about that, but he thought the acceptance of a black man in the world of baseball showed the beginnings of acceptance of all people. Tasa had worried about how Jews were regarded in America if people were angry about Negroes, but it wasn't anything her uncle addressed. He did say that education was accessible, so maybe she'd continue her studies at a university.

But she was getting ahead of herself. She thought back to her new home and the upcoming reunion with her American family. She could envision sitting around a large living room with them. It was summer now, and the windows might be open to a light breeze coming off the same ocean taking her to this new land. In the mornings, she'd look forward to walks along the Atlantic City Boardwalk, a famous structure that Uncle Walter went to great lengths to describe. He called it a promenade, said it was lined with tall hotels and dozens of confection shops, many with the city's own salt-water taffy, whatever that was. The boardwalk was great for people-watching, but he told them that more than half of its original eleven kilometers had been destroyed in a terrible hurricane three years earlier, and many of the ocean piers were also damaged. When Tasa read about that natural disaster, her mind flipped to the war's destruction and she had to push away those recurring images. She hoped the beachfront was largely rebuilt by now so she could soon be walking on the sand, collecting shells, picking up stray stones, and having time to make sense of the many stirrings and thoughts that, like the water churning beneath the ship's hull, were swirling inside her.

That evening, Tasa stood on the aft deck. The dark night surrounded her as she watched the vessel's steady movement produce a flurry of waves, their whitecaps glistening. The waters had calmed since the morning, and winds from the north cooled her in the summer heat, evaporating the sweat collecting in the hollow at her throat. She wore an open-necked sundress and, earlier that evening, had reluctantly removed Danik's locket, placing it inside the book she was rereading, *Narcissus and Goldmund*, then tucked the novel in the small satchel she carried everywhere. She knew the past was moving further and further behind her, like that time before war when the world was contained and secure, her family beloved in their tiny rural village. And yet the tears that rolled down her cheeks still felt like those of the girl she'd left behind in Podkamien.

The wind gusts swept strands of her thick hair across her face. More than two years had passed since Danik's death. As she stared out at the expanse of water, her mind raced through many images, her lungs sucking in the sea air as if she were taking in every moment, place, and person now lost to her. She looked over at her father and mother, standing across the deck, quietly holding hands, gazing backward at the ship's wake. What were they were thinking? What world did they see behind them, and what did they envision ahead?

She opened her satchel and pulled out the photograph of her family, the one she had discovered in her Podkamien attic that long-ago winter morning and managed to keep all these years. It was a lifetime since that photo was taken, shortly before she was born. Fast-forward from there: A war had been fought. People had lived, loved, and perished. This rehearsal with death had to stand for something. *What is it?* she wondered. *That each moment is precious and fleeting? That we learn to go forward by understanding what came before?*

Tasa peered up at the sky—a black curtain flecked with so many stars blinking back at her. Through this sweep, she imagined all of Podkamien and Brody and Vienna and everyone who had peopled those places. She visualized that narrow attic window and her early view of the world outside. She remembered the extended family that filled her childhood: Grampa Abram. Uncle Judah, Aunt Ella, Danik, and Albert. Aunt Norah and Uncle Levi. Uncle Ehud, Aunt Sophia, Dalila, and Mela. Uncle Jakov, Aunt Sascha, and Tolek, with whom she hoped to reunite in America.

She could hear Frau's comforting words: *Now, this is something much bigger you have to manage. But you are a strong young lady, Tasa. You're a survivor, yes?* She closed her eyes and was back in Frau's house, and at Brody Catholic. She felt a sharp stab as she thought of Frau, of Ania and Irina, and of Joshua Fishel. Her heartbeat quickened as the running and hiding and anguish played out once again, but she pushed her thoughts to the Gnyps and, finally, to Wien—City of Waltz. Her losses were now part of her, layered and weighing on her like the sweaters and coats during Polish winters. Tasa craned her neck as she stared skyward, locating the brightest star. Thinking, *That's Danik.*

She recalled a summer night like this one, with Danik in Brody. Before he left for the city then called Lwow. An evening that portended the changes about to occur. In the film they watched, Jascha Heifetz performed Camille Saint-Saens's Introduction and Rondo Capriccioso, a composition of two parts, like her own life. For her, the first part was now history, the second part yet to be written. The musical composition swung from a free-flowing rhythm to a syncopated melody, from notes floating softly off the instrument to those crying out in a moment of passion or pleading. It paralleled Tasa's emotions that wistful night—abstract and confusing—just as it did now. As she called to mind the music's excitability and power, she once again found herself comforted.

And she wondered, are there places we're meant to walk, people we're meant to love, lives we're intended to have? Or not? Do we ever leave that person we were in our past? Or should we? She understood she could never know how her life might have been different, just that she now stood on this ship's deck as a survivor of war with a new life awaiting. She felt like she was floating. A sensation of weightlessness overcame her. A fullness, too. But of what? Of what?

She had to close her eyes in order to calm herself. Then a new picture came to her: a blank sheet before music is ever set onto its pages. The notes evolving as a melody is discovered. Music that is mesmerizing, that expresses a fully imagined scene and a life and a world. She understood she was facing that great blank page right then.

She suddenly became aware of laps of water against the ship's hull and could feel the waves shift course under her, could sense the vessel slowing. Land must be near! The constant speed over these past few weeks had masked what now felt like a vibration under her feet as the engines throttled back. Specks of light started to flicker in the distance ahead, barely enough for the vessel to get its bearings. There was a calming of the water around the boat as the movement of the crew became hyperactive, clearly in preparation for docking. Swarms of passengers began to gather alongside the railing at the side decks, watching as the glitter of tall buildings came into a fuzzy focus.

Tasa took a step away from the rail and heard a soft scraping noise beneath her foot. She looked down but didn't see anything. She took another step backward and it was then that she spotted it, glinting up at her from the deck. A gold coin? She bent down and picked it up, her hand trembling. Holding it between her thumb and index finger, she brought it close to her face, examining the embossed profile of Boleslaw Chrobry, the first king of Poland, a crown covering his head, a mustache waving out onto his cheek, the year 1925 carved along the perimeter. She turned it over, framed it between the fingers of both her hands. There was the crowned eagle, its spurred feet, perimeter markings confirming the golden coin as a 10 zloty of the Polish Republic.

She felt like she was ten again, peering out from the attic window, excited to explore the world beyond. Waiting to discover what was hidden under a stone, as her mother had promised. Before evil had overtaken an entire people. Before it had hurled her deep into herself, into darkness, like the thrust of an undertow. She knew at that moment she'd never return to Poland but would feel its absence like something just short of hunger and pain.

So now she was abandoning one life to begin another. The thought of filling in this blank page, composing this next chapter in her life, left an uneasy yet pulling sensation. She gazed back at that infinite sea, the ship's wake growing smaller. The swishing of water sounded to her like a prayer. Like the whispering of a new world. *Come, come . . .*

Acknowledgments

There may be one name on the cover, but every book is a collaborative sport. *Tasa's Song* is no exception.

The endurance player on my team is my husband, Frank, my first reader and biggest advocate. I am extremely lucky to have a selfless partner who has been so steadfast in his support and encouragement of my writing.

The motivation for this fictional story was the truth that inspired it. When I began collecting my family's history in 1980, my only intention, as a working journalist at that time, was to insure that future generations of our family would understand where they came from. It was my sister's prodding, decades later, to use this history for a private memoir—a gift to honor my parents' 60th wedding anniversary—that set this writing project in motion. It jelled a couple of years after that, when my husband and I visited our daughter during her college semester abroad in Berlin and took a side trip to Krakow. It was my first time in Poland and that experience grew into the vision that became *Tasa's Song*.

My deepest gratitude:

To Lee Martin, Ellen Lesser, and Nancy Zafris, whose extraordinary guidance and encouragement helped me to become a better novelist. And for their advice, expertise, and support: Lee K. Abbott, Fred Andrle, Matt Bondurant, Kevin Boyle, Amber Dermont, Jennifer

Fisher, Carole Gerber, Ann C. Hall, Ann Kirschner, Greg Michalson, Estelle Rodgers, and Margot Singer.

To the many experts with whom I consulted, and to all of my early readers—your feedback was invaluable. Special thanks to violinist Chas Wetherbee and Carpe Diem String Quartet.

To my trailblazing publisher, Brooke Warner, at She Writes Press, and all the talented professionals who played a role in transforming my manuscript from computer files to finished product: Barrett Briske, Krissa Lagos, Julie Metz, Mike Morgenfeld, Annie Tucker, and my diligent editorial manager, Lauren Wise. Heartfelt thanks to my publicist Caitlin Hamilton Summie, web designers Lucinda Dyer and Bryan Azorsky, and to Alex Baker, Lisa Hinson, Alex Kass, and Rick Summie.

To my extraordinary family, and to my family of friends, all of who nourish me every day.

To my Vienna-born father, Ernest Stern, for instilling in me a love of classical music, and to my endearing mother, Aurelia Rosaminer Stern, to whom this novel is dedicated. The details of her early life remain the foundation of truth underlying *Tasa's Song*.

Tasa's Song Playlist and Musical Reference

In the Blackness of the Night
Tchaikovsky: *Souvenir d'un Lieu Cher*, op. 42, Meditation
(Remembrance of a Beloved Place)

Podkamien
Ruggieri violin
Beethoven: Ode to Joy
Strauss: The Blue Danube Waltz
Tchaikovsky: simple versions of concertos
Paganini: Caprice no. 24 in A Minor
Chopin mazurkas and polonaises

Frau Rothstein
Rachmaninoff's Piano Concerto no. 3 in D Minor, op. 30
Bösendorfer grand piano
Violin and piano duos of Bach, Viotti, Chopin, Shubert, and
Smetana
Violin compositions of Tchaikovsky, Sibelius, and Paganini
Bach: Violin Concerto no. 2 in E Major
Sonatas by Viotti
Chopin: Nocturne for Violin no. 2 in E-Flat Major, op. 9

Gypsy Airs
Klezmer music
Johann Kulik violin from Prague, made in 1869
Pablo de Sarasate: *Zigeunerweisen*, op. 20 (*Gypsy Airs*)
Beethoven: Violin Sonata no. 5 in F Major (*Spring* Sonata), op. 24, second movement, adagio molto expressive

Denial
Schubert: *Die Schöne Müllerin*
Zoltán Kodály: Duo for Violin and Cello, op. 7

Kristallnacht
Pablo de Sarasate: *Zigeunerweisen*, op. 20 (*Gypsy Airs*)
Bedrich Smetana: *From My Homeland*: Duo no. 1 for Violin and Piano in A Minor

They Shall Have Music
Tchaikovsky: *Sérénade Mélancolique*
Mozart: Requiem in D Minor
Szymanowski: *Stabat Mater*
Mozart: *The Magic Flute*
Violinist Jascha Heifetz
Camille Saint-Saens: Introduction and Rondo Capriccioso
Stradivarius (played by Heifetz)

A Secret Pact
Karol Szymanowski: Violin Concerto no. 1, op. 35
Chopin: Nocturne for Violin no. 2 in E-Flat Major, op. 9
Shostakovich

The Thrill of Anxiety

Spohr: Six Songs for Baritone, Violin, and Piano, no. 1 (*Abendfeier*)

The Note

Smetana: *Má Vlast: Vysehrad* and *Sarka*

Chopin: Minuet Waltz in D-Flat Major, op. 64, no. 1

Chopin: Nocturne for Violin no. 2 in E-Flat Major, op. 9 (Sarasate arrangement for violin and piano)

Magen David

Tchaikovsky: *1812 Overture*

Vivaldi: *The Four Seasons*, "La Primavera"

Mozart: *Die Zauberflote* (*The Magic Flute*), Act I, Second Scene

Judenfrei

Chopin: Piano Sonata no. 2, op. 35, third movement, "Funeral March"

Darkness and Light

Mozart: *The Magic Flute*

Beethoven: "*Spring* Sonata," second movement

Gestapo Overhead

Chopin: Nocturne no. 7 in C-Sharp Minor

Prokofiev: *Peter and the Wolf*, op. 67

A Country Apart

Spohr: Violin Concerto no. 9 in D Minor, op. 55, second movement, adagio

Sibelius: Violin Concerto in D Minor, op. 47, third movement, allegro, ma non tanto

Keepsakes

Beethoven: Violin Romance no. 2 in F Major, op. 50, adagio

Answered Prayers

Vivaldi: *The Four Seasons*, Concerto no. 4 in F Minor, "Winter,"
first movement, allegro non molto

Kol Nidrei

Chopin: Polonaise in A-Flat Major, op. 53, *Military* Polonaise

Beethoven: Piano Sonata no. 14 in C-Sharp Minor
(*Moonlight* Sonata)

Brahms: Sonata for Violin and Piano in G Major, op. 78, second
movement, adagio

Tchaikovsky: Violin Concerto in D, op. 35, second movement,
andante

Bruch: *Kol Nidrei*, op. 47, adagio

Staatenlos

Mozart: *Die Zauberflote* (*The Magic Flute*)

Strauss: *Tales from the Vienna Woods*, op. 325, *G'schicten aus dem
Wienerwald*

Passage

Camille Saint-Saens: Introduction and Rondo Capriccioso

Reader's Guide

1. Discuss the role music plays in Tasa's life and in the novel. What significance did Klezmer music and Gypsy references bring to the novel?

2. Why do you think the author chose to tell the story from Tasa's point of view? Was this approach effective?

3. How does Tasa's character change over the course of the novel? Describe some of her unique qualities.

4. Share your thoughts about how the relationship between Danik and Tasa began and ended. Were there alternatives to the choices they made?

5. Discuss the role family plays in Tasa's life.

6. What was the significance of Frau Rothstein as a character in this story? Of Josef Gnyp?

7. What role does religion play in the lives of these characters? How does it help them deal with adversity and respond to anti-Semitism? Why do you think Salomon denied that their lives as Jews were in danger?

8. What is the significance of the zloty coin?

9. Discuss the novel's settings—Podkamien, Brody, Vienna. Did these locales feel authentic to you? How did they enhance the story for you?

10. How does Tasa keep her memories of her mother from fading during their five years of separation? How does their relationship evolve as the novel unfolds?

11. Explain why the teenagers' prank in Brody was critical to the narrative. What did it reveal about Tasa and her friends? About the Soviet occupation of eastern Poland?

12. Did you like reading the letters that were inserted at various points in the novel? Why or why not?

13. As the novel ends, what kind of future does Tasa imagine for herself in Atlantic City?

14. Did knowing that this novel is inspired by actual events affect your interest in, and attachment to, the characters? Which characters did you like best, and why?

Please visit www.lindakass.com for further information.

Credits

Excerpt from "Optimism, An Essay" by Helen Keller, in *The World I Live In and Optimism: A Collection of Essays* by Helen Keller, published by Dover Publications in 2009.

Excerpt from "Auguries of Innocence" by William Blake, in *The Complete Poetry & Prose of William Blake*, edited by David V. Erdman, published by Anchor Books, 1965.

"The Coming of the Ship" from THE PROPHET by Kahlil Gibran, copyright © 1923 by Kahlil Gibran and renewed 1951 by Administrators C.T.A. of Kahlil Gibran Estate and Mary G. Gibran. Used by permission of Alfred A. Knopf, an imprint of the Knopf Doubleday Publishing Group, a division of Penguin Random House LLC. All rights reserved. Any third party use of this material, outside of this publication, is prohibited. Interested parties must apply directly to Penguin Random House LLC for permission.

Excerpt(s) from THE OPEN DOOR by Helen Keller, copyright © 1957 by Helen Keller. Used by permission of Doubleday, an imprint of the Knopf Doubleday Publishing Group, a division of Penguin Random House LLC. All rights reserved. Any third party use of this material, outside of this publication, is prohibited. Interested

About the Author

© Lorn Spolter Photography

As a journalist, Linda Kass wrote for regional and national publications, including *Columbus Monthly, TIME* and *The Detroit Free Press*, early in her career. *Tasa's Song*, her debut novel, is inspired by her mother's life in eastern Poland during the Second World War. Linda lives in Columbus, Ohio. Learn more at www.lindakass.com.

SELECTED TITLES FROM SHE WRITES PRESS

She Writes Press is an independent publishing company
founded to serve women writers everywhere.
Visit us at www.shewritespress.com.

The Sweetness by Sande Boritz Berger
$16.95, 978-1-63152-907-8
A compelling and powerful story of two girls—cousins living on separate
continents—whose strikingly different lives are forever changed when the
Nazis invade Vilna, Lithuania.

All the Light There Was by Nancy Kricorian
$16.95, 978-1-63152-905-4
A lyrical, finely wrought tale of loyalty, love, and the many faces of resistance, told from the perspective of an Armenian girl living in Paris during
the Nazi occupation of the 1940s.

Portrait of a Woman in White by Susan Winkler
$16.95, 978-1-938314-83-4
When the Nazis steal a Matisse portrait from the eccentric, art-loving
Rosenswigs, the Parisian family is thrust into the tumult of war and sepa-
ration, their fates intertwined with that of their beloved portrait.

Shanghai Love by Layne Wong
$16.95, 978-1-938314-18-6
The enthralling story of an unlikely romance between a Chinese herbalist
and a Jewish refugee in Shanghai during World War II.

The Vintner's Daughter by Kristen Harnisch
$16.95, 978-163152-929-0
Set against the sweeping canvas of French and California vineyard life
in the late 1890s, this is the compelling tale of one woman's struggle to
reclaim her family's Loire Valley vineyard—and her life.

The Belief in Angels by J. Dylan Yates
$16.95, 978-1-938314-64-3
From the Majdonek death camp to a volatile hippie household on the East
Coast, this narrative of tragedy, survival, and hope spans more than fifty
years, from the 1920s to the 1970s.